SEX IS A SPIRITUAL ACT

DR. DALE H. CONAWAY

PURITY PRESS
PUBLISHERS

Packaged by ACW Press
5501 N. 7th Ave., #502,
Phoenix, Arizona 85013
www.acwpress.com
The views expressed or implied in this work do not necessarily reflect those of ACW Press. Ultimate design, content and editorial accuracy of this work is the responsibility of the author(s).

Published by Purity Press Publishers
P.O. Box 252
Okemos, Michigan 48864-0252
To order inside the U.S. call: 1-517-381-2373

Or reach us via the Internet at: http://members.nbci.com/sosm/

Printed in the United States of America

ISBN 1-892525-37-2

To my loving wife Carla Joy….
For your charity, purity and integrity of purpose.
May the Lord openly reward you for your faithfulness
and for the kindness that you have shown
to the "least of these."

To my children…
Chrisina Joy, Benjamin Joseph and Candace Destiny.
Your lives speak prophetically to me daily. May your
potential be fully unleashed in your generation as you
walk in the beauty of holiness.

Contents

About the Author

D r. Dale H. Conaway is President and founder of Sword of the Spirit Ministries, a non-profit, tax exempt organization established in 1985. An ordained minister, Dr. Conaway has devoted more than 20 years in personal research on the subject of biblical sexuality. The author's academic and educational experience include:

- a Doctorate in Veterinary Medicine
- a Master's degree in pathology
- cancer research
- scientific publications

In the author's first book, *Sex & The Bible: A Biblical Perspective Of Human Sexuality;* Treasure House Pub. (1996), Dr. Conaway introduces the reader to some of the "spiritual laws" that govern human sexuality. In this volume, *Sex Is A Spiritual Act*, the author continues to develop his primary thesis; "Sex is a spiritual act that is governed by spiritual laws." In these two volumes, the author establishes a solid foundation for biblical morality and provides detailed information about the sources and dangers of current sexual trends.

Some of the author's stated goals and objectives:

- Propagate a biblical perspective of human sexuality in such a manner that will promote the sexual integrity and stability of future generations.
- Promote the sexual healing and restoration of this generation.
- Provide instructional resource tools that are academically sound and biblically oriented that will aid parents, educators and church leaders in addressing the sexuality issue.
- Develop a sex education curriculum that will target grades 4-12.

Dr. Conaway has been married 16 years. He and his wife Carla have three children.

The author has traveled throughout the continental U.S. teaching seminars on biblical sexuality in a variety of settings. If your church, ministry or organization would like more information you may contact us at:

Web site:http://members.nbci.com/sosm
Phone: 517-381-2373

To the Sword of The Spirit Ministry Executive Board
- *Pastor Raphael Green*
- *Deacon Samuel J. Hosey Sr.*
- *Dr. Fredrick E. Tippett*

Thank you for standing with me in the "day of small things."

To Pastors Phillip and Patricia Owens and the Immanuel's Temple Community Church Family
Thank you for providing a church that has been a true ark of safety.

Preface

This book was written to further clarify and expand upon the concepts written in *Sex and the Bible: A Biblical Perspective of Human Sexuality* (henceforth referred to as Volume 1). The ideas and principles in Volumes 1 and 2 are not "new" per se. The underlying basis for these ideas are all biblically based. What is new is the understanding with which these ideas are presented. The presentation of these ideas were the results of approximately twenty years of personal Bible study, research and prayer that focused on the spiritual aspects of human sexuality. I make mention of this fact for two reasons:

1. To give God the glory and credit for His revealing what was hidden in His Word.
2. To make it known that some of these ideas and concepts are still being formulated and developed even now as I write.

I have had the opportunity to listen to some nationally recognized ministers teach on some of the ideas from Volume 1. Some of what I heard did not adequately express what I was trying to communicate. Hopefully, *Sex Is a Spiritual Act* will more clearly expound, explain and expand upon the original intent and meaning of the concepts in Volume 1.

As we move into the new millennium, the issue of sex and sexuality will continue to become more and more controversial. It is not a coincidence that the topic of sex, sexuality and sexual sin has dominated the media for the latter portion of the 1990's. It is not a coincidence that the only elected president to be impeached in the history of this nation has been impeached for much of which is directly related to his lack of sexual morality.

It is not a coincidence that this nation is currently struggling with the issue of same sex marriages, gays in the military, gay adoption and church ordination of homosexuals.

I believe that the timing of many of these sexual conflicts have been divinely orchestrated. God is speaking to this generation. Revelations concerning the sexual sins of our national leaders (spiritual and political) point to the fact that this country is suffering from a "sexual identity crisis." This crisis in sexual identity was birthed during the early to mid 60's when this nation's second Sexual Revolution came forth. In matters regarding sex and its divine purpose, this nation has lost its identity.

Issues regarding sex and sexuality will continue to be a major point of contention and controversy as we move through the year 2000 and beyond. The church will be bombarded by the homosexual agenda like never before. Issues like:

1. Ordination of homosexual priest and pastors.
2. Marriage of gay and lesbian couples.
3. Marriage benefits for live in heterosexual and gay couples.
4. Homosexual rights.
5. Gay adoption rights.

The issue of sexual morality in general—and sexual sin in particular—among so-called church leaders will continue to haunt and hinder many local assemblies. On a regular basis now, we hear of some type of sexual scandal involving clergy. More and more churches are caving in to the homosexual agenda.

The pornographic appetite of this nation is out of control and seems to be growing everyday. America is the number one producer and consumer of hard core pornography in the world. In the midst of all the confusion and turmoil, God is speaking and seeking to address the sexual confusion that we have been ensnared by. God is speaking. Sexual sin is high on His agenda in this new millennium.

God is challenging the local church to more effectively deal with the sexual sin in its midst. If we ignore the handwriting on the wall, our society will continue to suffer the consequences: a rise in 1) out of wedlock births, 2) teen pregnancy, 3) sexually transmitted diseases, 4) divorce rates, 5) high school drop-out rates and 6) family disintegration.

God will judge this nation for its sexual sin. The Baby Boom generation will not escape God's judgment for having embraced the 1960's Sexual Revolution. Almost forty years have come and gone since the second Sexual Revolution was birthed. In Scripture, the number forty is associated with trial, chastisement and probation. God has not forgotten. He will not allow unrepentant sexual sin to go unpunished. Baby Boomers will be held accountable for the ungodly sexual covenants and philosophies of the second Sexual Revolution.

We are living in a critical hour. Judgment has already begun in the house of God. Holiness and sanctification remain the godly standards for His people. One of the most important challenges that the millennial church must face is the sexuality issue. The church must address this issue in a more comprehensive fashion if it is to hold back the rising tide of sexual immorality and present herself as a bride without spot or wrinkle to a soon-coming Christ.

People do not realized that sex is a "spiritual act that is governed by spiritual laws." People are ignorantly entering sexual covenants that profoundly impact their lives. Parents are seeking answers and sadly, many churches are also struggling with this issue. This volume may be used as a reference guide by parents and teachers who desire to address the sexuality issue in a more comprehensive fashion.

For those church leaders who desire to effectively deal with the issue of sexual sin, this volume will serve as a helpful resource tool that can be used in conjunction with other resources. I trust and pray that this book will aid in the *perfecting of the saints*, the *equipping of the saints* and in strengthening the doctrine of holiness and sanctification which *was once delivered to the saints*. May this volume contribute to the building up of *God's army*, that it may stand in this evil day.

Dr. Dale H. Conaway
June 2000

Foreword

The subject of sex and humanity's pre-occupation with this sensitive issue is an age-old experience. The abuse, misuse, confusion and corruption of this most beautiful and holy creation of God has placed sex in the category of taboo, distrust and social secrecy.

Dr. Dale H. Conaway, in this volume of *Sex Is a Spiritual Act*, provides the reader with a practical, balanced, sensible and principle-centered approval of the subject.

This book is a must for everyone, especially those who desire to counsel others in this area. I highly recommend it!

Dr. Myles E. Munroe
Pastor: Bahamas Faith Ministries International

Chapter One

SEXUAL IDOLATRY
THE DECLINE AND FALL OF NATIONS

This chapter will highlight the following ideas:

- Worship (how people identify with or relate to God) affects a people's culture in profound ways.
- What or how a people worship is key in defining the moral standards of a society.
- When a people's system of worship encourages sexual immorality, their culture rapidly declines.

For so it was, that the children of Israel had sinned against the Lord their God, which had brought them up out of the land of Egypt, from under the hand of Pharaoh king of Egypt, and had feared other gods. And walked in the stat- ues of the heathen, *whom the Lord cast out from before the children of Israel, and the Kings of Israel, which they had made.*

2 Kings 17:7,8 (emphasis added)

I would like to focus on five words in this passage, "the statues of the heathen."

What were the statues of the heathen that the writer is referring to? The Hebrew word for statues here is *chuqqah* (2708)* which means customs or ordinances. Customs are the habitual practices of a people that have been established over a period of time. These habitual practices usually become the laws by which the people are governed.

Customs are those practices that flow from a people's culture. Culture has been defined as the sum total of all socially transmitted patterns of behavior. Culture embodies a people's belief system through which all other social activities evolve. It has been said that nothing takes place within a society apart from its culture.

In 2 Kings 17:8, the customs make reference to those habitual practices or activities that are rooted in the culture or religion (belief system). The key elements of the heathen belief system (cultural ideology) are outlined in 2 Kings 17:9-17. The key elements are highlighted in these verses:

> verse 9: "high places"
> verse 10: "images and groves"
> verse 11: "high places"
> verse 12: "idols"
> verse 15: "vanity"
> verse 16: "images, groves, host of heaven, Baal"
> verse 17: "divination, enchantment, pass through fire"

The above mentioned verses refer to practices or customs that were ingrained into the fabric of that society. The key point is that what and how they worshiped set the tone for their belief system, customs and cultural practices. *What and or how a people worship lays the moral, ethical and philosophical foundation of that people's culture.* Religion and culture are inseparable.

Verses 9 and 11 speak of the "high places." These were not places where people congregated to smoke dope. They were elevated sites, usually found on the top of a mountain or a hill, consecrated to the

---

* Unless otherwise noted, numbers in parentheses are taken from Strong's Exhaustive Concordance of the Bible number key.

worship of pagan deities. The average high place that was dedicated to Baal worship would have an altar (2 Kings 21:3; 2 Chronicles 14:3) with a wooden pole that represented Asherah, the female fertility god, and/or a stone pillar representing the male penis or Baal (2 Kings 3:2).

At these "high places" of worship the people sacrificed animals and/or children (Jeremiah 7:31), burned incense, prayed, ate sacrificial meals and engaged in sexual intercourse (homosexual and heterosexual) with temple prostitutes. Bestiality was often practiced at these sites as well. Most "high places" were part of Baal worship, but Molech (Ammonite god) and Chemosh (Moabite god) were worshiped in similar settings.

When the children of Israel came into Canaan, they were ordered to destroy the "high places" of the inhabitants (Exodus 23:24, 34:13; Numbers 33:52; Deuteronomy 7:5, 12:3). This action would prevent the Israelis from being tempted to worship these false gods.

The "images" and "groves" mentioned in verses 10 and 16 (2 Kings 17) again refer to the male penis (image) and the female fertility element (grove) or Asherah. This reinforces the sexual nature of the idolatry. Verse 12 mentions the "idols" which were small statues that were either in human or animal form. Verse 15 mentions "vanity," the emptiness and frustration that results from being led astray by sexual idolatry. Verses 16 and 17 mentions "Baal," "host of heaven," "divination," "enchantment" and "pass[ing] through the fire." These two verses are important because they connect sexual idolatry with astrology, witchcraft and child sacrifice (modern day abortion).

This passage helps us to understand how a people's customs and statues evolve from their system of worship. *Everything begins with worship.* The Bible teaches that who, what and how a people worship will ultimately determine social order or disorder. A detailed description of the "statues of the heathen" may be found in Leviticus 18:3-30.

STATUES OF THE HEATHEN

And the Lord spake unto Moses saying, Speak unto the children of Israel and say unto them, I am the Lord your God. After the doings *of the land of Egypt, wherein ye dwelt, shall ye not do: and after the* doings *of the land of Canaan, whither I bring you, shall ye not do: neither shall ye walk in their ordinances [statues].*

Leviticus 18:3 (emphasis added)

From a historical and spiritual standpoint, both the Egyptian and Canaanite cultures were heavily influenced by Baal worship. Baal worship was the deification of the sexual element with the incorporation of animal worship (see Romans 1).[1] This type of idolatrous worship was perverted, profane and (sexually) promiscuous.

To better appreciate ancient Egyptian and Canaanite culture, we should examine the history of these two nations. The Bible teaches that Noah had three sons: Ham, Shem and Japhet. Ham had four sons: Cush, Mizraim, Phut and Canaan (Genesis 10:6). Mizraim became the progenitor of the various Egyptian tribes. Canaan became the progenitor of the people who settled mainly in Palestine, Arabia, Tyre, Sidon and other parts of the land promised to Abraham.

Historically speaking, Egypt was one of the most advanced civilizations ever. The Egyptians built some of the greatest and most enduring architectural structures ever known to man. Even today, the pyramids still inspire awe and amazement. The Egyptians were highly advanced in science, mathematics, astronomy and biology. It is highly probable that techniques for embalming and preserving dead bodies originated among the Egyptians. Ancient Egyptian culture and civilization was second to none.

On the other hand, the Canaanites were a less sophisticated people. Their contributions to the advancement of world civilization were few, if any at all. Here we see two peoples and two cultures on opposite extremes regarding social and scientific advancement.

It is important to note that, as these civilizations evolved, both cultures somehow became infected by the same perverted system of worship that led to their eventual ruin and oblivion. The point is that sexual perversion, once it infiltrates and poisons a culture, can destroy both great nations and obscure nations alike. Sexual sin can destroy a people and its culture.

> *Righteousness exalts a nation, but sin is a reproach to any people.*
>
> Proverbs 14:34

Both Egyptian and Canaanite civilization eventually succumbed to the destructive effects of corrupt worship and sexual idolatry in particular. In Leviticus 18, the Bible focuses on the specific nature of the sexual idolatry that corrupted and destroyed Canaanite culture and forced God to expel them from the land.

I would like to review and highlight some of the specific "statues" adopted and practiced by heathen nations of that day, beginning with incest (Leviticus 18).

I. INCEST

None of you shall approach to any that is near of kin to him, to uncover their nakedness: I am the LORD.

Leviticus 18:6 (emphasis added)

The Hebrew word for incest literally means "unclean" or "defiled." Leviticus 18:7-16 expands upon the specific incestuous sexual unions that are forbidden. These include sexual intercourse between: parents and children; grandparents and grandchildren; brothers and sisters; step-parents and step-children; half brothers and sisters; aunts and nephews or nieces and uncles; father-in-law and daughter-in-law or mother-in-law and son-in-law; and sister-in-law and brother-in-law.

In ancient Egyptian society, incest was very common. The Pharaohs would marry their sisters or even their own mothers. Apparently, they believed that these types of marriages strengthened their bloodlines and their hold on political power. We now know of the detrimental effects incest produces—which include birth defects—in children born to these unions. Incest is a breach of the sacred boundaries that God has established for personal and societal well being. One incest study found that one in three girls and one in five boys were sexually molested by age 18.[2]

Leviticus 18:6-30 is an important passage; in it God places specific boundaries upon the sexual activities of His people. These sexual standards were to mark the people of God as different (peculiar) from all other nations. One of the most important distinguishing traits between saint and sinner has to do with sexual attitudes and behaviors. The boundaries and restraints that God placed upon human sexuality are not repressive, they are culturally stabilizing and are necessary for social preservation.

In this passage of Scripture, we see the phrase "to uncover the nakedness." The literal meaning of this phrase is to "have sexual intercourse."[3] Jehovah God makes no distinction between the "naked-ness" of married couples. To uncover the nakedness of the wife was to uncover the nakedness of the husband. It is as if God views their "nakedness" as one and the same (no more twain but one flesh). God's Word affirms the sacred and spiritual nature of holy matrimony and seeks to maintain the purity and purpose of this sacrament. Incest is a serious breach of both the marital and parental bond.

II. STATUTORY RAPE

You shall not uncover the nakedness [genitals] of a woman and her daughter, neither shall you take her son's daughter or her daughter's daughter; it is wickedness.

Leviticus 18:17

The Hebrew word for wickedness (2154) is *zimmah* (lit. a sin of uncleanness; fornication, rape and/or incest in particular). The pri-mary idea conveyed in verse 17 is that an older (adult) man should not take sexual advantage of an adolescent girl. Here, we have the Bible propagating the spiritual and moral basis for "statutory rape" laws. By definition, statutory rape is the crime of having sexual inter-course with a person below the age of consent.

One of the problems with teens having sex is that more and more teens are having sex with adults. Federal and state surveys suggest that adult males are the fathers of 66 percent of babies born to teenage girls.[4] According to the Alan Guttmacher Institute, about 40 percent of fifteen-year-old mothers say the fathers of their babies are twenty years or older. For seventeen-year-old moms, 55 percent of the fathers are adults; for nineteen-year-olds, it is 78 percent.[5] In 1980, 48 percent of teenage moms were unmarried. Today, 65 per-cent of teenage moms are unmarried. These teens and their children are at high risk of poverty, school failure and welfare dependency.[6]

I believe that the 1960's Sexual Revolution helped to cultivate certain attitudes that led to laxity in the statutory rape laws in this country. In the 70's, some states lowered the age of consensual sex to 14.[7] These lax laws have, no doubt, contributed to the approximately one million teen pregnancies a year. A 60's-bred, sexually permissive society is partially responsible for unleashing these "sexual preda-tors" on society.

III. Pornography

Verse 17 of Leviticus 18 also speaks to another prevalent evil in contemporary society: *child pornography*. In this country, the child pornography industry is a multimillion-dollar industry. Even in Old Testament times, God condemns statutory rape and child pornography as wickedness.

Verse 18 forbids a man from having sexual relations with his wife's sister:

> *Neither shalt thou take a wife to her sister, to vex her, to uncover her nakedness [genitals], beside the other in her lifetime.*
>
> Leviticus 18:18

Note the "vexation" or emotional turmoil that is generated when this type of sexual competition is taking place.

Verse 20 forbids adultery, fornication and sexual relations with anyone other than your own spouse.

> *Moreover thou shalt not lie carnally with thy neighbor's wife, to defile thyself with her.*
>
> Leviticus 18:20

The key phrase here is "lie carnally." The Hebrew words used to describe this behavior are *shekobeth* and *zerah*. *Shekobeth* (7903) means to engage in unlawful sexual intercourse, such as dealing in prostitution. *Zerah* (2233), meaning to release seed, implies the use of any woman, other than your wife, for any kind of sexual gratification or sexual release. The behavior alluded to here makes reference not only to adultery (sex with anyone other than spouse) and prostitution, but also has broader applications that include the use of pornographic material for sexual release. Pornography is written, visual, or spoken material depicting or describing sexual activity or genital exposure that is arousing to the viewer.[8] This would include: *Hustler*, *Playboy*, *Playgirl* and *Penthouse* magazines; X-rated movies; adult pay per view; peep shows; live striptease clubs; soft porn or hard porn; phone sex; and computer (internet) porn.

This nation is inundated with hard core pornography. According to *Adult Video News*, an industry publication, hard core video rentals rose from seventy-five million in 1985 to 665 million in 1996.[9] It is estimated that Americans spent eight billion dollars on hard core videos, peep shows, sex magazines, etc. in 1996.[10] This is an astounding cultural development, because 25 years ago, the estimated revenue generated from pornography in this country was only between five and ten million dollars.[11] A leading sociologist has noted that the sexual content of American culture has changed more in the past twenty years than it had in the past 200 years![12] The United States is the world's leading producer of porn, producing about 150 new hard core videos a week.[13]

In 1998, internet users spent 970 million dollars on internet pornography. It is estimated that internet pornography revenues will rise to three billion dollars by the year 2003.[14] A recent study estimates that at least 200,000 Americans are hopelessly addicted to internet pornography.[15] Internet pornography is growing at such a rapid rate that the industry is poised to trade on Wall Street as any other Fortune 500 company.[16] Baal (sexual idolatry) and Mammon (material wealth) are companion deities that have captivated our culture!

IV. ABORTION

Verse 21 of Leviticus 18 strongly condemns the worship of Molech, one of the main Ammonite deities, and Chemosh, the Moabite counterpart. These deities were worshiped by offering children as burnt sacrifices. The modern day equivalent of this practice is abortion. Since the 1973 Roe v. Wade Supreme court decision, there have been an estimated thirty to thirty-five million abortions performed in this country. *There has always been a connection between sexual immorality and child abuse.* Often, the offspring of these immoral sexual unions are the victims of abortion, abandonment and abuse as they are figuratively sacrificed on the altars of Molech. If current trends continue, about 43 percent of American women will have an abortion in their lifetime. One survey found that approximately 80 percent of all abortions were "convenience" abortions.[17]

V. Homosexuality

Verse 22 of Leviticus 18 forbids homosexual relations. God's disdain for this particular perversion was manifest when he destroyed the cities of Sodom and Gomorrah (see Genesis 19). When studying Baalism, a religion based on sexual idolatry, one will discover a significant amount of homosexual activity within that religious cult. God uses the word "abomination" to describe His attitude toward this sin. The Hebrew word is *toevah* (8441). These are activities, behaviors and lifestyles that jeopardize the security and well-being of society in general. Some behaviors are personally destructive, while others are both personally and socially destructive.

There are those sexual sins that are not conducive to social stability or societal advancement. Without a doubt, certain lifestyles promote social decay and decline. Sexual abominations such as bestiality, incest, pedophilia, statutory rape and homosexuality are *socially destabilizing behaviors*. One reason these behaviors are strongly rejected by God is that they endanger society as a whole.

In the past two decades, American culture has become more accepting of the homosexual lifestyle. In 1991, only 17 percent of teens said that they were comfortable with homosexuality. A survey conducted in 1999 revealed that 54 percent of teens said that they were comfortable with it.[18] More evidence that homosexuality has won greater cultural acceptance is seen in the legislation, passed in Vermont, that allows gays to form "civil unions;" these unions amount to marriage in everything but name.[19]

VI. Bestiality

Verse 23 of Leviticus 18 forbids the practice of bestiality. Bestiality is, by definition, sexual intercourse with animals. The practice of bestiality in conjunction with many of the nature religions, Baalism in particular, is well documented.[20] The Hebrew word used in this verse for bestiality is *tebel* (8397), meaning "confusion." This word makes reference to the unnatural union of human and animal flesh.

Cultural Ruin

Leviticus 18:24 asserts that the Canaanite nations were "defiled" by all of the above mentioned practices. Both the Egyptian and

Canaanite cultures were permeated with these vile practices. It is important to note that the primary influence that led to the widespread dissemination of incest, statutory rape, child pornography, adultery, fornication, homosexuality and bestiality was a corrupt and perverted religious system of worship.[21]

In Romans 1, the apostle Paul sets forth some profound truths about corrupt worship and its relationship to social and cultural upheaval.[22] Leviticus 18 illustrates how rampant sexual idolatry contributed to the social, cultural and spiritual ruin of the inhabitants of Canaan (the Amorites). Ultimately, it was their corrupt system of worship, and the sexual sin that it bred, that led to God dispelling them from the land.

In Genesis God tells Abraham:

> *But in the fourth generation they shall come hither again:*
> *for the iniquity of the Amorites is not yet full.*
> Genesis 15:16

Amorites: Defilers of the Land

The Amorites were a desert and nomadic people who, over time, moved into Babylon and established a dynasty of their own that included Syria.[23,24] One of the most noted ancient Amorite kings was Hammurabi, who was remembered for a code of laws that he enacted. At the time of the Exodus, the Amorites were a people of Canaan and are often listed with the Hittites, Perizzites, Hivites and Jebusites as opponents of Israel (Exodus 33:2). When Israel prepared to invade Palestine, two Amorite kings stood in their way. The defeat of these two kings was the first stage of possessing the Promised Land and was looked upon as an important event in Israel's history.

It appears that organized worship of the so called "fertility deities" (sex deities) may have originated with the Amorites. The worship of these deities became embedded into Babylonian culture and eventually disseminated into Egypt and the rest of world. The worship of these sex deities may very well have been what Jehovah was referring to as the "iniquity of the Amorites" in Genesis 15:16. These iniquities include:

Homosexuality
Pedophilia

Prostitution
Incest
Infanticide
Idolatry (sex worship)
Adultery
Bestiality
Sorcery
Fornication
Rape
Witchcraft

In Abraham's day, the iniquity of the Amorites was not yet full. This means that their culture had not declined to the point in which the social order had to be actively judged by God. It is interesting to note that most of the "abominable customs" mentioned in Leviticus 18 are sexual in nature. God's warning to Israel in verse 30 is sobering:

> *Therefore shall ye keep mine ordinance, that ye commit not any one of these* abominable customs, *which were committed before you, and that ye defile not yourselves therein: I am the LORD your God.*
>
> Leviticus 18:30 (emphasis added)

ABOMINABLE CUSTOMS

Customs are those activities that flow directly from a people's culture. As stated earlier, customs are those social patterns of behavior that are accepted as normal and are rooted in tradition, religion and/or superstition. The Hebrew word for abominable is *towebah* (8441), meaning "disgusting or detestable in the eyes of God." Abominable customs are those social behavior patterns that have been rejected by God. Abominable customs are legally and socially accepted behaviors that originate from an abominable culture. Listed below are some activities the Bible classifies as abominable.

OLD TESTAMENT ABOMINATIONS

• Idolatry (Deuteronomy 7:25, 27:15, 32:16)
• Unjust weights and measures (Proverbs 11:1)
• Sexual uncleanness in general (Leviticus 18:22, 20:13; Deuteronomy 24:4)

- Incest (Leviticus 18:6-18)
- Lying with a woman in her menses (Leviticus 18:19)
- Adultery (Leviticus 18:20)
- Sodomy/homosexuality (Leviticus 18:22)
- Bestiality (Leviticus 18:23)
- Offering seed to Molech (Leviticus 18:21)
- Offering children in sacrifice (Deuteronomy 18:10)
- Sorcery, witchcraft, necromancy, and divination (Deuteronomy 18:10,11)
- The hire of a whore and price of a dog (sodomite) as a consecrated gift ("dogs and whores") (Deuteronomy 23:18).

Of the twelve abominable practices listed above, seven are sexual in nature. These practices are considered abominable because God Himself rejects them as such. God rejects these practices because of the following:

1. The spiritual impact that they have upon the individual practicing them.
2. The social destruction that these practices may inflict upon society.

Customs are the standards or social norms that serve to sanction a people's attitudes and behaviors. Customs not only sanction personal and public behavior, they also become the basis for which these behaviors become protected under the law. When abominable customs are being legally sanctioned and protected, one can be certain that the culture is on a collision course with God's judgment.

History teaches that abominable customs, if left unchecked, will eventually destroy a civilization. It took approximately 400 years for the "iniquity of the Amorites" to reach what I call the "critical mass of societal ruin." I am defining the "critical mass of societal ruin" as that point in time where societal sin has become so great that God's wrath initiates His judgment upon that society (see Romans 1:18).

The ancient Roman Empire is often sighted as an example of a once great civilization that deteriorated and collapsed as a result of moral and cultural decay. If the lifestyles of the Roman emperors who ruled Rome from about 46 B.C.–117 A.D. reflect the cultural and moral climate of ancient Rome, then there is little doubt that sexual idolatry played a great role in its decline and fall. Consider:

> **Julius Caesar** (49-44 B.C.): His sexual affairs with Roman women were said to be numerous. The most infamous of his many foreign mistresses was Cleopatra of Egypt.[25]
>
> **Augustus** (27 B.C.–14 A.D.): Committed adultery openly and often; engaged in homosexuality.[26]
>
> **Tiberius** (14-37 A.D.): A bisexual and a pedophile.[27]
>
> **Gaius Caligula** (37-41 A.D.): Habitually committed incest with all three of his sisters.[28]
>
> **Claudius** (41-54 A.D.): Married his niece (incest) and had three other wives.[29]
>
> **Nero** (54-68 A.D.): Entertained by prostitutes at his extravagant dinner parties; seduced young boys and married numerous women; went through a wedding ceremony with a young boy and treated him as his wife;[30] romantically linked to his own mother.[31]
>
> **Titus** (79-81 A.D.): Was bisexual.[32]
>
> **Domitian** (81-96 A.D.): Numerous affairs with married women and prostitutes.[33]

In the years prior to the reign of Julius Caesar, Rome was infiltrated by the so called "mystery" religions of the East (the Orient).[34] These religious cults, and the worship they inspired, encouraged gross sexual immorality. During the reign of Trajan (98-117 A.D.), there were 32,000 prostitutes in the city of Rome. During this same period, homosexuality was extremely common and even fashionable.[35] *The historical evidence seems to indicate that sexual idolatry played a key role in the moral and cultural decline of the ancient Roman Empire.*

POSSIBLE STEPS TO CUSTOM DEVELOPMENT

1. Cultural dissemination: Ideas and philosophies are generated and publicly disseminated.
2. Cultural desensitization: Ideas and philosophies are publicly practiced; "coming out of the closet."

3. Cultural assimilation: Ideas gradually become attitudes and behaviors that are accepted by the public as harmless or as having "social redeeming value."
4. Cultural indoctrination: Ideas and philosophies are further disseminated and propagated via educational institutions and the media.
5. Cultural legalization: Ideas and philosophies become law, and the behavior, no matter how socially destructive, is no longer punishable by law.

When a nation begins to sanction abominable customs, one can be sure that cultural decay, social disintegration and spiritual decline (moral rot) are all prevalent.

Deadly Customs

Righteousness exalteth a nation: but sin is a reproach *to any people.*

Proverbs 14:34 (emphasis added)

There are many contemporary examples of nations whose cultural beliefs and practices are dangerous and destructive to the social order of the nation as a whole. There are various ethnic groups whose customs bring a reproach upon those who practice them. Consider the plight of one African nation.

Uganda

This nation in central Africa has a population of about twenty million people. It is estimated that 10 percent of the population is HIV positive.[36] Since 1982, nearly two million Ugandans have died of AIDS.[37] According to Tom Kityo, a native Ugandan and manager of the AIDS Service Organization, there are certain *cultural practices* (customs) that aid the spread of HIV among the populace: for example, the groom's father can have sex with the bride or other tribal clan members may have sex with someone's wife. These are acceptable practices (customs).[38] Some tribal *traditions* dictate that a young woman must become "heir to her aunt." This means that a girl must take on the "wifely" duties of her aunt in the event that her aunt dies. There are other east African tribes where custom dictates that a married man is expected to let his brothers have sex with his wife.[39]

These traditions, cultural beliefs and practices have decimated Uganda and other so-called Third World nations whose sexual practices are traditionally more loosely defined.

I am reminded of an advertisement from one particular Central African nation that was promoting condom usage as a means of controlling sexually transmitted diseases (STDs). In the ad, the husband tells his wife that he must begin using condoms when he is on long trips away from home to protect himself, and her, from STDs that he may pick up from prostitutes. The wife approves and expresses her understanding of his plight. Most reasonable people would agree that *this condom advertisement represents a serious cultural flaw.*

It is not my intent to depict Third World nations as a bunch of immoral heathens. The point that I am making here is this:

1. Often, sexual behavior flows from cultural beliefs and traditions.
2. Sexual traditions that are not rooted in biblical truth can be deadly (individually and collectively).
3. No national, cultural, racial, or ethnic group is immune from the effects of sexual immorality.

Sin is a reproach to any people.

Proverbs 14:34

This sexual reproach that afflicts a nation has no regard to ethnicity, race, or region. Ancient Rome is a testimony of a once great nation that was basically destroyed from within. In Gibbon's, *The Decline and Fall of the Roman Empire*, the moral decline of Rome is well-documented as a contributing factor in the demise of that empire. There were cultural practices that emanated from the worship of Greek gods and goddesses. In worshiping these false deities, sexual perversion became widespread and proved to be socially destructive and destabilizing.[40]

Sexual sin was even a reproach to the children of Israel. It was the practice of Baalism (sexual idolatry) that led to cultural and social decline and the eventual exile of God's chosen people. Second Kings 17:7-23 recaps the sexual idolatry (Baalism) that led to the Israeli exile to Assyria.

> Blessed *is the nation whose God is the LORD; and the*
> *people whom he hath chosen for his own inheritance.*
>> Psalms 33:12 (emphasis added)

Historically, nations whose cultures were rooted in the worship of the God of the Bible were generally blessed with social, political and economic stability. On the other hand, nations whose cultures were rooted in sexual idolatry became socially, politically and economically unstable.

> *For the transgression of a land many are the princes*
> *thereof: but by a man of understanding and knowledge the*
> *state thereof shall be prolonged.*
>> Proverbs 28:2 (emphasis added)

In order to understand the sexual behavior that exist in many African nations, one needs to realize that *these sexual behaviors are largely determined by their religious attitudes.*[41]

This is an extremely important point because this is not only true of African nations, it is true of *all* nations. *Sexual attitudes and behaviors world-wide are largely determined by religion, which defines how a people identifies or relates to God.* This is the essence of worship. In this context, our concept of God is vital. In Volume 1, Chapter 3, we discussed the apostle Paul's thesis of how "corrupt worship" led to global sexual idolatry (Romans 1). When deadly customs are widely practiced within a society, the results can be socially devastating. The current AIDS situation that exists in Africa is only one example.

Sodom and Gomorrah

Sodom and Gomorrah is a classic example of an ancient society whose culture was given over to deadly customs and practices—so much so that God was forced to initiate active judgment upon its people. Apparently, a majority of the men in those two cities were either homosexual or bisexual. The whole region was infected by this perversion and came under (active) divine judgment (see Genesis 19:25). On a global scale, divine judgment was also manifest in Noah's day. In ancient biblical times, even as today, sexual idolatry was rampant and pervasive, and divine judgment came as a direct result of mankind's sin and rebellion (see Genesis 6 and 19). In the examples of the flood of Noah's day and Sodom and Gomorrah, cultural corruption produced deadly customs that eventually led to societal ruin.

> *But in the fourth generation they shall come hither again for the iniquity of the Amorites is not yet full.*
>
> Genesis 15:16

There comes a point in a society's evolution that the cultural corruption can no longer sustain a functional society. Concepts like justice, rule of law, equal protection under the law, equal rights and liberty, are no longer sustainable. Scientific advancement and technology usually suffer as well. When "iniquity becomes full," the land reaches a point of "critical mass." This happens when the land becomes saturated with the sin of the inhabitants (living and dead).

> *For all these abominations have the men of the land done, which were before you, and the* land is defiled.
>
> Leviticus 18:27 (emphasis added)

When the critical mass of sin is reached, God's wrath is activated, and His judgment is manifested.

> *And the land is defiled: therefore I do visit the iniquity thereof upon it, and the land itself* vomiteth out *her inhabitants.*
>
> Leviticus 18:25 (emphasis added)

> *That* the land spue *not you out also, when ye defile it, as it spued out the nations that were before you.*
>
> Leviticus 18:28 (emphasis added)

The Land Rejects and Ejects Its Corrupt Inhabitants

Scripture seems to indicate that the earth and the people that inhabit it share a special spiritual bond. It appears that the lifestyles (behaviors) of the land's inhabitants and the welfare of the land itself are linked, that is, share destinies. The cultural behaviors of a nation can either bless the land or curse it. The customs that people adopt are usually influenced by how, who, or what they worship. Customs (cultural practices) have a direct effect upon the land that the people inhabit. If the customs are godly and God-centered, the land will be at peace and will be blessed. *WORSHIP affects the CUSTOMS and the CUSTOMS affect the LAND* (see Leviticus 18; Deuteronomy 28:23; Matthew 24:7).

> *And all these blessings shall come on thee, and overtake thee, if thou shalt hearken unto the voice of the LORD thy God. Blessed shalt thou be in the city, and blessed shalt thou be in the field. Blessed shall be the fruit of thy body, and the* fruit of thy ground, *and the fruit of thy cattle, the increase of thy kine, and the flocks of thy sheep.*
>
> Deuteronomy 28:2-4 (emphasis added)

On the other hand, when the cultural practices are ungodly and sinful, the land becomes cursed:

> *And thy heaven that is over thy head shall be brass, and the earth that is under thee shall be iron. The LORD shall make the rain of thy land powder and dust: from heaven shall it come down upon thee, until thou be destroyed.*
>
> Deuteronomy 28:23,24

The land becomes defiled as a result of the cultural practices of the inhabitants. When this happens, the land itself "vomits out" (rejects) the sinful inhabitants.

> *Defile not ye yourselves in any of these things: for in all these the nations are defiled which I cast out before you: And the land is defiled: therefore I do visit the iniquity thereof upon it, and the land itself vomiteth out her inhabitants. Ye shall therefore keep my statutes and my judgments, and shall not commit any of these abominations; neither any of your own nation, nor any stranger that sojourneth among you: (For all these abominations have*

the men of the land done, which were before you, and the
land is defiled;) That the land spue not you out also, when
ye defile it, as it spued out the nations that were before you.

Leviticus 18:24-28

I would like to put forth a theory to partially explain what is actually taking place here. We all know that our physical bodies are composed of earth (Genesis 2:7). In this sense, we have our beginnings in the earth. When we die, it is ordained that we shall return to the earth from which we were created (Genesis 3:19). When wickedness and sin are perpetuated from generation to generation, transgressions accumulate back into earth. How? The land can register wickedness in two ways: from the physical bodies of the wicked dead that are buried into the ground at death and from the wicked and unrepentant behavior of the living inhabitants (1 Kings 18:17,18).

Physical Bodies of the Wicked Dead

When these bodies (of sin) are buried into the ground, the wicked deeds that have accumulated within these bodies are apparently accumulated within the earth. The unrepentant sin accumulates in the earth until "iniquity becomes full," that is, the land becomes saturated with sin and reaches a point of "critical mass." When this happens, the land spews out the inhabitants.

Through the bodies of the wicked dead, the land literally becomes saturated with sin and the land becomes cursed. In this manner, the land registers sin. We do know that the land holds us accountable to God for sins committed. There is a biblical foundation for this theory. Consider:

And he said, What hast thou done? the voice of thy brother's
blood crieth unto me from the ground. *And now art thou*
cursed from the earth, *which hath opened her mouth to*
receive thy brother's blood from thy hand.

Genesis 4:10,11 (emphasis added)

Do not prostitute thy daughter, to cause her to be a whore;
lest the land *fall to whoredom, and the* land *become full of*
wickedness.

Leviticus 19:29 (emphasis added)

For all these abominations have the men of the land done,
which were before you, and the land is defiled.
Leviticus 18:27 (emphasis added)

Even though these three Scriptures support the "accumulation of sin" theory, the most enlightening Scripture is found in the book of Job. In speaking of the wicked, this verse speaks powerfully:

His bones *are full of the sin of his youth, which shall lie down with him in the* dust.
Job 20:11 (emphasis added)

Here we are informed that the bones of the unrepentant wicked have accumulated the sins of his youth. Furthermore, his sins, having been collected in his bones, return to the earth when he is buried. When wickedness is continually perpetrated from generation to generation, it takes its toll upon the land that the wicked inhabit. If repentance is not sought and granted, the land becomes saturated with the sin of the wicked after a period of time. When the land reaches overload (critical mass), God will execute His judgment upon the land's unrepentant inhabitants.

This was the case described in Leviticus 18:24-30. Here we can clearly see that the land rejected the inhabitants because of the abominable customs that took place there generation after generation. Genesis 15:16 informs us that it took at least four generations (approximately 400 years) for the iniquity of the Amorites to become full.

But in the fourth generation they shall come hither again:
for the iniquity of the Amorites is not yet full.
Genesis 15:16

It took more than 400 years for the land to become "filled" (saturated) with the wickedness and sin of the Amorites. When this happened, God's judgment was set in motion, and a violent spiritual and natural reaction took place. We know from Leviticus 18 that the iniquity of the Amorites primarily consisted of sexual idolatry (perversion). It should be noted that God will not execute judgment until people have been given adequate time and opportunity to repent and sin has run its full course. Israel was warned to avoid these abominable practices at all cost (Leviticus 18:24). Sexual abominations are particularly devastating to the land and its inhabitants.

At least four generations of Amorites, with their abominable customs (cultural practices), caused judgment to be unleashed upon their descendents. Those descendents were eventually displaced by the Israelites. This illustrates the importance of living in harmony with the dictates of God's Word—for the sake of future generations, who may reap the curse of the unrepentant sins that are buried in the earth with their forefathers.

Wicked and Unrepentant Behavior of the Living

I believe that the unrepentant behavior of the living inhabitants reinforces the wickedness (curse) of succeeding generations. This is why repentance is so important; it can reverse and/or remove the curse of preceding generations and allow God to heal the land and forgive the inhabitant's sin. But when the inhabitants continue to perpetuate and propagate the wicked behavior of their forefathers, as in the case of the Amorites, the earth apparently "pleads" to God for relief and judgment.

> *And he said, What hast thou done? the voice of thy brother's blood crieth unto me from the ground. And now art thou cursed from the earth, which hath opened her mouth to receive thy brother's blood from thy hand.*
>
> Genesis 4:10,11

> *At that time, saith the LORD, they shall bring out the bones of the kings of Judah, and the bones of his princes, and the bones of the priests, and the bones of the prophets, and the bones of the inhabitants of Jerusalem, out of their graves: And they shall spread them before the sun, and the moon, and all the host of heaven, whom they have loved, and whom they have served, and after whom they have walked, and whom they have sought, and whom they have worshiped: they shall not be gathered, nor be buried; they shall be for dung upon the face of the earth.*
>
> Jeremiah 8:1,2

These two Scriptures further illustrate that the earth records the deeds of the inhabitants, living and dead. In Genesis 4, Cain's murderous deed is registered in the earth through the shed blood of his brother. In Jeremiah 8, the bones of the dead are dug out of their graves to answer for the wickedness of their past deeds.

> *For we must all appear before the judgment seat of Christ; that every one may receive the things done in his body, according to that he hath done, whether it be good or bad.*
>
> 2 Corinthians 5:10

> *And I saw the dead, small and great, stand before God; and the books were opened: and another book was opened, which is the book of life: and the dead were judged out of those things which were written in the books, according to their works. And the sea gave up the dead which were in it; and death and hell delivered up the dead which were in them: and they were judged every man according to their works.*
>
> Revelation 20:12,13

Second Corinthians 5 and Revelation 20 are New Testament illustrations that the works or deeds done in the body (earth) will be registered and accounted for (see also Matthew 12:36).

> *And I sought for a man among them, that should make up the hedge, and stand in the gap before me for the land, that I should not destroy it: but I found none. Therefore have I poured out mine indignation upon them; I have consumed them with the fire of my wrath: their own way have I recompensed upon their heads, saith the Lord GOD.*
>
> Ezekiel 22:30,31

> *If my people, which are called by my name, shall humble themselves, and pray, and seek my face, and turn from their wicked ways; then will I hear from heaven, and will forgive their sin, and will heal their land.*
>
> 2 Chronicles 7:14

Ezekiel 22 and 2 Chronicles 7 illustrate the importance of the living inhabitants' repentance in reversing the effects of wickedness committed by former generations. The living, by "standing in the "gap" for righteousness, can prompt God to forgive the sin and heal the land.

> *But let man and beast be covered with sackcloth, and cry mightily unto God: yea, let them turn every one from his evil way, and from the violence that is in their hands. Who can tell if God will turn and repent, and turn away from his fierce anger, that we perish not? And God saw their works, that they turned from their evil way; and God repented of the evil, that he had said that he would do unto them; and he did it not.*
>
> Jonah 3:8-10

The book of Jonah records the postponement of judgment on a generation because they chose to turn away from the wickedness of their predecessors and repent before God. This action taken by the Ninevites touched the heart of God and moved Him to forgive them and delay His judgment.

> *That the land spue not you out also, when ye defile it, as it spued out the nations that were before you.*
>
> Leviticus 18:28

I believe that this violent spiritual reaction is manifest in nature through droughts, earthquakes, pestilence, famine, violent storms, floods, plagues, volcanoes, political unrest, ethnic strife, war and other tribulations. God has a remedy to heal the land and reverse the curse. First and foremost, God's people were commanded to totally reject the Cannanite culture and its perverted religion (sexual idolatry).

> *And when the LORD thy God shall deliver them before thee; thou shalt smite them, and utterly destroy them; thou shalt make no covenant with them, nor shew mercy unto them: Neither shalt thou make marriages with them; thy daughter thou shalt not give unto his son, nor his daughter*

shalt thou take unto thy son. For they will turn away thy son from following me, that they may serve other gods: so will the anger of the LORD be kindled against you, and destroy thee suddenly. But thus shall ye deal with them; ye shall destroy their altars, and break down their images, and cut down their groves, and burn their graven images with fire.

Deuteronomy 7:2-5

The next important aspect of healing the land has to do with establishing a standard of righteousness in the land. Great civilizations spring forth from righteous cultures. Righteous cultures are the result of worship that is biblically based and God focused.

Righteousness exalteth a nation: but sin is a reproach to any people.

Proverbs 14:34

Chapter Summary

1. Worship, how a people identifies or relates to God, gives rise to customs (cultural practices). These customs define how a people identifies and relates to one another. Customs dictate whether a nation is blessed or cursed.
2. What and how a people worship lays the moral foundation of that people's culture.
3. Many ancient civilizations embraced sexual idolatry and incorporated ungodly sexual attitudes and behaviors within their cultures.
4. Sexual immorality can weaken a culture and destabilize a society.
5. When a nation's culture reaches a certain point of moral decay, the society will be actively judged by God. The destruction of Sodom and Gomorrah is one example.
6. Customs are those socially accepted patterns of behavior that flow directly from a people's culture or system of worship.
7. Abominable customs are derived from an abominable culture.
8. Of the twelve abominable customs mentioned in Deuteronomy, Leviticus and Proverbs, at least seven are sexual in nature.
9. Abominable customs, if allowed to spread unchecked, will lead to the eventual decay, decline and destruction of a civilization.

10. If you want to change a nation's customs (behavior), you must first change their culture (system of worship).
11. Sexual behaviors and attitudes ultimately flow from culturally instilled beliefs and traditions.
12. Sexual customs that are not rooted in Bible doctrine can be personally and socially destructive.
13. No nation, race, or ethnic group is immune from the destructive effects of sexual immorality.
14. The land and the people that inhabit it share a special spiritual bond.
15. The land registers the sins of its inhabitants and cries out to God for judgment.
16. Customs (culturally derived behaviors) that a people practice can either bless the land or cause it to be cursed.
17. When iniquity (sinful customs) "fill" the land, the unrepentant inhabitants are in danger of the judgment of God.
18. God's spiritual judgment upon the inhabitants of the land may be manifest in the form of:
    droughts
    famine
    plagues
    war
    earthquakes
    violent storms
    volcanic eruptions
    ethnic strife
    pestilence
    floods
    political instability
    economic collapse
19. If a nation repents of its sin and turns to God, judgment can be avoided.

If my people, which are called by my name, shall humble themselves, and pray, and seek my face, and turn from their wicked ways; then will I hear from heaven, and will forgive their sin, and will heal their land.

2 Chronicles 7:14

Chapter Two

A Righteous Gene Pool

A Note to the Reader

The reader should keep in mind that the concept of "spiritual DNA" that I have introduced here is a theoretical one. I believe that there is scriptural evidence that supports the existence of "spiritual DNA" but there is no objective way that I can prove it. Therefore, this concept need not become a point of theological contention. The idea of "spiritual DNA" is being presented here in an attempt to explain:

- How certain spiritual heritages may be passed on from one generation to the next.
- How spiritual covenants may be initiated and perpetuated in our children.
- The importance of establishing and maintaining godly covenants for the sake of future generations.

The reader may choose to agree or disagree with this particular concept without affecting his/her position in Christ.

And I will establish my covenant between me and thee and thy seed *after thee in their generations for an everlasting covenant, to be a God unto thee, and to thy seed after thee.*

Genesis 17:7 (emphasis added)

The purpose and intent of this chapter is to:

1. Explain the corrupting effects that sin had upon man's physical and spiritual nature. In doing so I will use certain biological terms:

   DNA—Deoxyribo Nucleic Acid. It contains the "blueprint" for all of the characteristics of each person. The DNA will "instruct" the body to make the specific proteins that will determine eye color, hair texture, etc.

   gene—A small portion of DNA

   genome—The total amount of DNA present within the cells of a particular species. For example, the human genome is the total amount of DNA present in the human race.

   gene pool—All of the genes (DNA) present within all of the individuals of the same family line.

   chromosome—Small structures in the cell nucleus made up of compact DNA and proteins.

All of these terms refer to the biologic material that is present within each person and responsible for passing on our physical characteristics to our children.

I will also use the biblical term "seed." The seed also refers to those elements carried within each person that may also be passed on to our children. In essence, the terms seed, DNA, genes, genome, gene pool and chromosome carry the same basic meaning. The important difference is that when the Bible uses the term "seed," it has both a physical and a spiritual meaning. The Bible affirms that not only our physical traits, but our spiritual traits can be passed on to our children as well. This chapter will highlight the theoretical idea that there exists within us both a physical seed and a spiritual seed. There is *physical* DNA, and there is *spiritual* DNA.

For everything that exists in the natural realm, there is a spiritual prototype that exists in the realm of the spirit. DNA is real, both natural and spiritual. If natural DNA transfers our physical traits on to our children, then spiritual DNA transfers a spiritual heritage on to our children. I am *not* suggesting that I fully understand *how* spiritual DNA works, but the idea of the existence of spiritual DNA is a position that is in harmony with holy Scripture. The apostle Paul even makes a distinction between the physical seed of Abraham and the his spiritual seed (Romans 4; Galatians 4). In the book of John, chapter 8, Jesus rejected the assertion of the wicked leaders who claimed that Abraham was their "father." They may have been of the *natural seed* of Abraham, but they were certainly not of his *spiritual seed*. Jesus clearly stated that their spiritual father was the devil.

2. Discuss how this corruption may have affected fallen man's genetic make-up (naturally and spiritually).
3. Explain the role of human sexuality in shaping historical events and how spiritual covenants are transferred from generation to generation.
4. Discuss God's divine strategy in establishing a "righteous gene pool" (RGP) in the earth.
5. Discuss the controversial issue of the "gay gene."

Spiritual Corruption

The earth also was corrupt *before God, and the earth was filled with violence. And God looked upon the earth, and, behold, it was corrupt; for all* flesh *had* corrupted *his way upon the earth. And God said unto Noah, The end of all flesh is come before me; for the earth is filled with violence through them; and, behold, I will destroy them with the earth.*

Genesis 6:11-13 (emphasis added)

God's decision to destroy mankind must have been an agonizing one. God is not irrational or vindictive. His destruction of the earth was not just an exercise to "get even" or to pay back mankind for the evils he had committed. If there had been any way to avoid this global holocaust, surely God would have done it. The fact of the matter is that God had no other option. He had to wipe the slate clean and start over. Why? This key phrase helps to explain why God had to take such drastic measures:

> *And God looked upon the earth, and behold, it was corrupt for all* flesh *had* corrupted *his* way *upon the earth.*
> Genesis 6:12 (emphasis added)

The earth became corrupt as a result of fallen man's corrupt nature. Mankind is connected to God's created order in such a way that when man's way became corrupt the rest of God's created order became corrupt (Romans 8:20-22).

What was this corruption and how did it come about? The Hebrew word for flesh used in the above Scripture is *basar* (1320). It has a strong sexual connotation as it is sometimes used to refer to the male sex organ (penis). In Ezekiel 23:20, the prophet rebukes Judah for her whoredom and ungodly fascination with the *basar* of her lovers).[1]

Fallen man's corrupt nature is connected to his sexuality. This corrupt nature is passed on to his offspring via sexual intercourse. Each succeeding generation has this corruption present within their seed, (that is, their gene pool, both natural and spiritual). This spiritual corruption was compounded by fallen man's unrestrained sexual immorality, which in turn seemed to worsen and magnify his fallen state. Man's fallen nature was passed on from one generation to the next. Mankind's spiritual gene pool (seed), the means through which his spiritual nature was generationally passed on, was now corrupt. I believe that there is scriptural evidence that supports the idea that the great Flood was precipitated by widespread sexual idolatry which had a corrupting influence on man's gene pool and society at large. Let's review the specific event to which I am referring.

> *And it came to pass, when men began to multiply on the face of the earth, and daughters were born unto them, That the sons of God saw the daughters of men that they were fair; and they took them wives of all which they chose. And the LORD said, My spirit shall not always strive with man, for that he also is flesh: yet his days shall be an hundred and twenty years. There were giants in the earth in those days;*

and also after that, when the sons of God came in unto the
daughters of men, and they bare children to them, the same
became mighty men which were of old, men of renown.
And GOD saw that the wickedness of man was great in the
earth, and that every imagination of the thoughts of his
heart was only evil continually.

Genesis 6:1-5

In this passage, the Bible records the events that led to the great
Flood. We are told that men began to multiply upon the face of the
earth. Introduced into this narrative are the "sons of God."[2] The
important thing to point out here is that sexual idolatry was rampant
and universal.

The Law of Marriage, given by Jehovah God to govern sexual relations, was rejected (Genesis 2:24). The result of this widespread sexual idolatry was the birth of a predatory race of ruthless, murderous
tyrants who inflicted chaos and destruction upon the whole face of
the earth. These individuals and the children that they birthed were
totally alienated from God as:

And God saw that the wickedness of man was great in the
earth, and that every imagination of his thoughts was only
evil continually.

Genesis 6:5

Adam's fall presented a problem, but God had a plan for his
restoration. The "Restorer" was to come through the "seed" of the
woman (Genesis 3:15). Rampant sexual idolatry jeopardized God's
plan of salvation and restoration—first, because of the corrupting
influence of sexual sin and secondly, because the offspring of these
ungodly sexual unions were totally alienated from God. Their
thoughts were "continually evil." These ungodly individuals were
apparently not willing to commune with God on His terms. The pre-
Flood race was a generation so corrupt and perverse that they were
not capable of preparing the succeeding generation for the promised
Redeemer.

Out of that entire generation only Noah found grace in God's
sight. Could it have been that, if God had not destroyed that wicked

generation, Noah would have eventually been murdered or corrupted as well? God needed a people through whom His plan of salvation could be revealed and propagated. God needed a "righteous gene pool" in the earth. He would begin again—with Noah.

> *These are the* generations *of Noah: Noah was a just man and perfect in his* generations, *and Noah walked with God.*
> Genesis 6:9 (emphasis added)

Through the entire biblical narrative, emphasis is placed on the importance of a people who are in fellowship with God and who are living separated from the world. Through Shem, Noah's second son, we see the divine plan unfolding as God calls out one of Shem's descendents to walk with Him. That individual was Abram (Abraham). God challenged Abram to leave his father's homeland, the idolatrous nation of Chaldea, and follow Him. God revealed Himself to Abram as the one and only true God in existence. Abram had to reject the polytheism (multiple god theology) of his day and all of the philosophical "relativism" that it fostered.

The corruption mentioned in Genesis 6 came about as a direct result of man's rebellion and disobedience. Adam's rebellion in the Garden of Eden initiated spiritual alienation from God. Later, Adam's offspring magnified and hastened the corruption through their rampant sexual idolatry and their rejection of the Law of Marriage (outlined in Genesis 2:24).[3]

> *Therefore shall a man leave his father and his mother, and shall cleave unto his wife: and they shall be one flesh.*
> Genesis 2:24

The corruption spoken of in Genesis 6 affected man's spirit, soul and body. As a result, the succeeding generations were becoming more and more alienated from God. It has always been God's intent that the older generation would proclaim to the younger generations His glory and power (Deuteronomy 6:7; 11:19). This clearly could not happen, as each succeeding generation (gene pool) was becoming more wicked than the one that had preceded it. If this was allowed to continue, the plan and purpose of God would have never unfolded on the earth.

Even though God is sovereign, He uses obedient vessels through which he can work to shape history. God has ordained the sex act as an important tool in the shaping of history. It is important then, that God is allowed to influence our sexual choices through His Word. Monogamous, heterosexual marriage, as outlined in Genesis 2:24, was God's way of working through Adam and Eve to influence historical events. God instituted marriage to prevent sexual exploitation, perversion, corruption and to preserve a righteous seed (gene pool): a seed that would preserve and pass on the true knowledge of God to the next generation. The Law of Marriage[4] in Genesis 2:24 provided the proper safe guards, controls and means whereby God could preserve a holy seed (righteous gene pool) in the earth. In the midst of universal sexual idolatry, there was total corruption. The personal and societal impact that sexual idolatry had upon Noah's generation is described in Genesis.

> *There were* giants *in the earth in those days; and also after that, when the sons of God came in unto the daughters of men, and they bare children to them, the same became* mighty *men which were of old, men of* renown. *And GOD saw that the* wickedness *of man was great in the earth, and that every imagination of the thoughts of his heart was only* evil *continually.*
>
> Genesis 6:4,5 (emphasis added)

These "giants" were ruthless tyrants who attained positions of power and influence in the earth through their wicked and sociopathic behavior. Wholesale sexual idolatry ruled the day. It was so widespread that it seemed to accelerate and exacerbate mankind's fallen condition. Noah's generation was a generation whose culture was completely saturated with sexual idolatry and incapable of transferring the knowledge of God to the next generation. In the midst of this corruption, Noah was found to be righteous in his generation (gene pool). Within Noah's spiritual DNA God found elements of righteousness that He could use to preserve His plan of restoration. (God always has a ram in the bush!)

"They Chose"

As free moral agents, Adam's offspring chose to reject any restraints that God had placed upon them. Through sex, God had ordained that mankind would work in conjunction with Him in shaping history through future generations. In rejecting the sexual restraints outlined in Genesis 2:24, fallen man rejected God's hand in influencing history. In effect, man was saying, "We don't need or want you to influence our destiny and future; we want to shape our own destiny, to be our own god." In multiplying wives, Satan, through fallen man, was attempting to derail God's plan for man's future redemption.

A Special Seed

Throughout the story of Abraham, special importance is placed upon his seed in the fulfillment of God's eternal plan.

> And I will establish my covenant between me and thee and thy seed after thee in their generations for an everlasting covenant, to be a God unto thee, and to thy seed after thee. And I will give unto thee, and to thy seed after thee, the land wherein thou art a stranger, all the land of Canaan, for an everlasting possession; and I will be their God. And God said unto Abraham, Thou shalt keep my covenant therefore, thou, and thy seed after thee in their generations.
>
> Genesis 17:7-9

In biological terms, the seed contains all of the information that will determine the nature and character of the offspring. In spiritual terms, the seed contains all the elements that will determine the spiritual disposition (nature) and character of the offspring. In the following pages, I will seek to advance the idea that a "righteous seed" can be produced in parents who obey the righteous dictates of God's Word. Righteous parents can pass on those elements of righteousness, in part, by teaching Godly precepts to their children. Apparently, walking in obedience to God's Word can somehow affect our spiritual DNA (seed). In this way, certain spiritual heritages can be passed on to our children.

In like fashion, wicked and sinful behavior is also incorporated into our spiritual DNA and passed on to our offspring. In the natural, we cannot choose our biological parents. In spiritual terms, we can change or choose our spiritual parents. How? By choosing to obey God's Word and by walking in His righteousness. The Bible asserts that we can be transformed from the children of darkness to the sons of light (1 Peter 2:8; Ephesians 5:8; Acts 26:18)

The Hebrew word for seed is *zera* (2233). It means fruit, plant, sowing time, posterity, or offspring. As stated earlier, the seed contains all of the necessary information that will ultimately determine the character and nature of the next generation. Let's look at an example from nature. We know that a peach seed will yield a tree that bears peach fruit. In other words, the seed determines what the tree will look like, what the tree will produce, how much fruit the tree will produce and when the tree will begin to produce. Questions concerning the nature or character of the fruit can ultimately be found within the seed.

> *For a good tree bringeth not forth corrupt fruit; neither doth a corrupt tree bring forth good fruit. For every tree is known by his own fruit. For of thorns men do not gather figs, nor of a bramble bush gather they grapes.*
>
> Luke 6:43,44

If the seed is corrupt, the tree will bring forth corrupt fruit. If a man is inwardly corrupt, he will bring forth corrupt works (behavior). Corrupt fruit can be harmful or detrimental to those who eat it. In like fashion, when Adam rebelled, his seed (gene pool or spiritual DNA) became corrupt and so did his offspring. When Adam's corrupt offspring began to build a system of sexual idolatry (corrupt worship) to please their corrupt nature, the result was cultural, social and global ruin.

> *And GOD saw that the wickedness of man was great in the earth, and that every imagination of the thoughts of his heart was only evil continually. And the LORD said, I will destroy man whom I have created from the face of the earth; both man, and beast, and the creeping thing, and the fowls of the air; for it repenteth me that I have made them.*
>
> Genesis 6:5,7

Fallen man's corrupt nature led him to construct a corrupt system of worship. This worship system laid the spiritual foundation for the corrupt, worldly philosophies that would eventually come forth (e.g. "If it feels good do it;" "Pleasure is the ultimate good in life," etc.). These worldly, hedonistic philosophies generated behaviors, attitudes and actions that were hostile to God and His nature.

When behavior is sinful (corrupt), certain spiritual laws are set in motion that lead to the judgment of God upon the sinner. Sinful behavior will always set God's judgment into motion.

> *Marriage is honourable in all, and the bed undefiled: but whoremongers and adulterers God will judge.*
>
> Hebrews 13:4

CIRCUMCISION

The primary objective in calling Abraham was to raise up a righteous gene pool. Through this seed, the "Restorer" would be revealed. There are many Scriptures that point to the importance of the "seed" (righteous gene pool). Once God established a righteous gene pool within Abraham's offspring, He placed a strict moral code on them. They were to maintain their sexual purity and separate identity from the world at large. The hallmark of this relationship was a surgical procedure known as *circumcision*, the removal of the foreskin of the penis.

For the Hebrew, circumcision was a necessary symbol of identification with Jehovah God. This act "marked" the male Jew as God's property; it sanctified his sexuality as belonging to God. Circumcision was symbolic of Jehovah's sovereignty over the male Jew's sex drive. From a logical standpoint, God could have cut Abraham anywhere on his body. Why Abraham's penis? As we all know, God never does anything just for the sake of doing it. There is a purpose and plan in every act that He performs. In a world wholly given to sexual idolatry and sexual sin, God was in need of a sexually sanctified people through whom the "Restorer" would eventually come.

For this plan to succeed, Abraham had to submit his sex drive to the dictates of God's will. Abraham had to agree to let Jehovah become personally involved in his sex life. In so doing, God could orchestrate the unfolding of history through Abraham's righteous gene pool (seed). We see then that circumcision was a highly symbolic act performed to keep both the natural and spiritual "gene pool" from spiritual defilement (corruption). It is important to note that a covenant relationship with God begins at the level of your sexuality.[5]

As I read the Old Testament, two things are impressed upon me:

1. The importance of living sexually pure (living in accordance with the laws God established to govern our sexuality).
2. The spiritual warfare that surrounded establishing and maintaining a righteous gene pool (seed).

Godly sexual relations conducted within biblical guidelines were established to aid in the propagation and development of a righteous gene pool. When we examine the Old Testament, we can see God placing strong emphasis on holiness (sexual purity), sanctification and separation of His chosen people. Why was this so? Is God a segregationist? Absolutely not! God never endorsed separation based on skin color or ethnicity (Moses was married to an Ethiopian woman; see Numbers 12:1). God's separatist laws must be viewed in the spiritual context of His overall plan, strategy and purpose for fallen mankind. Sexual purity and separation was necessary for the propagation of a righteous gene pool, a gene pool through which He could:

1. Reveal Himself.
2. Manifest Himself.
3. Reproduce Himself.

In Old Testament culture, genealogies, (family bloodlines) were traced through the father (Abraham beget Isaac, Isaac beget Jacob, etc.). Through scientific advancement, we now know that this cultural practice has a biologic basis. The presence of the Y chromosome (gene) determines that a child will be born male as opposed to being born female. The Y chromosome is only inherited from the father and, unlike other genes, can be passed down from generation to generation unchanged and unaltered.[6] Mankind's history can be traced through the DNA (genes). Specifically, the Y gene contains important historical information . By examining the Y gene, one can trace back a man's male ancestry for centuries.[7] This is precisely how it was shown that President Thomas Jefferson likely fathered at least one son by his female slave, Sally Hemings.[8] By analyzing their Y chromosome, it has been reported that members of a Jewish priesthood have traced their ancestry back 3,300 years to Aaron, Moses' older brother.[9] This is just one example of how biblical truth and biological fact agree.

Genes not only contain information about one's past, genes also contain information about one's present. For example, the presence of certain genes can predict whether a person will have certain health problems. Sickle cell anemia and cystic fibrosis are two disorders that can be traced to genetic disorders.[10] What do our genes tell us about our future? Could it be that within the genome (DNA) of each person God has encoded the details of our *origin, purpose* and *destiny*?

Having been created in the "image of God," mankind carries and transfers this image within his DNA (Romans 1:19). Every living person is a living testimony of God's power, grace and mercy. As we shall later see, sin has distorted that image.

THE BIRTHRIGHT

In studying the lineage of Jesus Christ, one can detect evidence of the "righteous" traits that were necessary to qualify a person as a forefather of the Messiah. After the Flood, this righteous lineage began with Abraham. In a sense, Abraham can be viewed as the beginning of the *righteous gene pool* (RGP). For our purposes, we will define a gene pool as all the genes (DNA) of all the individuals within a family line. A righteous gene pool, then consists of all of the righteous (godly) elements that exist within the bloodline of a defined group of people. Abraham was the "father of the faithful." Through his seed the Messiah was revealed to the world in the person of Jesus Christ. The Messiah could only be revealed through a righteous seed. Abraham was chosen as the father of the RGP because God saw righteous elements within Abraham—elements that qualified him to be the forefather of Messiah.

The Old Testament refers to the means of the Messianic inheritance as the "birthright." In Bible times, the birthright was the right, privilege, or possession to which a person, especially the firstborn son, was legally entitled to. In Israel, the firstborn son enjoyed a favored position. His birthright included a double portion of his father's assets upon the father's death (Deuteronomy 21:17). Part of the firstborn's benefits were a special blessing from the father and the privilege of leadership of the family (Genesis 43:33).[11] The birthright tradition was initiated in Abraham and was continued through Isaac. It was rejected by Esau and opportunistically seized by Jacob. When Reuben lost it, Joseph and Judah attained it (1 Chronicles 5:1,2).

From a political and governmental standpoint, King David embodied the Messianic promise, for his kingdom was to be "established forever." It appears that King Saul, the first king of Israel, had the opportunity of being in the spiritual lineage of the Messianic inheritance, but he was rejected due to his disobedience and rebellion. Consider the following Scriptures:

> *And Samuel said to Saul, Thou hast done foolishly: thou hast not kept the commandment of the LORD thy God, which he commanded thee: for now would the LORD have established thy kingdom upon Israel forever. But now thy kingdom shall not continue: the LORD hath sought him a man after his own heart, and the LORD hath commanded him to be captain over his people, because thou hast not kept that which the LORD commanded thee.*
>
> 1 Samuel 13:13,14

> *And when he heard that it was Jesus of Nazareth, he began to cry out, and say, Jesus, thou* Son of David, *have mercy on me. And many charged him that he should hold his peace: but he cried the more a great deal, Thou* Son of David, *have mercy on me.*
>
> Mark 10:47,48 (emphasis added)

The passage in 1 Samuel 13 helps us understand the nature of the RGP. The presence of a RGP is manifest, in part, by one's willingness to: choose obedience to the Word of God, accept and obey God's revealed truth and submit to the will of God.

In 1 Samuel 13 God rejects King Saul because of his disobedience. Saul's rebellion greatly undermined his destiny. In Mark chapter 10, blind Bartimeus appeals to Jesus for help. In doing so,

Bartimeus addresses Jesus as the "Son of David." This title has messianic implications. By using this title, Bartimeus caught Jesus' attention and received a miracle of healing. The issue I want to raise here relates to King Saul's tragic destiny, and how it may have been different from what he experienced.

I would like to ask a theoretical question. If King Saul had chosen obedience to God's will as opposed to rebellion, is it possible that blind Bartimeus (about one thousand years later) might have been saying: "Jesus thou son of Saul, have mercy on me"? Even though Saul was not of Judah's lineage, the prophetic word spoken to Saul by the prophet Samuel appears to have messianic overtones.

> ... "for now would the Lord have established thy kingdom upon Israel forever."
>
> 1 Samuel 13:13e

I pose this theoretical question to highlight the importance of choosing righteousness, obedience and submission to God as opposed to choosing evil, wickedness and rebellion. The present day choices that we make will ultimately affect our position in history. Like King Saul, most people don't consider the *long-term* consequences of their sin and rebellion.

Reuben: Birthright Lost

As one studies the life of Joseph, one can see a spiritual conflict unfolding. This conflict is directly related to the birthright that God established as the means of revealing Himself to the world through the Jewish people. Joseph ultimately endured the suffering that often comes with the birthright. As a result, he also experienced the blessing that comes as a result of obedience to the God of the birthright. Judah, his older brother, also prevailed and attained a portion of the spiritual inheritance of the birthright (1 Chronicles 5:1,2). This included the privilege of having the Messiah born with his tribal name. Jesus was referred to as the Lion of the "tribe of Judah."

The fact that Joseph and Judah attained such high honor was made possible by the failure of Reuben, Jacob's first-born son (1 Chronicles 5:1,2). From a legal standpoint, the first-born male had special privileges and responsibilities. These included:

1. A double portion of his father's earthly goods.
2. Becoming head of the family upon the death of the father.
3. Exercising considerable authority over other family members.

> *Reuben, thou art my firstborn, my might, and the begin-
> ning of my strength, the excellency of dignity, and the excel-
> lency of power: Unstable as water, thou shalt not excel;
> because thou wentest up to thy father's bed; then defiledst
> thou it: he went up to my couch.*
>
> Genesis 49:3,4 (emphasis added)

> *Now the sons of Reuben the firstborn of Israel, (for he was
> the firstborn; but, forasmuch as he defiled his father's bed,
> his birthright was given unto the sons of Joseph the son of
> Israel: and the genealogy is not to be reckoned after the
> birthright. For Judah prevailed above his brethren, and of
> him came the chief ruler; but the birthright was Joseph's.*
>
> 1 Chronicles 5:1,2 (emphasis added)

The key point that I want to make here is that Reuben lost his opportunity to receive the birthright and its associated blessings because of *sexual sin*. This is an important spiritual lesson! Sexual sin can disqualify an individual from certain spiritual blessings and privileges.

CORRUPTION OF THE GENE POOL

Sexual sin has a corrupting effect upon humanity. This corruption goes deeper than the eye can see.

> *Flee fornication. Every sin that a man doeth is* without *the
> body; but he that committeth fornication sinneth* against *his own body.*
>
> 1 Corinthians 6:18 (emphasis added)

Sexual sin (fornication) is unique from all other sins. The word "against" in the context of this Scripture means "into" or "within." No other sin penetrates "*into*" the depths of our being like sexual sin.

Sexual sin penetrates and affects us at the core of our being in ways we don't fully understand. *Wickedness and sin can penetrate to the level of our DNA (spiritual and natural) and exert an effect upon future generations in profound ways.* I will scripturally support this point of view later.

In the case of Noah, he "found" grace in the sight of God. The fact that Noah found grace seems to imply that he dedicated himself to searching for God's grace. I believe that Noah engaged in activities and behaviors that placed him in God's favor. Noah was a rare find in a corrupt generation completely given over to sexual idolatry.

> *But with thee will I establish my covenant; and thou shalt come into the ark, thou, and thy sons, and thy wife, and thy sons' wives with thee.*
>
> Genesis 6:18

Noah and his family clan may have been the only people of that generation who were:

1. Abiding by Genesis 2:24.
2. Not given to sexual idolatry.
3. Practicing monogamy.

The Scripture states that all flesh, except Noah, had corrupted his way. The speed and thoroughness in which sexual idolatry had disrupted the social order was phenomenal. In less than two or three generations, the social destruction was complete. It is a testimony to the devastating effects that sexual sin can have upon a culture and society. When the 60's Sexual Revolution began, there were three or four commonly reported Sexually Transmitted Diseases. Thirty years later—approximately one generation later—there are more than thirty known pathogens that are sexually transmitted.[12] Some of these pathogens are incurable (e.g., genital warts, genital herpes, human papilloma virus, Hepatitis B and AIDS). Sociologists are now pointing to the rise in violent crime, child poverty, teen pregnancy, divorce rate and the breakdown of the traditional family as being directly related to the Sexual Revolution of the 1960's.[13]

Marriage: God's Way

God has a vested interest in who you have sex with and how you go about having sex, that is why He instituted covenant marriage. We must remember that *copulation* establishes *population*. Populations shape historical events. *Whom you copulate with, and the circumstances surrounding that copulation, matters to God!* God did not want unrestricted, unbridled sexual passion to be unleashed in the earth.

God knew, based on how *He* designed sex, that if men and women did not have restraints placed upon their sex drive, fallen humanity would begin to worship sex and become controlled by it.[14]

DNA

And God said, Let the earth bring forth the living creature after his kind cattle, and creeping thing, and beast of the earth after his kind: and it was so.

Genesis 1:24

In 1953, American biochemist James Watson and British biophysicist Francis Crick announced their discovery of the "double helix" structure of DNA. They had discovered the molecule that carried the genetic information that is passed on from one generation to the next. Basically, DNA is a chemical molecule that contains codes for all of the biological information about an individual. DNA codes the information that will determine one's eye color, skin color, hair color, hair texture etc.

DNA determines every biological trait of a person. Every cell in the human body (except red blood cells) contains a copy of the same DNA. DNA makes up the chemical molecules that form genes. These genes contain the blueprint (instructions) that will determine all of the physical and biological characteristics mentioned earlier.[15] A gene is merely a portion of DNA. DNA has been referred to as the master molecule because it contains the blueprint of life. The word "*gene*ration" makes reference of the genetic information (DNA) that is transferred from the parent to child.

One very important principle in the Bible is that living creatures will reproduce after their own kind. You and I, as sexual creatures, will bring forth offspring of like genetic make up. As spiritual entities, we will also reproduce offspring that has our spiritual DNA.

This principle is clear throughout Scripture; both *spiritual* and *natural* traits are passed on from one generation to the next (see Genesis 18:19). Even as genes pass on our physical traits to our offspring in the natural, there is a type of spiritual DNA that can pass on spiritual traits and our spiritual heritage from generation to generation. The apostle Paul makes a distinction between those who are Abraham's natural seed and his spiritual seed (see Romans 4 and Galatians 4).

In humans, the passage of genes (DNA) from one generation to the next takes place primarily through heterosexual intercourse. The sexual covenants that we enter will result in the transference of certain information that will impact our offspring in profound ways. We should be very careful about the sexual covenants that we choose to enter because sexual covenants are *spiritual covenants*.[16] Spiritual covenants extend beyond the life of those who initiated them and can affect future generations.

> *Keeping mercy for thousands, forgiving iniquity and transgression and sin, and that will by no means clear the guilty; visiting the iniquity of the* fathers *upon the children, and upon the children's children, unto the third and to the fourth generation.*
>
> Exodus 34:7 (emphasis added)

> *And God said unto Abraham, Thou shalt keep my covenant therefore, thou, and thy seed after thee in their generations. This is my covenant, which ye shall keep, between me and you and thy seed after thee; Every man child among you shall be circumcised.*
>
> Genesis 17:9,10 (emphasis added)

In Exodus 34:7, we see that iniquity (ungodly covenants) is extended beyond the generation of those who initiated them. In Genesis 17:9,10, we see that godly covenants are also extended beyond the generation of the initiator. It is a fact (biological and spiritual) that sexual covenants will affect our offspring. In medical terms, there are certain disease conditions that are passed on from parent to child via the DNA (genes). There are approximately ten thousand disorders that are inherited as the result of one "bad" (mutant) gene.[17] There are approximately fifty to one hundred thousand genes in the human genome,[18] and one bad gene can cause serious health problems.

There are single gene (DNA) disorders that pose major health problems; for example, sickle cell anemia affects one in every 400 African Americans, and cystic fibrosis affects one in every 2000 White Americans.[19] In the natural, we know that certain disease conditions are passed on through the genes (DNA). But what about spiritually? What about those traits that are spiritually inherited? What is the biblical evidence for the existence of spiritual DNA?

> *Wherefore, as by one man sin entered into the world, and death by sin; and so death passed upon all men, for that all have sinned:*
>
> Romans 5:12 (emphasis added)

When Adam rebelled, something took place within his body. We know this to be a fact because on the day that he rebelled, his physical body began to decay (grow old) until he eventually died. There was another, unseen effect, that sin had upon Adam, but it did not manifest itself until the next generation when Adam's son Cain murdered his brother Abel. Not only had Adam passed on his physical nature to his offspring, but he had also passed on his fallen *sin nature* to his offspring. This is precisely what the Bible teaches. We are all sinners (have the sin nature) as a result of who our father was. It was passed on to us. The word "pass" used in Romans 5:12 means to "travel" or "walk through." Since the Garden of Eden, the sin nature has *traveled* down the Adamic gene pool (DNA). The corruption of Adam's gene pool was magnified and accelerated when sexual idolatry became rampant in the earth as outlined in Genesis 6.

Spiritual DNA

God found righteous elements within Noah's spiritual gene pool (DNA). This was evident by Noah's obedience to God's command to build the ark, a project that took about 120 years. Noah walked with God. This was also an outward sign that he had spiritual genes containing righteous elements. The fact that Noah could hear the voice of God and respond to that voice in strict obedience, is evidence of the righteous elements that existed within Noah's spiritual DNA. Even though Noah was a sinner, he chose to walk with a righteous God. He made righteous choices. Apparently, right choices (righteousness) can somehow effect our spiritual DNA in ways that we don't fully understand.

> *And as I may so say, Levi also, who receiveth tithes, payed tithes in Abraham. For he was yet in the* loins *of his father, when Melchisedec met him.*
>
> Hebrews 7:9,10 (emphasis added)

This passage of Scripture makes reference to the incident recorded in Genesis 14 in which Abraham gave tithes to Melchisedec, king of Salem. The important point to note here is the effect that Abraham's *action* had upon Levi, who was not yet born. This righteous covenant that Abraham entered affected the future generations that were still in his loins. Indeed, covenants, be they righteous or wicked, can affect those who are still in our loins. How does this happen? How can decisions that we make affect our offspring generations from now? The answer lies in one's spiritual DNA. It is the existence of spiritual DNA that transfers the effects—good or bad—of spiritual covenants from one generation to the next. Let me illustrate this using a chart.

Spiritual DNA in the loins of Abraham transferred to Levi's generation.

Abraham	Isaac	Jacob	Levi

1st Generation	2nd Generation	3rd Generation	4th Generation

The spiritual covenant that Abraham entered was still in effect long after his death. Scripture states that Levi paid tithes while he was yet in the "loins" of Abraham. In Volume 1 we discuss how a man enters sexual covenants with his penis. The testicles, which contain future generations, "witness" these covenants and are thus affected by the sexual covenants that their fathers entered.[20]

The covenant that Abraham entered into with Melchisedec was still functional after four generations.[21] This generational blessing highlights the importance of entering righteous covenants for the sake of future generations. In this case, the (righteous) spiritual activity of the great-grandfather (Abraham) was enough to justify God blessing the great-grandson (Levi).

It works pretty much the same way with unrighteous covenants. They are generationally transferred as well. Whether we realize it or not, we pass on a biological and spiritual heritage to our offspring. It is so important that we do right, talk right, walk right, live right, think right and be right! Abraham believed God, and it was counted to him as righteousness. The effect that this had upon his seed was eternal in scope.

A Gay Gene?

A National Institutes of Health study, authored by Dean Hamer, reported the existence of a genetic marker that predisposed people to homosexual behavior, essentially a "gay gene."[22] This was good news to gay activists because they believed that scientific evidence of a gay gene would mean social acceptance of homosexual behavior. Shortly after the publishing of this paper, it was revealed that Hamer was a homosexual activist with an agenda of his own. Hamer's research was found to be flawed in both its methodology and basic assumptions. It was later shown that many of the gay men in Hamer's study did *not* have the gene that he said was linked to gay behavior.[23] There is *no evidence* that proves the existence of a gay gene. Why? Because there is *no gay gene!*

Genes have a function. They function to instruct special mechanisms within the cell to produce a specific protein.[24] Some proteins help determine what activities will take place within the body. Sex hormones are proteins.

The basic concept is this: A specific testosterone gene will orchestrate the production of a specific testosterone protein. Testosterone is involved in creating the desire or urge to engage in sexual intimacy (libido). In this case, a specific gene led to the formation of a specific protein (hormone) which is designed to affect the way we feel or function.

That's essentially *all* the gene does. It provides the blueprint and gives instructions to make a specific protein. The protein may affect the way you feel, but the *decision* to *act* upon those feelings are a function of your *will*. It has nothing to do with a gene. Genes may make the protein that gives you the urge to have sex, but the gene does not *make* you engage in sex. The gene does not make you go to a motel, pull off your clothes and get in bed with another person!

Genes do not produce decisions, they produce proteins. The decision as to who you get in bed with or what hotel you may go to is your *choice*. The gene does not make the choice of who you have sex with, where you have sex, when you have sex, or how you have sex. These choices are manifestations of your *free will*. How you choose to use the testosterone, produced by the gene, is up to you. You may choose to have sex with a woman, man, boy, girl, horse, or a cow. (Disclaimer: I am not advocating sex with minors or animals, it is both illegal and immoral). You may even choose *not* to have sex at all! There is *no* homosexual gene, *no* bisexual gene, *no* pedophilia gene, *no* bestiality gene, *no* sadomasochist gene, *no* necrophilia gene, *no* lesbian gene, *no* incest gene, *no* adultery gene, *no* masturbation gene, *no* transvestite gene and *no* kinky freak sex gene!

What does exist is a gene that either makes you male or female. The gene that determines if you are male is the Y chromosome, and the gene that determines if you are female is the X chromosome.

Male *and* female *created He them.*
Genesis 1:27 (emphasis added)

Genes do *not* produce homosexual behavior—or heterosexual behavior for that matter. *Behavior is a function of a free will that exercises the power of choice.* The gene may produce the hormone that may make you feel like "doing it," but if you are in right relationship with the God of the Bible, you will choose to "do it" the biblical way—within the confines of covenant marriage. There is *no* gay gene!

FAMILY SEXUAL PERVERSIONS

Unrighteous covenants produce generational curses that run through family bloodlines. I have seen families where all of the men were either on drugs or were alcoholics. I have seen other situations where most of the family was in prison or had past criminal records. These are typical manifestations of generational curses.

Some families have various sexual perversions that are prevalent from generation to generation. This is a manifestation of a generational curse. One of the most devastating events that has been responsible for the propagation of ungodly sexual covenants was the so-called Sexual Revolution of the 1960's. Ungodly sexual covenants that were forged decades ago still affect people in profound ways today.

> *When* Judah *saw her, he thought her to be an* harlot; *because she had covered her face. And he turned unto her by the way, and said, Go to, I pray thee, let me come in unto thee; (for he knew not that she was his* daughter in law.*) And she said, What wilt thou give me, that thou mayest come in unto me? And he said, I will send thee a kid from the flock. And she said, Wilt thou give me a pledge, till thou send it? And he said, What pledge shall I give thee? And she said, Thy* signet, *and thy* bracelets, *and thy* staff *that is in thine hand. And he gave it her, and came in unto her, and she* conceived *by him.*
>
> Genesis 38:15-18 (emphasis added)

Genesis 38 gives the account of Judah and his illicit sexual affair with Tamar. I just want to highlight several important items. Tamar was Judah's daughter-in-law; therefore, this was an illegal and unlawful act of incest. It is also important to note the three items that Judah surrendered to Tamar in exchange for sex.

1. His signet (family ring): These were symbols of *authority* and were often used in the transacting of business.

2. His bracelets: Bracelets were worn as symbols of *identity*, and they often had the family name engraved on them.
3. His staff: The symbol of spiritual guidance and *protection*.

Here we see that sexual sin robs a person of: their God-given authority, as symbolized by the signet (ring); their identity, as symbolized by the bracelet; and their protection (safety) or spiritual covering.[25]

I'm using the example of Judah to illustrate how past sexual sins (unrighteous covenants), such as this case of incest, can creep into the family bloodline and affect one's descendants. Note what happens ten generations later during the reign of King David, a descendent of Judah:

• David commits adultery with Bathsheba (2 Samuel 11:4).
• David's son Amnon rapes his sister (2 Samuel 13:14).
• David's son Absalom sleeps with David's wives (2 Samuel 16:22).
• David's son Adonijah seeks to marry one of his father's wives (1 Kings 2:17).

The last three of these examples speak of incestuous relations, that is, sexual relations between close family members. Among the most common forms of incest are sexual relationships between brothers and sisters and fathers and daughters. Here are some factors that may contribute to incestuous relationships:[26]

1. Crowded living conditions.
2. Low moral standards.
3. Personality maladjustment in an adult.
4. Adolescent curiosity.

DORMANT SINS ACTIVATED

We see here that this incestuous curse resurfaces in the eleventh generation of Judah's lineage. This is not a coincidence. David's sin with Bathsheba seems to have activated that incestuous curse (spirit) that was dormant (asleep) within his family bloodline. This curse was initiated in the days (loins) of Judah. This highlights the fact that ungodly covenants, initiated by foreparents, can have a deep and profound impact on future offspring. It also points to the importance of fathers in activating certain curses that are dormant in their family bloodlines. This is a key point. The Bible presents fathers as both *activators* and *initiators* of certain curses and/or blessings that are resident within family bloodlines. We saw this principle with the illustration of Abraham and Levi.

There are dormant sins in each of our family histories that are waiting to be activated. In the old "Count Dracula" movies, the ashes of the count would lay dormant and harmless in his coffin. The ashes would be "activated" when blood was poured on them. At this point, Dracula would be "resurrected" and begin his murderous rampage. I use this example only to illustrate that there are dormant sins within family lines that are activated when parents engage in certain ungodly covenants.

How we conduct our sex life is extremely important. Dormant sins of the past can be reactivated through sexual sin.

Generational curses that are present because of past ungodly covenants must be dealt with. If these ungodly sexual covenants are not broken, Satan may use these hidden covenants to ensnare our children and our children's children, from generation to generation.

Ungodly Sexual Covenants

Thus were both the daughters of Lot with child by their father. And the first born bare a son, and called his name Moab: *the same is the father of the* Moabites *unto this day. And the younger, she also bare a son, and called his name* Benammi: *the same is the father of the children of* Ammon *unto this day.*

Genesis 19:36-38 (emphasis added)

As a result of these incestuous sexual unions, two children were born to the daughters of Lot: Moab and Benammi. As Scripture indicates, they became the progenitors of the Moabite and Ammonite peoples. The Moabite people were a people given to sexual idolatry. Their favorite deity was Baalpeor.[27] As you may recall, it was the Moabite women who infiltrated the Israeli camp as they dwelt at Shittim and introduced them to the sexual idolatry of Baalpeor. This sin brought a curse on Israel and twenty-four thousand people died in one day. The Ammonite people, Lot's seed through his younger daughter, are believed to have started the worship of Molech. Molech was worshiped by sacrificing young children on altars of fire.

Here again we can see the effect of ungodly sexual covenants upon the offspring. In this case, the Ammonite and Moabite people were affected and infected with the sexual idolatry (incest) of their parents.

DNA: The Blueprint of Life.

Before a house can be built, the builder needs a "blueprint" (plan) detailing the specifications of that house. The blueprint will determine what the house will ultimately look like. It is the responsibility of the "architect" to fashion the blueprints and give them to the builder. In this simple analogy, God, as man's creation, is the "architect" and "builder." The DNA is the "blueprint" that God uses to build.

*The human body contains about 75 trillion cells. Inside most cells is a nucleus that contains a complete set of the body's **blueprints**. Those blueprints are compacted into 46 packets called **chromosomes**. 23 **chromosomes** are inherited from the father and 23 **chromosomes** are inherited from the mother. When these chromosomes are united they make up the 46 chromosomes in the typical human cell.*

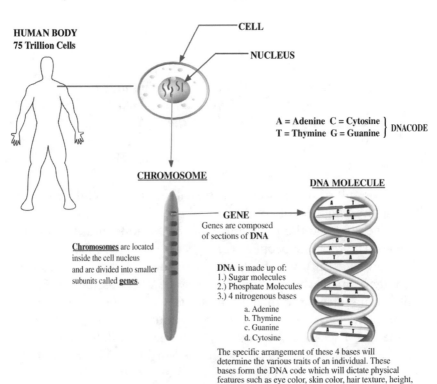

HUMAN BODY
75 Trillion Cells

CELL

NUCLEUS

A = Adenine C = Cytosine
T = Thymine G = Guanine } DNA CODE

CHROMOSOME

DNA MOLECULE

GENE
Genes are composed
of sections of **DNA**

Chromosomes are located
inside the cell nucleus
and are divided into smaller
subunits called genes.

DNA is made up of:
1.) Sugar molecules
2.) Phosphate Molecules
3.) 4 nitrogenous bases

a. Adenine
b. Thymine
c. Guanine
d. Cytosine

The specific arrangement of these 4 bases will
determine the various traits of an individual. These
bases form the DNA code which will dictate physical
features such as eye color, skin color, hair texture, height,
etc...

Human Genome Project

The human genetic pattern is a biologic map of three billion pairs of chemicals that make up the DNA in each human cell. These four chemical pairs are thymine-adenine and guanine-cytosine. These chemical pairs are arranged in specific ways to create about one hundred thousand human genes. These genes form the actual blueprint for the production and assembly of proteins, which, in turn, determine the formation and the function of the cells and organs within the body.

The Human Genome Project is an international scientific collaboration that began decoding the genes about ten years ago. The goal is to gain a basic understanding of the entire genetic blueprint of a human being. This genetic information is found in each cell of the body, encoded in the chemical deoxyribonucleic acid (DNA). The project is intended to:

1. Identify all the genes in the nucleus of a human cell.
2. Establish, by a process known as mapping, where those genes are located on the chromosomes in the nucleus.
3. Determine, by a process known as sequencing, the genetic information encoded by the order of the DNA's chemical subunits.

In the year 2000, it is estimated that molecular biologists will complete the first draft of the sequence of the entire human genome.[28] With the completion of this project, mankind will, in theory, be able to manipulate and control his own biologic destiny.

A Corrupt Gene Pool

And God looked upon the earth, and, behold, it was corrupt; for all flesh had corrupted his way upon the earth.

Genesis 6:12

The Hebrew word for corrupt is *shachath* (7843), meaning "ruin." When something is ruined, it is in a fallen state. It is the irreparable damage or destruction that has come upon a thing. Ruin implies decay and disintegration from inside out. Such was the case of fallen man. His rebellion had led to complete corruption. This corruption affected him spiritually, mentally and physically. We know this to be the case because:

> GOD saw that the wickedness of man was great in the earth, and that every imagination of the thoughts of his heart was only evil continually.
>
> Genesis 6:5

Fallen man's flesh was affected. Every cell of his being had been infected, even down to the level of his DNA (gene pool). In the beginning, every cell inside Adam's body was programmed to live forever. When sin corrupted his flesh, his cells began to decay until physical death occurred.

> For dust thou art, and unto dust shalt thou return.
>
> Genesis 3:19

When Adam's flesh was corrupted, his DNA (genetic material) was corrupted. This meant that the corruption could be passed on to each succeeding generation. The sin nature (Adamic nature) would be passed on within the physical and spiritual DNA.

> Wherefore, as by one man sin entered into the world, and death by sin; and so death passed upon all men, for that all have sinned.
>
> Romans 5:12

Note how sin entered the world, or the "inhabitants" of the world. It (sin) entered Adam's body first and was then transferred to those in his loins. It was transferred to his children (offspring) via the process of sexual reproduction. We know this is true because sin reveals itself in the form of death, and all men will eventually die, no exceptions.

SPIRITUAL DNA

Adam's corrupt nature infects and affects all of his children. When the Bible speaks of the (corrupt) Adamic nature, it is referring to both his *physical* and *spiritual* nature. We, Adam's offspring, inherited both his corrupt physical and spiritual nature. Remember, Adam is more than a physical being, he is also a spiritual being. How did we inherit Adam's physical nature? Through his physical DNA. How did we inherit Adam's spiritual nature? Through his spiritual DNA.

> *For as by one man's disobedience many were made sinners...*
>
> Romans 5:19a

Physical DNA is involved in the transfer of physical traits from parent to offspring. Spiritual DNA is involved with the transfer of spiritual traits from parent to offspring. They are different in that one is natural and the other is spiritual. Jesus makes an interesting point in His conversation with Nicodemus:

> *That which is born of the flesh is flesh; and that which is born of the Spirit is spirit.*
>
> John 3:6

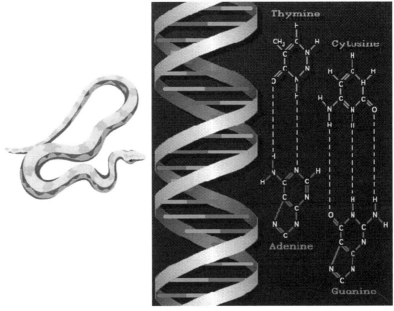

DNA Molecule

This passage from John illustrates the following:

1. There are at least two separate elements of human nature.
2. There are things that are conceived in the one's physical nature.
3. There are things that are conceived in one's spiritual nature (spiritual DNA).

You can be transformed from a "child of darkness" to a "child of light," from a "son of the devil" to a "son of God."
Note:

1. Righteousness has an affect upon our offspring.
2. Righteousness permeates the gene pool of the upright.
3. Righteousness can be transferred from one generation to the next.

> *But the* seed *of the* righteous *shall be delivered.*
>
> Proverbs 11:21b (emphasis added)

> *His* seed *shall be mighty upon earth: the* generation *of the* upright *shall be blessed.*
>
> Psalms 112:2 (emphasis added)

THE LAW OF REGENERATION[29]

In Volume 1 I made reference to what I called the Law of Regeneration. The word "regeneration" occurs twice in the Bible—in Matthew 19:28 and Titus 3:5—and is composed of two Greek words. They are *palin* (3825), meaning to "renew again," and *genesis* (1078), meaning "nativity" or "nature." Together, these Greek words create *paliggenesia* (3824), that is, regeneration.

In Scripture, regeneration speaks of attaining a new spiritual nature (life). It is the inward transformation that causes a complete revolution of the individual from inside out. Regeneration is an important aspect of the gospel message. As children of Adam, we are alienated from the life of God (Ephesians 4:18). We are alienated from God and have a corrupt nature. The type of spiritual transformation that the Bible speaks of represents a "rebirth" or being "born again."

Jesus answered and said unto him, Verily, verily, I say unto thee, Except a man be born again, he cannot see the kingdom of God.

John 3:3 (emphasis added)

Our first birth represents all that we are in Adam. At birth, we each begin to outwardly express the genes that we received from our parents at conception. Having been born in Adam, we have all been conceived in sin (Psalms 51:5) and have inherited his fallen nature. We have inherited Adam's "spiritual DNA." In that sense, we have inherited a "bad set" of spiritual genes. In regeneration, a miracle takes place. The born-again believer receives a new set of spiritual genes. This is the essence of regeneration; through the power of God, an individual is "re-gened." This means that:

1. We have a new spiritual nature.
2. We have a new spiritual life (Romans 6:4).
3. We have a new spiritual father (John 1:12).

The born-again, transformed and regenerated individual comes forth with a new set of "spiritual genes" that have been inherited from the heavenly Father. Note what the apostle John states:

For whatsoever is born of God overcometh the world: and this is the victory that overcometh the world, even our faith.

1 John 5:4 (emphasis added)

The word "born" as used here is *gennao* (1080), and it means "to procreate, beget, conceive, or gender." It also makes reference to the supernatural regenerative process wrought in the born-again believer by the Holy Spirit. This inward transformation brings about an outward transformation in one's lifestyle, actions and attitudes (2 Corinthians 5:17). It is important to note that re-*gene*ing is a spiritual transformation that goes beyond behavioral reformation.

But as many as received him, to them gave he power to become the sons of God, even to them that believe on his name.

John 1:12

Chapter Summary

1. DNA (genetic material) is the means whereby specific physical traits are transmitted to the next generation. There is biblical evidence of the existence of "spiritual" DNA whereby spiritual traits and covenants are transferred to the next generation.

2. Fallen man's corrupted state was made worse by widespread sexual idolatry that produced offspring who were:
   a. Alienated from God.
   b. Unwilling to commune with God.
   c. Unable to prepare the next generation for God's redemptive plan.

3. The great Flood was precipitated by widespread sexual idolatry that had a corrupting influence on man's natural and spiritual gene pool (DNA) and society at large.

4. Noah walked with God and did righteous deeds. He found grace and favor with God and as a result:
   a. His spiritual gene pool (DNA) was chosen by God to save humanity.
   b. He built an ark and saved himself and his family from destruction.
   c. He was able to preserve and transfer God's redemptive plan to future generations.

5. God shapes history and future events through the sex act. Therefore God has a vested interest in how, when and where people engage in sexual intercourse.

6. Marriage was instituted so that:
   a. God could exert His divine influence upon the shaping of future events.
   b. A righteous gene pool could be reestablished in the earth.
   c. Fallen man's sex drive could be properly regulated.

7. Sexual idolatry is fallen man's attempt to shape his own destiny and future, apart from God.

8. A man's "seed" contains the genetic information (DNA) that will be passed on to the next generation. The Bible places special importance on the seed and its role in the fulfillment of God's divine plan.

9. Abraham's seed was to be the means whereby the whole world would be blessed. Abraham had both a natural and a spiritual seed (Romans 9:4-8).
10. It appears that righteous behavior, words and actions have an effect upon the individual's spiritual DNA.
11. By means of the spiritual DNA, both righteous and unrighteous covenants can be passed on to future generations.
12. There are dormant iniquities that reside in family bloodlines that can be activated when people choose to commit sin.
13. The Law of Regeneration makes provision for fallen mankind to be spiritually re-gened through the born-again experience. Regeneration grants the sinner a:
   a. New life.
   b. New name.
   c. New father.
   d. New destiny.
   e. New spiritual DNA.

Chapter Three

THE JEZEBEL SPIRIT.
WHAT SHE REALLY WANTS

*Notwithstanding I have a few things against thee, because
thou sufferest that woman Jezebel, which calleth herself a
prophetess, to teach and to seduce my servants to commit
fornication, and to eat things sacrificed unto idols.*

Revelation 2:20

In Old Testament days, Jezebel was a symbol of witchcraft, sorcery,
satanic domination, manipulation, false worship and sexual idolatry. This chapter highlights the destructive affects that the "spirit of
Jezebel" had upon ancient Israel. Today, this same spirit is under-
mining the contemporary church. This chapter will explore the devastation that Jezebel can inflict upon an individual, a local church
and a society.

*And they went to bury her: but they found no more of her
than the skull, and the feet, and the palms of her hands.
Wherefore they came again, and told him. And he said,*

> *This is the word of the LORD, which he spake by his servant Elijah the Tishbite, saying, In the portion of Jezreel shall dogs eat the flesh of Jezebel: And the carcass of Jezebel shall be as dung upon the face of the field in the portion of Jezreel; so that they shall not say, This is Jezebel.*
>
> 2 Kings 9:35-37 (emphasis added)

Second Kings 9 records the death of a woman who was responsible for leading Israel into its darkest period of idolatry to date: Jezebel. Even in New Testament times her very name stood for all that was false, manipulative, detestable and destructive. Elijah, the prophet of God, prophesied her end: "Dogs shall eat the flesh of Jezebel." But as Scripture points out, she was not totally consumed. It is important to note that her *skull*, *feet* and *hands* were left behind. I want to focus your attention on what was *left* of her, because I believe it has spiritual significance and is relevant for the church today. Even though Jezebel may be physically dead, her "spirit" (skull) is still with us, her "mission" (feet) has not changed or diminished and her works (hands) remain. Every local church that has been ordained by God, sooner or later, must deal with the spirit of Jezebel. Who is Jezebel? What is her mission? What does she come to do? How does she affect the church today? In order to answer these questions, let us take a brief look at her life.

JEZEBEL: HER SPIRIT, MISSION AND WORKS

Jezebel came from Phoenicia, an ancient land northwest of Palestine on the eastern shore of the Mediterranean Sea. Phoenicians were known for their trade, commerce and skills as a seafaring people. Phoenicians were also known for Baal worship. Jezebel's father, Ethbaal, was a high priest of the temple of Astarte.[1] Astarte was the female goddess of sexual love. Ethbaal, whose name means "Baal is with him," later became king of Tyre and Sidon after murdering his brother and ascending to the throne.[2]

The Phoenician idolatrous system of worship was powerful indeed. In Ezekiel 28, the Bible symbolically associates the king of Tyre with Satan himself by referring to him as the "anointed cherub." This leads me to believe that Tyre was a major satanic stronghold and that the kings who ruled that city where under strong satanic control and influence.

Ethbaal raised and trained his daughter Jezebel in the ways of wickedness and satanic worship through occult Baalism. Under his tutelage, Jezebel became intimately familiar with the power of sexual idolatry, sorcery and witchcraft (2 Kings 9:22). Much like her father, Jezebel became a ruthless, reckless, cold-blooded tyrant. She was totally committed to propagating her father's religion. Her love and devotion for her religion made her intolerant to the point of destroying anyone who opposed her gods.

The first mention of Jezebel in Scripture is her marriage to Ahab, the eighth king of Israel. Truly, this was a match made in hell. Ahab's father was king Omri, of whom it was said:

> *But Omri wrought evil in the eyes of the LORD, and did worse than all that were before him.*
>
> 1 Kings 16:25

Omri was a weak, idolatrous king. Consequently, his son was also weak and uncommitted to the things of Jehovah God. As a matter of fact, Ahab was even weaker and more idolatrous than his father. It should be noted that weakness breeds weakness. Weak fathers breed weak sons.

> *And Ahab the son of Omri did evil in the sight of the LORD above all that were before him.*
>
> 1 Kings 16:30

Marrying Jezebel was probably an act of political expediency. These types of marriages were common and often took place to establish military and/or political alliances with other nations. Whatever the motivation may have been, in the marriage of Ahab to Jezebel we see *weakness* and *wickedness* united. When this happens the results can be devastating. In Israel's case, it proved to be very destructive.

IDOLATRY: UNITING BAAL AND ASTARTE

Jezebel went to work immediately. Using all of her skill, and with no resistance from Ahab, she established Baal worship on a grand scale. Not only was Baal (symbolized by the male penis) worshiped, but so was Astarte (symbolized by the female sexual element). Never before in Israel had there been an individual who had the will and the skill to unite these two sex deities on this scale. At her table sat 450 prophets dedicated to Baal and another 400 prophets dedicated to Astarte. These false, idolatrous prophets were all supported and financed by the state.

> *And he reared up an* altar for Baal *in the* house of Baal, *which he had built in Samaria. And Ahab made a* grove; *and Ahab did more to provoke the LORD God of Israel to anger than all the kings of Israel that were before him.*
>
> 1 Kings 16:32,33 (emphasis added)

Baalism replaced the worship of Jehovah as the official state religion. The true prophets of Jehovah were either slain or went into hiding. Look at what Ahab, under Jezebel's influence, did.

1. He reared up an altar for Baal, a place of public sacrifice. There is no doubt that this altar was a huge replica of the male organ that was deified and worshiped.[3]
2. He built a "house" for Baal. These so-called houses were places of sexual indulgence. In these "houses" one could engage in various forms of sexual sin. The prophets and priestesses of Baal were consecrated to this service. It is important to note that these were not just places of prostitution alone, but were places of worship and identification with the Baal deity.
3. He made a "grove," literally "ashera": a temple or area of worship where the female sexual element was deified and worshiped.
4. He allowed the persecution of the true prophets of Jehovah God.

In combining these two forces, Israel became the breeding ground for every type of abominable sexual sin practiced.

This is an important point because it highlights, in part, what the spirit of Jezebel has come to do, namely, to propagate sexual idolatry and all of those philosophies and movements that support sexual idolatry. The spirit of Jezebel (sexual idolatry) seeks to:

1. Influence the political arena.
2. Infect society with sexual immorality.
3. Influence the cultural climate.
4. Infiltrate and weaken the true church.

In contemporary America we can see the spirit of Jezebel at work.

- Recently, President Clinton was impeached as a result of the most publicized sex scandal in American history. As a result of this sex scandal, there appears to be more social tolerance for adulterous behavior.
- Since the Sexual Revolution of the 1960's, our culture has yielded to the philosophical notion that sexual sin and perversion is normal, acceptable and without meaningful consequences.
- The church has even been infiltrated and weakened by this Jezebelian spirit. Consider:
  a. Homosexual priests and pastors are being ordained in some denominations.
  b. Same sex couples are being married and sanctioned as biblical.
  c. Sex scandals have reached the highest echelons of national church leadership.
  d. Sexual scandal among pastors and local church leaders is rampant. Every year scores of church leaders succumb to sexual sin and have to resign.
  e. Gay and lesbian groups are quick to attack preachers and ministers who take a biblical stand against homosexuality as intolerant bigots who lack compassion.
  f. Many churches tacitly condone homosexuality by allowing openly gay individuals to function in important ministries (such as, ministers of music).
  g. An Episcopal church commission set up to study same sex unions has declined to take a stand on the issue.
  h. About three years ago, a state bishop of a large Pentecostal denomination publicly stated that there was

nothing wrong with young people engaging in "petting" (sexual touching). A pastor of that same denomination told me that he endorsed masturbation as an alternative to fornication.

   i. Some churches now view domestic partners ("shacking up") as equal to heterosexual marriage.

   j. A recent *Kansas City Star* article reports that Catholic priests may be contracting the AIDS virus at a rate four times that of the general population.[4]

This weakening that we see in the church is due to what I call *reverse evangelization*, that is, the world evangelizing the church. The church should be evangelizing the world, but now it appears that the reverse is happening. Many churches are becoming more "worldly," rather than the world becoming more "churchly."

As we move into the new millennium, I believe that the conflict surrounding sexual immorality will escalate. More and more we will see society pressuring the church to remain silent or become more tolerant and compassionate of the sexual preferences of others. Many churches will continue to succumb to the social, cultural and spiritual pressure to become politically correct. Even so, there will remain some "Elijah" churches that will not bow to Baal or kiss his image. There will be some ministries who will not be intimidated by the spirit of Jezebel.

There will be those ministries who will not yield to the doctrine of political correctness and preach the truth. God did not call and establish the church to be politically correct but biblically correct. For the true church, the Bible is the standard, not the political pundits or the latest CNN poll!

JEZEBEL'S MISSION:
CULTURAL, ECCLESIASTICAL AND PERSONAL

Now therefore send, and gather to me all Israel unto mount Carmel, and the prophets of Baal four hundred and fifty, and the prophets of the groves four hundred, which eat at Jezebel's table.

1 Kings 18:19

Cultural Effects

At the cultural level, the spirit of Jezebel seeks to influence society to embrace sexual idolatry and immorality as the normal, acceptable standard. Baal is the male fertility deity symbolized by the male organ (penis). The groves mentioned in 1 Kings 18:19 were actually references to Ashtoreth (Venus), the female goddess of sexual love. In uniting these two deities, Jezebel unleashed a powerful force that captivated the culture and held the nation of Israel in spiritual bondage.[5] As a result of this sexual idolatry, the Assyrians led the nation of Israel into captivity.

> *In the ninth year of Hoshea the king of Assyria took Samaria, and carried Israel away into Assyria, and placed them in Halah and in Habor by the river of Gozan, and in the cities of the Medes. For so it was, that the children of Israel had sinned against the LORD their God, which had brought them up out of the land of Egypt, from under the hand of Pharaoh king of Egypt, and had feared other gods.*
> 2 Kings 17:6,7

In ancient biblical times, the spirit of Jezebel had a tremendous impact upon the culture. In today's contemporary society, the spirit of Jezebel is still impacting the culture. If we study the cultural effects of the 1960's Sexual Revolution, we can readily see the spirit of Jezebel at work. Consider that over the past thirty years:

- The marriage rate has declined steadily.
- The number of heterosexual couples "shacking up" has increased nearly 6 percent.[6]
- The divorce rate has doubled (approximately 50 percent of all first time marriages now end in divorce).
- Reports of child abuse have increased fivefold.
- The out of wedlock rate has increased from 9 percent to 30 percent.
- The number of known STDs has grown from three (commonly reported in 1964) to more than thirty (in 1994).

Also, consider the following:

- In some communities, 66 percent of children are born out of wedlock.
- Approximately one and a half million abortions are performed each year.
- Three million new cases of STDs among teens are reported each year.
- More than one million teens become pregnant each year.
- About fifteen million Americans contract an STD yearly.

These are just a few examples of how our culture has suffered from the sexual idolatry that the spirit of Jezebel propagates. Directly related to this sexual idolatry are other signs of social decay. For example, over the past twenty-five to thirty years;

- Violent crime has risen 600 percent.
- SAT scores have fallen by eighty points.
- Poverty has shifted from the old to the young (today approximately 40 percent of the nation's poor are children).
- Out of wedlock births have risen more than 500 percent.

The laws of this nation are becoming more and more accommodating to the sexual idolatry that has overtaken it. Consider:

- Laws making it easy to get a divorce (no fault divorce).
- Ordinances recognizing domestic partners as equivalent to married couples.
- Legislation trying to legalize homosexual marriages.
- Laws allowing gay couples the right to adopt children.

In effect, we now have a culture (society) that encourages ungodly covenants and discourages godly covenants. This is precisely what the spirit of Jezebel has come to do.

Ecclesiastical Effects

How has the spirit of Jezebel affected the church? For whatever reason, the church has not adequately addressed the 60's Sexual Revolution. Because of this, the same spirit of sexual idolatry (Jezebel) that we see in the world has creeped into the church. Consider:

- The ordination of homosexual priests (both male and female) by some denominations.
- The alarming number of pastors and priests that are falling into sexual sin on both the local and national level.
- Approximately fifteen hundred pastors leave the ministry each month nationwide, in part due to moral failure.[7]
- Approximately 18 percent of abortion patients describe themselves as born-again or evangelical Christians.[8]
- The number of teen pregnancies and out of wedlock births in many local assemblies are similar to secular society as a whole.
- Experts estimate that clergy misconduct lawsuits, which began appearing in the mid 80's, now number in the thousands.[9]
- 60 percent of Catholic priests said they knew of at least one priest who has died of AIDS or has the virus that causes AIDS.[10]

The church doctrine regarding sexual behavior has been watered down considerably. A few years ago I was invited to a Pentecostal youth convention to share some of the principles out of Volume 1. After I shared, one of the state bishops publicly declared that there was nothing wrong with "petting" (sexual touching). He said this to an audience of teenagers and young adults. This epitomizes the weakened doctrinal stance that many local churches have tolerated. A weak doctrine produces weak, vulnerable saints. We can see that the spirit of Jezebel, to a great degree, has seduced and weakened the church itself.

According to a spokesman from one of the nation's leading insurers of religious organizations, at least five incidents of clergy sexual misconduct are reported weekly in the state of Wisconsin alone.[11] Sexual misconduct has become such a problem that many major religious denominations in America have formed committees with full-time staff charged with educating clergy about sexual misconduct.[12]

It is a sad day when church leaders have to be taught that sexual misconduct is unacceptable behavior. All of the aforementioned facts highlight what happens when the church does not effectively deal with issues related to sexual immorality. Indeed, the spirit of Jezebel has had a tremendous impact on the spiritual and cultural climate of the church.

> *Notwithstanding I have a few things against thee, because thou sufferest that woman Jezebel, which calleth herself a prophetess, to teach and to seduce my servants to commit fornication, and to eat things sacrificed unto idols. And I gave her space to repent of her fornication; and she repented not. Behold, I will cast her into a bed, and them that commit adultery with her into great tribulation, except they repent of their deeds.*
>
> Revelation 2:20-22

Personal Effects

Jezebel symbolizes whoredom at its worst. Through her cunning and sheer will of determination, she was responsible for uniting the two primary sexual deities of her day, Baal and Ashtoreth (Venus).

> *So he erected an altar for* Baal *in the house of Baal, which he built in Samaria. And Ahab also made the* Asherah. *Thus Ahab did more to provoke the LORD God of Israel than all the kings of Israel who were before him.*
>
> 1 Kings 16:32,33 NAS (emphasis added)

In uniting with these two deities, the spiritual covenant with Jehovah was severed and a new spiritual covenant was established.[13] On the personal level, the spirit of Jezebel seeks to cause a disruption of the fellowship and union that we have in Christ. Jezebel seeks to bring us into the bondage of, and in allegiance with, another lord (spirit).

> *Flee fornication. Every sin that a man doeth is without the body; but he that committeth fornication sinneth against his own body. What? know ye not that your body is the temple of the Holy Ghost which is in you, which ye have of God, and ye are not your own?*
>
> 1 Corinthians 6:18,19

The apostle Paul states that the body is a temple. Temples were built for sacrifice and worship. In fact, the most important activity surrounding a temple is worship. Most temples have altars upon which various sacrifices can be made. Symbolically speaking, the sexual organs are the most sacred "altars" in the body temple.[14] Worship may be defined as showing reverence or devotion toward a deity. In worship we become:

1. Allied with the deity worshiped (Romans 6:16).
2. Identified with the deity worshiped (Psalms 135:18).
3. Unified with the deity worshiped (1 Corinthians 6:16).

In effect, Jezebel seeks to alter your spiritual *allegiance* and destroy your *identity*. Through idolatrous (sexual) unions, Jezebel seeks to disrupt or delay your eternal *destiny*.

The Inheritance of the Fathers[15]

Not only does Jezebel want to alter your eternal destiny, she also wants to steal your inheritance. First Kings sheds light on this principle.

> *And it came to pass after these things, that Naboth the Jezreelite had a vineyard, which was in Jezreel, hard by the palace of Ahab king of Samaria. And Ahab spake unto Naboth, saying, Give me thy vineyard, I may have it for a garden of herbs, because it is near unto my : and I will give thee for it a better vineyard than it; or, if it seem to thee, I will give thee the worth of it in money. And Naboth said to Ahab, The LORD forbid it me, that I should give the* inheritance my fathers *unto thee.*
>
> 1 Kings 21:1-3 (emphasis added)

In Bible days, inheritances from forefathers, which had been passed on for many generations in the same family, were priceless.[16] The Law of Moses maintained that property of this type had to remain within the family who had inherited it. To part with such an inheritance was like parting with life itself. Naboth refused to give up his inheritance because he realized the multigenerational effect it would have on his offspring. To surrender his inheritance would not only affect him, it would also affect his children and his children's children. But watch Jezebel:

> *And Jezebel his wife said unto him, Dost thou now govern the kingdom of Israel? arise, and eat bread, and let thine heart be merry:* I will give thee the vineyard of Naboth *the Jezreelite*
>
> 1 Kings 21:7 (emphasis added)

The important thing to consider here is the focus of the conflict: the *inheritance*. Jezebel uses all of her treacherous skills to take away Naboth's inheritance. Let's examine the highly symbolic nature of this conflict. The name Naboth literally means "fruit." The Hebrew word for inheritance also means "heritage," "property," or "possession." The Scripture states:

> *Lo, children are an* heritage *of the LORD: and the* fruit *of the womb is his reward.*
>
> Psalms 127:3 (emphasis added)

Now it becomes clear what Jezebel was really after. She not only wants to destroy your life, she also wants your "seed" or the "fruit" of your body, your children. Jezebel wants to steal and control the "field" in which your "seed" is planted, grows and ripens. She does this via sexual immorality and sexual sin. In this sense, your "field" is your sexuality or sex life. If she can seize and control it, she can steal your fruit and destroy your inheritance.

The message is clear: Jezebel, via sexual sin, wants to take possession of your life, your destiny and your fruit (children). Sexual sin robs and prevents you from fulfilling your God-ordained purpose. This passage further illustrates the effect that sexual sin can inflict upon future generations; sexual sin can have a multigenerational effect.

Shedding Innocent Blood

Jezebel has no problem with shedding innocent blood through her guile and treachery. As we have pointed out, Naboth means "fruit." Destroying innocent fruit is Jezebel's specialty. I liken this to modern day abortion.

In 1973, the U.S. Supreme Court issued a ruling that established a woman's constitutional right to an abortion (Roe v. Wade). Since that time, there have been an estimated thirty to thirty-six million abortions performed in this country. The U.S. has one of the highest rates of unplanned pregnancy and abortion in the industrialized world.[17] Consider the following facts about abortion:[18,19]

- About 1.4 million American women have abortions each year.
- 89 percent of these abortions are performed before the twelfth week of pregnancy.
- 82 percent of these women are unmarried or separated.
- 44 percent have had at least one previous abortion.
- Catholic women have them at a higher rate than do Protestant women.
- Of the estimated 1.8 million abortions performed in 1996, approximately 18 percent were done on women who described themselves as born again or evangelical.[20]
- At current rates, 43 percent of American women will have an abortion in their lifetime.
- More than twice as many women have an abortion as get college degrees.
- 11 percent of women having abortions never used birth control.
- 55 percent of women having abortions are under the age of twenty-five.
- 22 percent of abortions are performed on teenagers.
- 33 percent of abortions are performed on women between the ages of twenty and twenty-four.
- 45 percent of abortions are performed on women over the age of twenty-five.
- 1,210,883 abortions were performed in 1995.
- In 1995, almost 20 percent of all pregnancies in the U.S. ended in abortion, the highest rate of any Western industrialized country.

Why Women Get Abortions

- 76 percent said that they were concerned about how having a baby could change their lives.

- 51 percent had problems with a relationship or wanted to avoid single parenthood.
- 13 percent cited health of the unborn.
- 7 percent cited health of the mother.
- 1 percent cited rape or incest.[21]

According to the statistics, most abortions occurring in the twentieth week or later were not related to the health of the unborn child or the mother. Of those clinics responding to the survey, 90 percent of these types of abortions were for nonmedical reasons. In countries like China, a child may be aborted because it is the wrong sex.

In the book of 1 Kings, Naboth was killed because his presence proved to be an *inconvenience* and a hindrance to what Ahab wanted. Today, the unborn are destroyed in the womb—most of the time—because they are simply an inconvenience.

Partial Birth Abortion

The technical medical term for this barbaric procedure is "intact dilation and extraction" (D&X). This procedure is used in pregnancies that are too advanced to be terminated by suction. It is performed by bringing the unborn, feet first, into the birth canal. The skull is then punctured with a sharp instrument, and the brain is sucked through a catheter. This procedure is so controversial that even a pro abortion senator has described it as "too close to infanticide."[22]

There is something desperately wrong in a society that would allow attacks of this nature on innocent human life. The destruction of "innocent fruit," while still in the womb, is an indication that Jezebel's *skull*, *feet* and *hands* are still with us. The spirit of Jezebel is alive and fully functional in contemporary America.

Accountability of the Church

Notwithstanding I have a few things against thee, because thou sufferest that woman Jezebel, which calleth herself a prophetess, to teach and to seduce my servants to commit fornication, and to eat things sacrificed unto idols.

Revelation 2:20

I want to conclude our discussion on Jezebel by carefully dissecting this Scripture. Even though the spirit of Jezebel has wrought much confusion and destruction, the Lord does not absolve the church from its responsibility in contributing to that confusion. Here in Revelation 2:20, the Lord seems to be indicting the church:

> *Notwithstanding I have a few things against thee, because thou* sufferest *that woman Jezebel....*
>
> Revelation 2:20a

According to Strong's Concordance, the Greek word for sufferest has several meanings, including: "forsake," "lay aside," "leave," "omit," or "to let" (Greek 863). In this context, it means "to allow or permit." Jesus is accusing the church of allowing Jezebel to spread her destructive doctrine unchallenged and unopposed; she was allowed to infiltrate and poison this church, thereby weakening it. This accusation is relevant today because the Sexual Revolution of the 1960's was not sufficiently addressed by the church. As a result, we are seeing the destructive effects of that "revolution" in society and in the church as well. Mainline Christian denominational churches are struggling with issues of sexuality and sexual sin.[23]

The Lord is holding the church accountable for its negligence in allowing Jezebel's doctrine to go unchecked and unchallenged. The church needs to launch a counterattack that should begin within its own four walls! Passivity and acquiescence is no longer an option. The church can no longer afford to standby while condoms and birth control pills are being passed out to teens in schools. The church cannot afford to allow the homosexual indoctrination of our children on the joys of the gay lifestyle. We must respond with truth. What we see today is the same thing that took place in the church of Thyatira: an unopposed invasion of the spirit of Jezebel into many local assemblies.

Teach and Seduce

What is the church allowing Jezebel to do? Two things: to *teach* and to *seduce*. Jezebel teaches by *precept* and by *example*. Sadly, many who have assumed leadership positions in a large number of our churches are simply not qualified to lead. Their lives are not good examples to those they seek to lead. The divorce rate (and the rate of extramarital affairs) among clergy is alarming. When those who are pastoring are unable or unwilling to live in accordance with scripture, the unspoken lesson that it communicates will ultimately weaken the followers. The church is in desperate need of godly leaders who are willing to make the sacrifices necessary to uphold a high moral standard in their public and private lives. More than anyone, spiritual leaders teach more by what they *do* than by what they *say*. False instruction and satanic seduction go hand in hand.

Above all else, Jezebel is a seducer. The word "seduce" (4105) means to "cause to roam or stray," "to deceive," "to err." Jezebel's primary method of leading people astray is the lure of fornication. Fornication is sexual idolatry and can include many expressions of sexual sin including:

- Premarital sex
- Extramarital sex
- Homosexual sex
- Pedophilia
- Incest
- Bestiality

Any deviation from truth leads to *err*, but fornication is one of the greatest deviations from the truth there is. It is a sin that is shrouded in deception. Deception often involves distorting perception, disrupting the reasoning capacity of the individual. The deceived person has a problem with perception, that is, the ability to correctly interpret what he sees. For example, a deceived person can *see* a rattle snake on the ground, but due to a perception malfunction, he may attempt to rub the snake because he *perceives* it to be a cat. The deceived person's vision is fine; his problem is that he is not correctly *interpreting* what he sees.

This is a dangerous position to be in. One can go through life deceived: seeing, but lacking the ability to properly interpret the things seen. When this happens, wrong seems right, up appears to be down, darkness appears to be light. In the case of sexual sin, the deceived is deluded into thinking that it is harmless and without lasting consequences. Note the attitude and philosophy of the adulterous spirit:

Such is the way of an adulterous woman; she eateth, and wipeth her mouth, and saith, I have done no wickedness.
                                    Proverbs 30:20 (emphasis added)

The seducer will have you believe that you can partake of "forbidden sacrifices" without being punished. All you have to do is "wipe away" the physical evidence of the "meal" (sexual sin) and go your way. Get rid of the physical evidence by: using a condom; using birth control pills; or getting an abortion. The solution she presents seems so simple. *Eat and wipe.* Unfortunately, it is never that simple. The spiritual, psychological and emotional scars that are inflicted upon those who "eat forbidden meals" (sexual sin) are deep and lasting.

The seducer tries to convince you that you may enter into unlawful sexual covenants and nothing will be required of you. Please note: Every sexual covenant you enter must be given account of. The seducer tells you, "Be discreet, and you won't get caught. Besides, what you choose to do in your private life, is nobody's business!" These are the typical lies and deceptions that Jezebel uses to seduce and lead people astray. In fact, the illegal sexual covenants into which people enter have personal, social, generational and eternal consequences.

For she hath cast down many wounded: yea, many strong men have been slain by her. Her house is the way to hell, going down to the chambers of death.
                                    Proverbs 7:26,27

That ye abstain from meats offered to idols, and from blood, and from things strangled, and from fornication: *from which if ye keep yourselves, ye shall do well. Fare ye well.*
                                    Acts 15:29 (emphasis added)

The teaching of Jezebel includes a philosophy that tempts the individual into "eating things sacrificed to idols." Jezebel is intent on getting the church to partake in activities that have been consecrated to demons and rejected by God. Fornication is a sacrifice that is dedicated to devils. It is also a sacrifice that has been rejected and cursed by God. It is forever settled in heaven: God rejects sexual sin. God understands that we are weak, but He also understands that through His strength, we can be strong! It is important to note that God will:

- Forgive you of sexual sin.
- Deliver you from sexual sin.
- Cleanse you from sexual sin.
- Help you avoid and overcome sexual sin.

But He will *never, ever* allow you to habitually practice sexual sin and then accept you into heaven after you die! This is basic and fundamentally sound Bible doctrine.

> *Know ye not that the unrighteous shall not inherit the kingdom of God? Be not deceived: neither* fornicators, *nor idolaters, nor* adulterers, *nor* effeminate, nor abusers of themselves with mankind, *Nor thieves, nor covetous, nor drunkards, nor revilers, nor extortioners, shall inherit the kingdom of God.*
>
> 1 Corinthians 6:9,10 (emphasis added)

Chapter Summary

1. Jezebel will forever stand as a symbol of treachery, sorcery and sexual immorality.
2. The spirit of Jezebel lives on to hinder the New Testament church today.
3. The spirit of Jezebel seeks to promote sexual idolatry by infiltrating the local church with worldly philosophies and ungodly lifestyles that tolerate sexual sin.
4. "Reverse evangelism" is defined as the world evangelizing the church. This is manifest when the church embraces worldly standards, methods and philosophies. In essence, the church becomes more worldly, rather than the world becoming more churchly.
5. There will always be true churches that will not be seduced by Jezebel nor bow down to Baal.
6. On the personal level, Jezebel, through sexual sin, seeks to:

    a. *Destroy* your identity.

    b. *Delay* your destiny.

    c. *Deny* your spiritual inheritance.

7. The spirit of Jezebel, through treachery and deceit, seeks to slay the innocent.

8. Like the church of Thyatira, many present day local churches have been invaded by the spirit of Jezebel.

9. One cannot habitually practice sexual sin and be considered a true believer in Christ. The habitual practice of sexual sin will deny you a place in heaven.

10. Any sexual act that violates the revealed Word of God is nothing more than phallic worship or sexual idolatry. The list includes, but is not limited to:

    a. Adultery (Greek, *moicheia*): Sexual relations with someone other than your spouse (Matthew 15:19; Mark 7:21).

    b. Bestiality: Sexual relations with animals; closely associated with zoophilia, which is the sexual attraction to animals (Leviticus 18:23, 20:13; Deuteronomy 27:21).

    c. Fornication (Greek, *porneia*): Illicit sexual intercourse in general; mainly refers to unmarried individuals who engage in sexual intercourse.

    d. Homosexuality (Greek, *arsenocoites*): Same sex unions (Leviticus 18:21, 20:13; Romans 1:26; 1 Corinthians 6:9; 1 Timothy 1:10).

    e. Incest (Hebrew, *zimmach*): Sexual relations with close family members.

    f. Necrophilia: Sexual contact with dead bodies.

    g. Pedophilia: Adults engaging in sex with children.

Chapter Four

PHINEHAS:
RESISTING SEXUAL IDOLATRY
IN THE
LOCAL CHURCH

Phinehas, the son of Eleazar, the son of Aaron the priest, hath turned my wrath away from the children of Israel, while he was zealous for my sake among them, that I consumed not the children of Israel in my jealousy.

Numbers 25:11

And they journeyed from mount Hor by the way of the Red sea, to compass the land of Edom: and the soul of the people was much discouraged because of the way.

Numbers 21:4

This stretch of the wilderness journey proved to be the most dangerous, difficult and distressful leg of the trip thus far. It was a period of extreme hardship, misery and suffering. Consider the events that had unfolded:

1. Miriam, sister of Moses, dies in the Kadesh wilderness (Numbers 20:1).

2. Moses speaks ill with his lips, strikes the rock at Meribah (meaning strife), and is banned from the Promised Land (Numbers 20:10-12).

3. The Edomites deny the Israelites permission to pass through their territory and threaten all-out war (Numbers 20:20,21).

4. Aaron, brother of Moses and the first high priest dies upon Mt. Hor (Numbers 20:28).

5. Once again, the children of Israel murmur against God and His leadership. Fiery serpents are sent among the congregation, and many are bitten and die (Numbers 21:6).

As the pressure and stress of these events mounted, the people come to a point of spiritual and physical exhaustion, but the worst was yet to come! This weary and worn people became frustrated, bitter and impatient. They were now vulnerable to Balak's scheme.

And the children of Israel set forward, and pitched in the plains of Moab on this side Jordan by Jericho. And Balak the son of Zippor saw all that Israel had done to the Amorites.

Numbers 22:1,2

As the Israelites settled into the plains of Moab, they came under the watchful eye of Balak, the king of Moab. The scheme that he implemented, with the help of a Midianite prophet by the name of Balaam, dealt a crippling, almost fatal blow to the Israelites. The Hebrew word *Balak* (1111) means "to annihilate" or "to make waste." This leaves no doubt as to his intent and purpose regarding the nation of Israel. Annihilation of God's people was his ultimate goal.

In Numbers 22–24 we witness a life and death spiritual struggle as Balaam, using witchcraft and sorcery, attempts to curse the nation of Israel for Balak. His witchcraft and magic are powerless, for every time he tries to curse Israel, God forces him to pronounce a blessing upon them. It appears that Balaam and Balak abandon their attempt to curse and annihilate Israel:

And Balaam rose up, and went and returned to his place: and Balak also went his way.

Numbers 24:25

In reality, the fight was just beginning. The New Testament points out three aspects of Balaam's ministry:

1. The "error"of Balaam (Jude 11).
2. The "way" of Balaam (2 Peter 2:15).
3. The" doctrine" of Balaam (Revelation 2:14).

I want to focus on the doctrine (teaching) of Balaam because it was this doctrine that proved to be the downfall of the Israelites. As a result of this doctrine, twenty-four thousand men died in one day (Numbers 25:9).

THE DOCTRINE OF BALAAM

The doctrine of Balaam was obviously designed to weaken and corrupt the nation of Israel from within. This doctrine was designed to alienate Israel from her God. Where Balaam's witchcraft and sorcery failed, his doctrine succeeded. What exactly was the doctrine of Balaam?

> Behold, these caused the children of Israel, through the counsel *of Balaam, to* commit trespass *against the LORD in the matter of Peor, and there was a plague among the congregation of the LORD.*
>
> Numbers 31:16 (emphasis added)

The doctrine of Balaam was designed to cause the people of God to commit "trespass" against Him. The word for trespass used here is *ma'al* (4604), meaning "treachery" or "falsehood." Treachery is behavior characterized by betrayal, disloyalty and unfaithfulness. It is the breaking of one's allegiance with a trusted ally. It is the same type of betrayal that an adulterous spouse exhibits when he or she has sexual relations with someone other than their spouse.

Balaam's doctrine, first and foremost, was designed to cause the people of God to break their covenant with Him and betray Him. It is the propagation of spiritual adultery and high treason against God. Since Balaam could not do anything that would turn God against His people, Balaam, through his doctrine, seduced the people of God to do things that would turn the people against God. Balaam's doctrine encourages the type of ungodly behavior that will bring the wrath of God upon His people.

Balaam discovered that a curse cannot be implemented against God's people without due cause (Proverbs 26:2). God does not change and He cannot be bought off. Balaam had made a tactical error in his first attempt, but now he came to the conclusion: "If I can't get Jehovah to turn His back on Israel, maybe I can get Israel to turn its back on Jehovah." In joining themselves to Baalpeor, this is precisely what happened. Israel forced Jehovah to actively judge them for their sexual sin. God will judge sexual sin, be it in the church or in the world.

Revelation 2:14 gives us more information concerning the doctrine of Balaam.

> But I have a few things against thee, because thou hast there them that hold the doctrine of Balaam, who taught Balak to cast a stumblingblock before the children of Israel, to eat things sacrificed unto idols, and to commit fornication.
>
> Revelation 2:14 (emphasis added)

Here we see that this doctrine is a "stumblingblock." The word John uses here is the Greek word *skandalon* (4625) from which our word "scandal" arises. A scandal is that which discredits or defames. Balaam's doctrine of sexual sin is designed to destroy the credibility of the people of God. In order to be an effective witness for Jesus, a Christian must have credibility. Without credibility, your witness is ineffectual. A stumbling block is that which causes one to fall. When the saint "falls" into sin, they loose their credibility to witness for Jesus.

The word "stumblingblock" (*skandalon*) has another interesting meaning. This word is also used to describe a trap or a snare. More specifically, it is the part of the trap that is used to lure or attract the prey into the trap. In practical terms, it is the worm on the hook that attracts the fish. The lure is always positioned in such a way as to hide the real danger; it is deceptively designed to hide the deadly hook that will lead to the eventual destruction of the prey.

Revelation 2:14 also states that Balaam's doctrine encourages God's people to eat things offered to idols. Partaking of idolatrous sacrifices is a serious offense.[1] When partaking of food that has been offered up to a particular deity, the partaker was symbolically communing or becoming identified with that deity. This usually preceded the act of fornication, which is the essence of Balaam's doctrine.

The word translated "fornication" (4203) here refers to unlawful sexual conduct. It is inclusive of a number of forbidden sexual practices including, but not limited to: premarital sex, extramarital sex, adultery, incest, homosexuality, pornography, pedophilia and polygamy. In essence, it is any sexual activity that takes place outside the bonds of holy matrimony.

THE DOCTRINE OF BALAAM: COMPROMISE, COMPLICITY, COMPLACENCY AND COMPLIANCE

The doctrine of Balaam is a doctrine of *compromise* with sin, *complicity* with sinners, *complacency* toward sin and *compliance* with the world.

Compromise

The doctrine of Balaam encourages the church to lower its standards. It seeks to weaken or water down Bible doctrine. It's that voice that says, "It really doesn't take all of that to be saved. You should not be so dogmatic and fanatic when it comes to holiness."

While many are compromising and lowering the standards, the Word of God speaks clearly concerning His standards:

> *Go through, go through the gates; prepare ye the way of the people; cast up, cast up the highway; gather out the stones; lift up a* standard *for the people.*
> Isaiah 62:10 (emphasis added)

One reason so many churches are suffering from a lack of credibility is because they have lowered the biblical standard. Currently, some mainline denominational churches are wrestling with the doctrine of Balaam as it relates to the issue of homosexuality and its place in the church.[2]

Complicity

The doctrine of Balaam encourages the church into complicity with sinners. This simply means that the church has become a partner in sinful activity. It's that voice that says, "It's okay to engage in pre-marital sex because God knows we are all weak; every now and then we all must sin; God understands."

When there is complicity with sin and sinners, the church loses its credibility and moral authority. When believers commit the same acts as the sinner, it is tantamount to "having a form of godliness, but denying the power thereof." (2 Timothy 3:5)

Complacency

The doctrine of Balaam encourages the church to be satisfied with things the way they are. It's the voice that says, "Young people are gonna do it (have sex) no matter what. You can't change people, so you may as well leave well enough alone."

Compliancy

The doctrine of Balaam encourages the church to give in to worldly ways and allow the culture of the world to enter the church. It is the voice that says, "If you can't beat 'em, join 'em." Compliance is born out of shame for who we are and what we are called to be, that is, salt and light. No wonder Paul states:

> For I am not ashamed of the gospel of Christ: for it is the power of God unto salvation.
>
> Romans 1:16 (emphasis added)

A Critical Hour

The doctrine of Balaam has conditioned the church to more readily yield to the forces of sexual immorality in the world. The spirit of the age is one of complacency, complicity, compliance and compromise with the world. In the area of sexual conduct, many churches are struggling. Consider these facts:

- Ordination of gay and lesbian priest and ministers.
- Church sanctioning of homosexual marriages.
- Approximately 18 percent of the estimated 1.8 million abortions performed in 1996 were done on women who described themselves as born again or evangelical.[3]
- Both local and national church leaders are falling into sex scandals at alarming rates.

- Teen pregnancy and out of wedlock birth rates in many local churches are about the same as they are in secular society;
- Catholic priests are contracting AIDS at a rate four times that of the general population.[4]
- Clergy face about twice the risk of dying of AIDS as white males in all occupational groups combined.[5]

This is a critical hour for the church. As we enter the twenty-first century, doctrinal issues of sexual purity will be challenged and debated more and more. Could it be that 1 Timothy 4:1 is being fulfilled in this hour?

> *Now the Spirit speaketh expressly, that in the latter times some shall depart from the faith, giving heed to* seducing *spirits, and doctrines of devils.*
>
> 1 Timothy 4:1 (emphasis added)

The church is in desperate need of leaders who will not compromise on scriptural teachings. Jude writes:

> *Beloved, when I gave all diligence to write unto you of the common salvation, it was needful for me to write unto you, and exhort you that ye should earnestly* contend *for the faith which was once delivered unto the saints.*
>
> Jude 1:3 (emphasis added)

The church needs *contenders*, not pretenders! In Numbers 25 we have such an individual.

Phinehas: A Contender for the Faith

And when Phinehas, the son of Eleazar, the son of Aaron the priest, saw it he rose up from among the congregation, and took a javelin in his hand; And he went after the man of Israel into the tent, and thrust both of them through, the man of Israel, and the woman through her belly. So the plague was stayed from the children of Israel.

Numbers 25:7,8

In the intense atmosphere described in Numbers 25, a man appears on the scene, seemingly from out of nowhere, to address this crisis. The individual was a man by the name of Phinehas. Very little is known about him until this "sexuality crisis" threatened the Israeli nation. Who was this man? How is his life significant for the church today?

In the midst of this devastating sexual revolution, Phinehas, grandson of Aaron, arrived on the scene. This young man was very focused in executing his assignment. His assignment was threefold:

1. Stop the devastating plague that threatened the Israeli nation.
2. Execute judgment (swift and uncompromising) upon the spirit of sexual idolatry and harlotry (doctrine of Balaam).
3. Call the church to repentance and implement God's healing for the wounds brought about by ungodly sexual covenants.

The satanically inspired plan to infiltrate the tabernacle worship of Jehovah with Baalism (sexual idolatry) had to be stopped. In doing so, Phinehas represented the spirit of godly zeal that is anointed and equipped to deal with this spiritual invasion. In dealing with sexual sin in the church, Phinehas had to address the *sexual revolution* that was destroying his generation.

> *And when Phinehas, the son of Eleazar, the son of Aaron the priest, saw it, he rose up from among the congregation, and took a javelin in his hand; And he went after the man of Israel into the tent, and thrust both of them through, the man of Israel, and the woman through her belly. So the plague was stayed from the children of Israel.*
>
> Numbers 25:7,8

The sexual idolatry that had infiltrated the ranks of the church had a devastating effect. The destruction was swift. In one day, approximately twenty-four thousand Israelis died of a deadly plague. At this rate, all fighting-aged men would have been dead within about three weeks.

Phinehas' ministry was extremely important. His name means "mouth of brass." Brass is a hard metal that is durable and lasting.

Likewise, the word that God placed in his mouth was a "hard" and perhaps unpopular one. Phinehas represented:

- The spirit of righteous indignation unleashed to effectively address sexual idolatry (doctrine of Balaam) in the church.
- The launching of a major counteroffensive against a sexual revolution that threatened the church from within.
- Preparation of God's people for the next major spiritual move of God in his generation.

> *And, behold, one of the children of Israel came and brought unto his brethren a Midianitish woman in the sight of Moses, and in the sight of all the congregation of the children of Israel, who were weeping before the door of the* tabernacle of the congregation. *And when Phinehas, the son of Eleazar, the son of Aaron the priest, saw it, he rose up from among the congregation, and took a javelin in his hand; And he went after the man of Israel* into the tent, *and thrust both of them through, the man of Israel, and the woman through her belly. So the plague was stayed from the children of Israel.*
>
> Numbers 25:6-8 (emphasis added)

I have highlighted the two phrases "tabernacle of the congregation" and "into the tent" to point out what was actually taking place here. I believe that this was a blatant attempt to turn the wilderness tabernacle into a shrine for Baal worship. This Israelite leader (Zimri), under satanic influence, was attempting to incorporate Baal worship with the worship of Jehovah God. He boldly brought this Baal prostitute (Cozbi) onto the sacred tabernacle grounds and attempted to become "one" with the Baal deity by engaging in sex with her.

Satan's strategy to defile the church with worldly philosophies and lifestyles has not changed. Many churches lack the doctrinal teaching that emphasizes the need to avoid sexual sin. As a result, sexual sin abounds in many local assemblies.

> *Now the name of the Israelite that was slain, even that was slain with the Midianitish woman, was* Zimri, *the son of*

> *Salu, a prince of a chief house among the Simeonites. And
> the name of the Midianitish woman that was slain was
> Cozbi, the daughter of Zur; he was head over a people, and
> of a chief house in Midian.*
>
> Numbers 25:14,15 (emphasis added)

Phinehas came against Zimri, whose name means "musical," or "music" (2174) and is associated with a Hebrew word which means to "celebrate in song." This symbolically speaks of Satan's attempt to corrupt the music by which we worship God. One of the main problem areas in many churches is the music department. Good musicians who are saved and committed to the things of God are hard to come by these days.

Phinehas also came against Cozbi, whose name means "false," "liar," or "deceit" (3579). Many churches have been deceived by false worldly philosophies. As the church compromises the Word of God, it is becoming more and more like the world. When the Word of God is not adhered to in a local assembly, worldly philosophies, attitudes and behaviors weaken that assembly.

The Ministry of Phinehas

As we examine the history of Phinehas' ministry, we can see the relevance for the contemporary church.

- Phinehas withstood the spirit of whoredom and sexual idolatry that had invaded the camp and stayed the plague (Numbers 25:7).
- Phinehas was dispatched by Moses as part of an army sent to destroy the Midianites, who had ensnared Israel into sexual idolatry (Numbers 31:6).
- Phinehas spoke a prophetic and strategic word that initiated the civil war against the "men of Gibeah." As you may recall, the men of Gibeah were bisexuals who attempted to rape another man but settled for raping his concubine to death. They symbolize a spirit of sexual perversion that had infiltrated the land (Judges 20:28).
- Phinehas brought forth a strategic word that avoided a civil war over the possibility of idolatrous practices within the tribes of Rueben, Gad and Mannasah (Joshua 22).

I believe that this man's life and ministry bears prophetic significance for the church in this hour. I believe that God is unleashing the "spirit of Phinehas" to boldly stand against the tide of sexual idolatry that is weakening the church. He represents God's desire to deal, head-on, with the issue of sexual sin within the house of God.

> *For the time is come that judgment must begin at the house of God.*
>
> 1 Peter 4:17a

Millennial Outpouring

The ministry of Phinehas was important in that the second census (Numbers 26) could not take place until he had done what God had raised and anointed him to do: resist the spirit of sexual idolatry that had infiltrated the church and implement God's healing to a generation that had been deeply wounded by ungodly sexual covenants. The second census was in preparation for what God was about to do *next*.

In Numbers 25, God sent Phinehas forth to address the sexual idolatry that had infiltrated the Old Testament church. Today, God is calling and sending forth the spirit of Phinehas to address the sexual sin that has infiltrated many present day churches. The spirit of Phinehas will be essential in preparing the people of God for the next major spiritual event for this generation.

As we enter into a new millennium, the church is at a great crossroad. It appears that we are on the brink of a great spiritual move of God.

Three Major Cycles

We are on the threshold of entering one of the most crucial and pivotal eras of world history. The world is poised for global change. World economies are merging. Technological and scientific discoveries are rapidly changing the way we live. As we enter into a new millennium, we will witness the end and the start of three major cycles that are spiritually relevant: a *100-year cycle*, a *1000-year cycle* and a *2000-year cycle*.

100-Year Cycle

One hundred years ago, the church was on the threshold of what church historians now recognize as one of the greatest Pentecostal outpourings since the days of Acts chapter 2.[6] In the late 1800's, God was preparing the church for a revival that was to begin in 1906. Today, I believe that God is trying, once again, to prepare the church for another significant event. In Scripture, the number 100 is associated with God's grace or His divine enablement.[7] Will this next 100-year cycle be the beginning of an outpouring of God's grace (enablement) upon the church? We won't have to wait long for an answer.

Historical Parallels

One hundred years ago, this nation was in the midst of the the Industrial Revolution. During this period, there was systematic application of scientific knowledge to the manufacturing process. The Industrial Revolution rapidly transformed this nation from a predominantly farm-based economy to a manufacturing-based economy. In the midst of this era of technological change, God was preparing the church for one of the greatest revivals the church in America has witnessed. It was called the Azusa Revival.[8]

One hundred years later, we are in the midst of another great technological revolution. Computer technology has changed the world. Every five years, our knowledge base increases more than two-fold. This computer-driven technological revolution has changed and will continue to change our society. Every aspect of our lives will be affected as this knowledge explosion accelerates.

Millennial Mission

> *And he called his ten servants, and delivered them ten pounds, and said unto them,* Occupy *till I come.*
>
> Luke 19:13 (emphasis added)

The church must realize that its ability to serve God will be greatly affected by this technological revolution. The word "occupy" means to busy oneself, to trade, or to do business. The challenge for the church now, as always, is to work and function within this world system without becoming a part of it. Many churches have neglected the mandate to occupy by failing to stress academic excellence and educational achievement. The church must be prepared to harness some of this knowledge and technology and use it to build the kingdom of God. As we enter the new millennium, the church can no longer afford to go to the world to build God's kingdom. The church doesn't need to be placed at the mercy of those who couldn't care less about God's work.

We need more than anointed preachers, pastors and evangelists. We also need anointed architects, teachers, economists, engineers, scientist, researchers, physicians and mathematicians. The church, as it seeks to God's will, needs the anointing and the power of God like never before. The church also needs expertise and education like never before. The churches that endeavor to successfully combine these—anointing, power, expertise and education—will be in a position to be greatly used by God throughout the new millennium.

As I see it, the millennial mission should include the need to achieve academic excellence. This can and should be done without compromising the standard message of sanctification and holiness. One of the big problems in many churches is that *neither* sanctification nor academic achievement is stressed or preached! In the midst of this technological revolution, God is preparing the church for another great revival move. As we enter the new millennium, our "millennia motto" should go something like this:

Salvation that leads to sanctification and education that leads to occupation!

The church must begin to "breed" a generation of spirit-filled, sanctified achievers who are academically and educationally equipped to occupy the kingdom until the Lord returns.

1000-Year Cycle

In Scripture, the number 1000 is connected with divine completeness and the glory of God.[9] What is God planning to reveal concerning His glory in this next 1000-year cycle? One thousand years ago, the world was on the brink of unprecedented change. It was a time of great achievement and terrible misery.[10] Will the new millennium bring suffering and misery? One thing is certain, the world is changing at a rapid pace. The words of Jesus in Matthew 24:5-7 need to be studied carefully.

And ye shall hear of wars and rumors of wars: see that ye be not troubled: for all these things must come to pass, but

> *the end is not yet. For nation shall rise against nation, and*
> *kingdom against kingdom: and there shall be famines, and*
> *pestilences, and earthquakes, in divers places.*
>
> Matthew 24:5-7

As the world moves closer to its appointed destiny, the signs Jesus spoke of in this Scripture will take on new meaning. I am not attempting to predict when Christ will return, but, as the next millennium unfolds, the signs of His return will become more and more evident. In explaining one of the features of the "end time," the angel tells Daniel that knowledge shall increase (Daniel 12:4). In the midst of this knowledge explosion and great achievement, will there be unprecedented misery and global chaos? The third millennium will present challenges and crises that only God can solve.

2000-Year Cycle

Two thousand years ago, Jesus Christ died on a Roman cross and rose from a borrowed tomb three days later. Two thousand years later, the church is about to enter a new era of prophetic (and historical) significance. I believe that the apparent shift in the heavenly constellation is speaking to this generation. Let me explain. Scripture states:

> *The heavens declare the glory of God; and the firmament*
> *sheweth his handywork.*
>
> Psalms 19:1

There is a biblical and scientific basis for suggesting that the major constellations, planets and stars are vehicles of God's natural revelation to mankind. The most common heavenly body in which most are all familiar with is the "Star of Bethlehem." Two excellent books that the reader may want to reference are *The Witness of the Stars* by E.W. Bullinger and *The Gospel in the Stars* by Joseph A. Seiss (Kregel Publications). Both of these books convincingly set forth the theory that the whole gospel message of Christ can be seen in the stars.

I want to briefly expand upon this idea that the "heavens declare the glory of God; and the firmament sheweth his handywork." In light of what happens every 2000 years within the heavens, this truth is significant. The constellations are twelve groups of stars visible in the night sky (see illustration below). These constellations (figures) can be seen on the inner surface of a huge sphere surrounding the earth, the so-called celestial sphere.[11]

As the earth spins on its axis, it slowly reverses direction, and this cycle (direction reversal) is completed every 2000 years. Consequently, there is a shift in the constellation that dominates the celestial sphere. The constellation that has dominated our celestial sphere over the past 2000 years has been the sign of the "fishes," also known as Pisces. As we enter this next 2000-year period, the constellation that will dominate the celestial sphere will be the sign of the "water bearer," also known as Aquarius. Aquarius represents the figure of a man who has a great bucket of water in his hand. From this bucket he is pouring out from the heavens a great stream of water that flows forth like a mighty river upon the earth.[12]

THE GREAT OUTPOURING OF THE 2000-YEAR CYCLE[13]

I believe that this 2000-year celestial shift is "prophetically" speaking of a great outpouring that awaits this third millennia generation.

> *And it shall come to pass afterward, that I will* pour out *my spirit upon all flesh; and your sons and your daughters shall prophesy, your old men shall dream dreams, your young men shall see visions: And also upon the servants and upon the handmaids in those days will I pour out* my spirit.

> Joel 2:28,29 (emphasis added)

Will the year 2000 be the beginning of the Aquarius outpouring of church revival?

If we look at these three cycles with a spiritual eye, we will see that this generation is on a collision course with an event of tremendous spiritual magnitude.

- 100 speaks of *grace and divine enablement.*
- 1000 speaks of the *glory of God revealed.*
- 2000 speaks of a *prophetic outpouring* coming upon the church.

I believe that this generation is on the threshold of a great out-pouring of God's grace and enablement. It will be an era of the glory of God being revealed to His people like never before. The essential question is, will the church be ready for this outpouring? Will the church be prepared for this next major move of God? Weak, sin-infested churches will not endure this next move of God in the earth. This is why the spirit of Phinehas is so important in this hour. If the church is to be prepared for this next move of God, the issue of sex-ual idolatry must be addressed within the local church. We must, in the spirit of Phinehas, slay the spirit of Zimri and Cozbi and neu-tralize the doctrine of Balaam that seeks to defile and undermine the church.

As we rapidly move into the twenty-first century, God will con-tinue to demand accountability for hidden, ungodly sexual covenants. He will continue to demand that His church be an exam-ple of sexual purity and godliness. Through the spirit of Phinehas, God will continue to challenge the church to reject the world's sex-ual standard, resist the doctrine of Balaam and uphold the biblical standard for sexual morality.

CHAPTER SUMMARY

1. The issue of sexual idolatry and sexual sin will be one of the most divisive and controversial issues that will reach crisis proportions for the church in the twenty-first century.
2. Phinehas represents the spirit of righteous indignation that is unleashed to address the sexual sin that has come to weaken and destroy the church.
3. The doctrine of Balaam represents those worldly ideas and philosophies that come to weaken the Bible doctrine regarding moral purity and sanctification.
4. The doctrine of Balaam is a doctrine of compromise with sin, complicity with sinners, complacency toward sin and compliance with worldly standards.
5. The doctrine of Balaam comes to condition the church to more readily yield to the forces of sexual immorality.
6. The doctrine of Balaam is manifest in these ways:
   - Ordination of gay and lesbian priest and ministers.
   - Church sanctioning of homosexual marriages.
   - Approximately 18 percent of the estimated 1.8 million abortions performed in 1996 were done on women who described themselves as born again or evangelical.
   - Both local and national church leaders are falling into sex scandals at alarming rates.
   - Teen pregnancy and out of wedlock birth rates in many local churches are about the same as they are in secular society.
7. Phinehas was called, anointed and equipped to address the sexual revolution that had infiltrated the wilderness church, and was destroying his generation.
8. The judgment of God against sexual idolatry was unleashed upon the church. Twenty-four thousand men perished in one day. At this rate, all fighting-aged men would have been dead within about three weeks.
9. The ministry of Phinehas was important in that the second census could not take place until he had done what God had raised and anointed him to do: resist the spirit of sexual idolatry (doctrine of Balaam) and implement God's healing to a generation that had been wounded by ungodly sexual covenants.

10. The church is at a great crossroad. The church is on the brink of a great spiritual move of God. Before this move can be fully implemented, the issue of sexual sin within the church must be addressed.

11. As we enter the new millennium, we will witness the end and the beginning of three major cycles that are spiritually relevant: a 100-year cycle, a 1000-year cycle and a 2000-year cycle.

12. These three cycles speak to this generation prophetically.
    100 speaks of grace and divine enablement.
    1000 speaks of the glory of God revealed.
    2000 speaks of a prophetic outpouring coming upon
    the church.

13. As we rapidly move into the twenty-first century, God will continue to demand accountability for hidden sexual covenants. He will continue to demand that His church be an example of sexual purity and godliness.

Chapter Five

HOMOSEXUALITY AND THE CHURCH

Thou shalt not lie with mankind, as with womankind: it is abomination.

Leviticus 18:22

And likewise also the men, leaving the natural use of the woman, burned in their lust one toward another; men with men working that which is unseemly, and receiving in themselves that recompense of their error which was meet.

Romans 1:27

This chapter is *not* being written to:

1. "Bash" practicing homosexuals (gay bashing).

I am not interested in "bashing" anyone. My job is to present biblical truth and focus this truth upon the sexuality issue. In presenting truth, we are often compelled to take an uncompromising stand on the issues.

2. Convince homosexuals to stop practicing homosexuality.

I have found that people are going to do what they want. In such cases, it is not my intent to try and convince people against their own will. People have a God-given, God-ordained right to make personal choices. My job is to *warn* people of the spiritual consequences of those choices.

3. Make a political statement about homosexuals or homosexuality.

I have no interest in politics per se. I am not a politician. I am a veterinarian by profession, a scientist by training and a *preacher* by calling. Herein lies my motivation: to preach and proclaim the life-changing, sin-purging gospel of Jesus Christ. I realize that the issue of homosexuality has, over the years, become a political issue as homosexuals have sought to gain legal status for their lifestyle choices. Be that as it may, I am still compelled to call sin, sin—even at the expense of being called a homophobic bigot and "politically incorrect."

4. To stir up hatred against homosexuals.

It is not my desire to stir up hatred toward the homosexual anymore than it is my desire to stir up hatred toward the prostitute, adulterer, pedophile, or fornicator. As a preacher of the gospel, if I preach against adultery, does that mean I want people to go out and kill adulterers? If I preach that prostitution is a sin, does that mean that I want people to go out and start killing prostitutes and their "johns"? Of course not! The intent is to communicate the life changing gospel of Jesus Christ to those who see the need and want to change.

5. To promote homophobia.

By definition, homophobia is the fear of homosexuals. Homosexuals are not to be feared. They are to be loved like any other sinner, just as God loves the sinner but does not love the sinner's sin. God loves the homosexual but does not love homosexuality. God loves the adulterer but does not love adultery. God loves the prostitute, but He does not love prostitution. If I "feared" the homosexual, I would be afraid to tell them biblical truth.

6. Hurt gays or lesbians.

If you are one who is inclined to hate, hurt, or harass homosexuals because of their sexual choices, then you need to repent and seek the forgiveness of the God of the Bible. The Bible states that "God so loved the world that He gave His only begotten Son." The love that God has for the world includes the gays and the lesbians. God never endorsed hating the homosexual or any other sinner. Through His compassion and power, we are to preach the truth of God's Word in a spirit of love and humility. The truth is this: God loves the homosexual, but He rejects the sin of homosexuality.

A homosexual is a person who has sexual relations with other individuals of their own gender. The word "homosexual" is composed of the prefix "homo," meaning "same," and the word "sexual." Thus, the literal meaning of homosexual is "same sex." One of the words used to describe Jehovah's disdain for this particular practice is "abomination." The Hebrew word here is *toebah* (8441), which is often used to describe the kind of activity that is rooted in the worship of false gods. Homosexuality was a common practice in the worship of Baal.[1] These customs are particularly abhorrent in the mind and heart of God. Jehovah's disdain for this particular custom (sodomy), was made evident when He destroyed the cities of Sodom and Gomorrah (Genesis 19).

Biblical Perspective

Lesbianism

The term "homosexual" applies to both males and females who are sexually intimate with individuals of the same gender. For female homosexuals, the term "lesbian" is also used. This word is also of Greek origin. The Greek poetess Sappho, who lived around 600 B.C., wrote sexually explicit poetry to women. Sappho lived on the island of Lesbos, from which the term lesbian is derived.

The apostle Paul wrote:

> *For this cause God gave them up to* vile affections: *for even the women did change the natural use to that which is* against nature.
>
> Romans 1:26 (emphasis added)

Paul characterizes the practice of lesbianism (women having sex with women) as a "vile" affection. The word translated "vile" here is *atimia* (819), meaning "shameful, disgraceful and/or dishonorable." These are those inward passions or impulses that dishonor God's original intent for humanity. From the New Testament, biblical perspective, homosexual practices are vile, shameful, disgraceful and dishonorable.

Even though Paul is a man of great intellectual capacity, his argument in condemning the sin of lesbianism is not an intellectual one. He condemns this activity on the basis of what is universally accepted as "natural" law. Simply stated, it (homosexuality) is not natural. It is not consistent with the divine laws that govern the natural universe. In the natural order, males were designed to sexually engage females for the purpose of reproduction.

This natural principle is found throughout the animal kingdom. If homosexuality was to be universally adopted, life on earth, as we know it, would cease. In lesbianism, the woman's physical body is used in a manner that it was not designed for. Paul is saying that the female sex organs are functioning in a way that violates its physical and natural design. This unnatural change in function is "against nature."

"Against Nature"

The Bible teaches that homosexual activities are contrary to the natural order. This behavior opposes nature's scheme. The word "nature" as used here is *phusis* (5449), meaning to "germinate" or grow by germination or natural production.

Germination is the growth and development of a "seed" after it has been planted. Paul is alluding to the fact that a woman's body was designed to:

1. Be impregnated with a man's "seed".
2. Nurture and nourish that seed.
3. Allow that seed to grow until it is birthed nine months later.

God designed and equipped the woman with the "tools" that would allow implantation, growth and development (germination) of her husband's seed. This growth and germination process cannot take place when two women are having sex. It is not nature's design or intent. Paul's argument is clear: If every woman engaged exclusively in lesbian practices, there would be no germination or growth of the human population. This lifestyle would lead to the universal annihilation of the human race. This lifestyle choice is a choice that people have a right to make, but, clearly, Bible doctrine does not support or encourage this choice.

Paul's argument is simple, yet irrefutable. This 2000-year-old argument is so effective that the homosexual community began to adopt it themselves when they proclaimed that homosexuals were "born that way." There are those that would have us believe that sexual orientation is a matter of "genetic destiny" and not a matter of personal choice. These proponents say that homosexuality is as natural or as normal as heterosexuality.

Twenty years ago, the gay community successfully argued that sexual orientation was a lifestyle "choice." More recently, the gay community has insisted that homosexuality is a genetically inherited trait and not a "choice" after all.[2] The gay community takes the argument a step further: Since homosexuality is a biologically inherited trait, homosexual behavior should have legal protection under the law. Even though there is no scientific evidence of the existence of a "gay gene," there are those who continue to use the "nature" argument in defense of their lifestyle choice. Paul's argument against lesbianism still stands as strong today as it did 2000 years ago.

> *For even their women did change the natural use into that which is against nature.*
>
> Romans 1:26 (emphasis added)

The Effeminate and the Abusers: Unseemly Behavior

> *And likewise also the men, leaving the natural use of the woman, burned in their lust one toward another; men with men working that which is unseemly, and receiving in themselves that recompense of their error which was meet.*
>
> Romans 1:27 (emphasis added)

> *Know ye not that the unrighteous shall not inherit the kingdom of God? Be not deceived: neither fornicators, nor*

idolaters, nor adulterers, nor effeminate, *nor* abusers of themselves with mankind.

1 Corinthians 6:9 (emphasis added)

Homosexuality is the abandonment of the natural male/female sexual relationship in order to engage in unnatural sexual intercourse with another male. Once again, Paul speaks of the "natural use" of the woman, making reference to the physical design of the woman. God designed the female vagina to accommodate the male penis. It is the natural order and basis for male/female sexual relations.

> *So God created man in his own image, in the image of God created he him;* male and female *created he them.*

Genesis 1:27 (emphasis added)

On the other hand, the rectum was *not* designed to accommodate the penis. Paul speaks of "working that which is unseemly." In Greek terminology, the word "unseemly" (808) is a direct reference to the male or female genitals or human nakedness. The word is also translated as "shame" or "indecency". In using this word within this context, the apostle Paul is making reference to the indecent and shameful use of the genitals when they are used in homosexual sex. This may also be Paul's way of describing sodomous activity between two men. Sodomy is contrary to the natural order that God established in the beginning.[3] Divine order speaks out loudly against the practice of homosexuality.

> *For this cause God gave them up unto vile affections: for even their women did change the natural use into that which is against nature: And likewise also the men, leaving the natural use of the woman, burned in their lust one toward another; men with men working that which is unseemly, and receiving in themselves that recompense of their error which was meet.*

Romans 1:26,27

> *And likewise also the men...*

Romans 1:27a

In the same manner, Paul asserts that men followed suit in their pursuit of same sex relations even as the women had done. Paul classifies male on male sex in the same category as female on female sex, that is, as "vile affections."

> *...leaving the natural use of the woman....*
>
> Romans 1:27b

Men forsook or rejected the natural use of the woman. This rejection is rooted in fallen man's rejection of God Himself. The word translated "natural" here is the Greek word *phusikos* (5446) meaning "physical, inborn, or instinctive." It has to do with those patterns of behavior that do not have to be taught or instructed in order to be learned. These are naturally acquired behavioral patterns. The key thought is that God, in creation, "designed" a man to sexually desire a woman. A woman was designed in such a way as to attract and captivate a man spiritually, emotionally and physically.

These instinctive, inborn propensities are responsible for the male and female courtship and mating patterns. It should be pointed out that a *man was not "designed" (born instinctively) to sexually desire another man.* Many who practice homosexuality claim that they were "born that way." This position is unbiblical, unscientific and unnatural. The fact of the matter is this, *we were all born sinners, but we "choose" the sin that appeals to our fallen humanity.* Homosexuality is one choice among many sins that a sinner may or may not choose to practice or commit.

What does Paul mean when he speaks of the natural use of the woman? In this case he is specifically addressing the issue of sexual intercourse and the design of the woman's body to be employed for this purpose, including conception, gestation and lactation. Paul speaks of the *use* of the woman, not *abuse* of the woman. The word "woman" in the Greek is *thelus* (2338). The prefix *thele* means "nipple" or "to give suck." In using this word, Paul is making reference to the God given ability of the woman (mature female) to birth forth life and sustain that life. It also speaks of the anatomical and biological differences that God has ordained in man and woman from creation. The homosexual act may produce an orgasm, but it cannot produce a human life; and it will never glorify God the Creator who designed sex with reproduction in mind.

By rejecting the natural course of human sexual relations, the homosexual rejects:

1. God's spiritual law.
2. God's natural law.
3. The instinctive and innate mechanisms of attraction to the opposite sex.
4. The divine plan for sexual fulfillment.

...burned in their lust one toward another...

Romans 1:27c

The word "burned" used here is *ekkaio* (1572), meaning "to inflame," "to kindle," "to set ablaze," or "to set on fire." This is an important word that gives us significant insights into sexual sin in general and homosexuality in particular. The word *ekkaio* is built from the prefix *ek*, meaning "outward" or "outside," and *kaio*, meaning "to set ablaze" or "to set on fire." The prefix *ek* is significant because it denotes the origin of the "fire." The sin of homosexuality is kindled (initiated) by *external factors*. In other words, it is *not* innate or something one is born with. It is a behavior that is *learned or acquired* at some point *after* birth. Many people will testify that an older individual initiated them into homosexuality, oftentimes when they were young, vulnerable and impressionable. They were initially "set ablaze" (*ekkaio*) by external forces that have, over a period of time, developed into personal lifestyle choices. In fact, there are those sexual-reorientation therapists who report high rates of molestation in the early childhood of their homosexual clients.[4] We don't fully understand why people make the choices that they make, but we do know that sexually abused children are more likely to become an abuser in adulthood.[5]

The Greek word for lust is *orexis* (3715). It means "excitement of the mind." Sexual sin and perversion, including homosexuality, is often initiated and perpetuated by the continuous exposure of the mind to those elements that propagate illicit sexual behavior. This is why it is so important to avoid pornographic and sexually explicit material that is designed to incite lust.

… men with men working that which is unseemly…

Romans 1:27d

This passage refers to men engaging in sodomous activity (e.g. oral or anal sex). The Greek word for man is *arsen*. In 1 Corinthians 6:9, Paul uses the word *arsenokoites* to describe male homosexual activity. Arsenokoites is a graphic depiction of a man who penetrates (anally or orally) another male. This is the sinful act of a man who approaches and uses another male sexually, as if he were a woman. The apostle goes on to say that this type of behavior is "unseemly"(808). This word refers to the genitals and the shameful way in which they are used. Contrast this statement of shame with the pride exhibited by many gay rights activist who claim that the Bible supports their sex style.

> *…and receiving in themselves that recompense of their error which was meet.*

Romans 1:27e

When a man engages in this type of activity, spiritual laws are violated. When spiritual laws are violated, spiritual penalties result. In God's justice system, the punishment will always fit the crime, and the only "plea bargain" is repentance. In the case of the homosexual, the penalty is "received in themselves," that is, in their physical bodies. More often than not, the homosexual lifestyle leads to sickness, disease and a premature death.[6]

Paul speaks of "their error." The Greek word used here is *plane*, meaning "fraudulent," "deceit," "delusional," or "deception." Clearly, by biblical standards, this sex style is fraudulent. Any person who engages in homosexual activity and thinks that it is an act to be proud of is deceived in their heart and delusional in their thinking. Any church or denomination that ordains homosexual pastors or priests or sanctions homosexual weddings is under the strong influence of a spirit of deception (delusion).

> *And for this cause God shall send them strong delusion, that they should believe a lie: That they all might be*

damned who believed not the truth, but had pleasure in unrighteousness.

2 Thessalonians 2:11,12 (emphasis added)

Spirit of Deception

In 1 Corinthians 6:9, Paul explains that sexual sin, including homosexuality, is rooted in deception.

Be not deceived.

1 Corinthians 6:9

The word "deceived" used here means "to be swayed by false impression, delusional (in one's) thinking, or to mentally stray." Sexual sin is one of the most powerful tools of deception there is. When one is under the influence of a spirit of homosexuality, that person is greatly deceived. This level of deception is dangerous because the one being deceived has reached a point in which their ability to reason properly has, apparently, malfunctioned. You see, deception has little to do with *what you see*; it has to do with your ability to correctly *interpret what you see.* The deceived is unable to reason and come to the proper conclusion, even after thorough inspection of the factual realities. It is difficult to convince the deceived differently because of an apparent malfunctioning of reasoning capacity. To the deceived, up becomes down, wrong becomes right, good becomes evil and darkness becomes light. In the case of the homosexual, sodomy with another man becomes a perfectly normal, healthy and legitimate alternate sex style. It is one thing to commit sin covertly, but to commit sin openly and boldly proclaim how proud you are in doing so, is deception at its worst.

Among the ancient Greek and Roman elite, homosexual love was considered to be on a higher spiritual plane than heterosexual love. Pederasty, sodomy between an adult male and a young boy, was openly practiced by a number of Roman emperors, including Nero.[7] Throughout ancient Greece, Sparta and Rome, there were public laws sanctioning pederasty.[8] In a recent article published by the American Association of Psychologists (APA), the claim was made that adult-child sex with willing children may not be harmful, and may even be beneficial.[9] This is merely the first step in trying to desensitize the public to the idea that pedophilia, incest, child sexual abuse and the seduction of minors is a culturally and socially acceptable behavior that should be sanctioned and legalized.

When Paul wrote the book of 1 Corinthians, not only was there a temple in Corinth dedicated to Venus (Aphrodite), the goddess of sexual love,[10] there was also a temple dedicated to the god Apollo, where male homosexual prostitutes were employed for those who engaged in homosexual acts. The sin of homosexuality was by no means confined to the Graeco-Roman world. It was practiced, generally in association with idol worship, the world over.

OLD TESTAMENT PERSPECTIVE

In the Old Testament, homosexuality was considered an abominable act.

> *Thou shalt not lie with mankind, as with womankind: it is abomination.*
>
> Leviticus 18:22

> *If a man also lie with mankind, as he lieth with a woman, both of them have committed an abomination: they shall surely be put to death; their blood shall be upon them.*
>
> Leviticus 20:13

Under the Law of Moses, homosexuality, as with many other transgressions, was punishable by death. We are no longer under this aspect of the law; therefore, *to perpetrate violence upon people because of their sexual preference is no longer acceptable to God.* This Scripture reference is merely being used to affirm Old Testament doctrine against the practice of homosexuality.

> *There shall be no whore of the daughters of Israel, nor a* sodomite *of the sons of Israel".*
>
> Deuteronomy 23:17 (emphasis added)

The woman shall not wear that which pertaineth unto a man, neither shall a man put on a woman's garment: for all that do so are abomination unto the LORD thy God.

Deuteronomy 22:5

The Old Testament reinforces God's disapproval for homosexual behavior in the infamous story of Sodom and Gomorrah (Genesis 19). It is the city of Sodom that the word "sodomy" (anal intercourse) is derived. For centuries now, Sodom has been the symbol of the divine retribution that await those who indulge in the sin of homosexuality. The fiery destruction of these two cities is an eternal reminder of God's rejection of this sex style.

It should be pointed out that homosexuality was probably rejected by the Jews because of its association with the worship of idol gods.[11] Homosexuality was indeed a common sacrifice among the worshipers of the sex god Baal.[12] In the mind of the Jew, rejecting homosexuality was the equivalent of rejecting idolatry in its worst form. They viewed homosexuality as an act of spiritual apostasy, which meant leaving Jehovah for another god. There is not one single reference in the Old Testament that condones or encourages homosexuality.

New Testament Perspective

New Testament doctrine is in harmony with Old Testament Scripture in its rejection of the sin of homosexuality. Here are three scriptural references that specifically refer to male homosexuality.

And likewise also the men, leaving the natural use of the woman, burned in their lust one toward another; men with men working that which is unseemly, *and receiving in themselves that recompense of their error which was meet.*

Romans 1:27 (emphasis added)

Know ye not that the unrighteous shall not inherit the kingdom of God? Be not deceived: neither fornicators, nor idolaters, nor adulterers, nor effeminate, *nor abusers of themselves with mankind, Nor thieves, nor covetous, nor drunkards, nor revilers, nor extortioners, shall inherit the kingdom of God.*

1 Corinthians 6:9,10 (emphasis added)

Knowing this, that the law is not made for a righteous man, but for the lawless and disobedient, for the ungodly and for sinners, for unholy and profane, for murderers of fathers and murderers of mothers, for manslayers, For whoremongers, for them that defile themselves with mankind, for menstealers, for liars, for perjured persons, and if there be any other thing that is contrary to sound doctrine.

1 Timothy 1:9,10 (emphasis added)

In each of these passages, the apostle Paul uses explicit language to describe those who engage in the homosexual act. I believe that he does so to leave no doubt in the mind of the reader, present and future, as to what he is talking about. For example, in 1 Corinthians 6:9 he uses the words "effeminate"(Greek *malakos*) and "abusers of themselves with mankind" (*arsenokoites*). Those who translated these words from the original Greek really toned down the force of language that Paul was using. In a sense, many in our culture would find Paul's language to be quite offensive. The "effeminate" is the man who allows himself to be sexually used as a woman, that is, a man who allows himself to be sodomized (anally penetrated) by another man. The *arsenokoite* is a man who actually sodomizes (penetrates) another man. In essence, Paul is incriminating both the anally "penetrated" (effeminate) and the "penetrator" (*arsenokoite*).

In 1 Timothy 1:9,10, Paul groups homosexuality along with other sins that are "contrary to sound doctrine." This is an important point of consideration for what is becoming a growing controversy in the church. There are major Christian denominations that are now ordaining gay and lesbian priests and ministers. In many churches, homosexuality is now tolerated and accepted as if it were a biblically endorsed behavior. What we are seeing is a gradual polluting of the "doctrinal" purity that makes for a called out and separated people (Jude 3).

There is much debate as to who will inherit the kingdom of God. Major denominations are struggling with ordaining homosexual priests. Currently, mainline denominational churches (Episcopal, Lutheran, Methodist, Presbyterian and United Church of Christ) are deeply divided over this issue.[13]

In justifying the ordination of homosexual ministers, some argue that the New Testament is not really clear on this issue. This argument is untrue. Paul uses very clear language in addressing homosexuality. They also argue that Jesus never really addressed the issue. This argument implies that if He (Jesus) had openly condemned homosexuality, those who are practicing homosexuality would not do so. This, of course, is not the case.

In refuting this weak argument, I would simply say that Jesus' silence on this issue does not mean he approved of the behavior. The same argument can be made that Jesus never addressed or openly condemned the smoking of crack cocaine, selling dope, or pimping women. Also, Jesus never addressed the sin of pedophilia (sexually molesting children). Does His silence on these issues mean that He approved of the practice of these sins? No. This is a very foolish and empty argument. Jesus' silence does *not* imply Jesus' approval.

The main reason that Jesus never addressed homosexuality is because there was no *need* to address this sin within the cultural context of His day. In Jesus' day, among his Jewish contemporaries, homosexuality was a taboo that was consistently and fervently rejected. From a cultural standpoint, homosexuality was thoroughly rejected and discouraged in the Jewish society of Jesus' day. Unlike our present day culture, there were no "gay pride" parades and homosexual rights organizations to contend with. For all practical purposes, it was not a sin that was prevalent in the culture of Israel in Jesus' day. Why should He go about preaching against that which was virtually nonexistent? Jesus addressed those issues and sins that were pressing and relevant to the culture and times in which He lived.

Adokimos: *Mental Depravity*

> And likewise also the men, leaving the natural use of the
> woman, burned in their lust one toward another; men
> with men working that which is unseemly, and receiving
> in themselves that recompense of their error which was
> meet. And even as they did not like to retain God in their

knowledge, God gave them over to a reprobate mind, to do those things which are not convenient.

Romans 1:27,28 (emphasis added)

A reprobate mind results from:

1. The (willful) psychological rejection of God and the things He represents.
2. God rejecting the sinner.
3. God surrendering the rejected sinner over to the perversion of his or her choice.

Paul seems to be implying that the homosexual sex style is a depraved condition that warranted God's complete rejection. When our thoughts reach this level of depravity, it presents a serious spiritual problem.

> *And GOD saw that the wickedness of man was great in the earth, and that every imagination of the thoughts of his heart was only evil continually.*

Genesis 6:5

When the mind becomes alienated from God, the potential for depraved behavior is great. A reprobate mind works to the detriment of the sinner in two ways. First, God gives the reprobate over to those spiritual entities that are ensnaring his or her soul. God literally removes any protective hedge and allows that person space and opportunity to indulge in his sin. Secondly, the reprobate becomes ensnared in a vicious, downward cycle of sin and depravity.

> *But every man is tempted, when he is drawn away of his own lust, and enticed. Then when lust hath conceived, it bringeth forth sin: and sin, when it is finished, bringeth forth death.*

James 1:14,15

The reprobate, try as he may, will never satisfy his insatiable lust because this lust is spiritual in nature. Problems that are spiritual in nature cannot be solved by natural means alone. In his futile attempt to fulfill his lust, he reaps the destructive spiritual and physical *consequences of his sin.*[14]

> And thou mourn at the last, when thy flesh and thy body are consumed.
>
> Proverbs 5:11

The Demise of Man

For the wrath of God is revealed from heaven against all ungodliness and unrighteousness of men, who hold the truth in unrighteousness; Because that which may be known of God is manifest in them; for God hath shewed it unto them. For the invisible things of him from the creation of the world are clearly seen, being understood by the things that are made, even his eternal power and Godhead; so that they are without excuse: Because that, when they knew God, they glorified him not as God, neither were thankful; but became vain in their imaginations, and their foolish heart was darkened. Professing themselves to be wise, they became fools, And changed the glory of the incorruptible God into an image made like to corruptible man, and to birds, and fourfooted beasts, and creeping things. Wherefore God also gave them up to uncleanness through the lusts of their own hearts, to dishonour their own bodies between themselves: Who changed the truth of God into a lie, and worshiped and served the creature more than the Creator, who is blessed for ever. Amen. For this cause God gave them up unto vile affections: for even their women did change the natural use into that which is against nature: And likewise also the men, leaving the natural use of the woman, burned in their lust one toward another; men with men working that which is unseemly, and receiving in themselves that recompense of their error which was meet. And even as they did not like to retain God in their knowledge, God gave them over to a reprobate mind, to do those things which are not convenient; Being filled with all unrighteousness, fornication, wickedness, covetousness,

maliciousness; full of envy, murder, debate, deceit, malig-
nity; whisperers, Backbiters, haters of God, despiteful,
proud, boasters, inventors of evil things, disobedient to par-
ents, Without understanding, covenantbreakers, without
natural affection, implacable, unmerciful: Who knowing
the judgment of God, that they which commit such things
are worthy of death, not only do the same, but have pleas-
ure in them that do them.

Romans 1:18-32

Romans 1 accurately describes fallen man's spiritual, moral and cultural digression. As his relationship with the one true God deteriorated, so did his culture and his civilization. The destruction of his culture was in direct proportion to his rebellion against the one true God. At the heart of the cultural decay that many ancient civilizations experienced was a corrupt system of worship with its manifest sexual idolatry.

Ultimately, it was fallen man's corrupt disposition toward God's revealed truth that led to his cultural, social and personal demise. There are five key terms that are alluded to in Romans 1:18-32 that describe fallen man's attitude toward God's revealed truth. They are:

- *Subversion* of the truth: to overthrow or destroy; to undermine that which is already established.
- *Aversion* to the truth: the act of avoiding or turning away from.
- *Perversion* of the truth: to deviate from the norm; to distort, twist, or misinterpret; to change the meaning of.
- *Inversion* of the truth: to turn upside down; to reverse the order; to move in the opposite direction.
- *Diversion* from the truth: the act of distracting the attention.

Subversion of the Truth

For the wrath of God is revealed from heaven against all *ungodliness* and *unrighteousness of men, who hold the* *truth in unrighteousness.*

Romans 1:18 (emphasis added)

Ungodliness is *asebeia*, literally "corrupt worship."[15] Ungodliness (corrupt worship) produces unrighteous and irreverent (immoral) behavior. In order to justify their unrighteous behavior, ungodly men "hold the truth" in unrighteous. The word "hold," as used here, literally means "to suppress." The apostle Paul is saying that those who persist in immoral behavior suppress the truth. To suppress means to restrain or hold down by force. In other words, ungodly men restrain, block, or otherwise try to prevent the truth from rising to its proper place. In effect, the truth is subverted. As long as the truth of God is suppressed or subverted, it will never be able to do what it was designed to do: convert the soul, renew the mind and save the sinner.

Aversion to the Truth

> And even as they did not like to retain God *in their knowl-edge, God gave them over to a reprobate mind, to do those things which are not convenient.*
>
> Romans 1:28 (emphasis added)

Aversion means to avoid something because of hatred or dislike. Ungodly men, in their fallen state, rejected God's truth because they "did not like to retain God" in their knowledge. In turning away from God, they refused to even recognize and acknowledge Him in their thoughts. After careful consideration of the self-evident truths of God, they discarded Him from the minds. They simply did not like what they saw in God. They avoided thinking about God and the things that pleased Him.

> And this is the condemnation, that light is come into the world, and men loved darkness rather than light, because their deeds were evil.
>
> John 3:19

Fallen man's love for the things of darkness alienated him from the light of God's truth. When one's eyes have grown accustomed to darkness, light becomes uncomfortable and is often avoided.

Perversion of the Truth

> *For this cause God gave them up unto* vile affections: *for even their women did change the natural use into that which is against nature.*
>
> Romans 1:26 (emphasis added)

Perversion is deviation from the natural use of a thing. Perverted behavior is the result of corrupt worship. The word "vile" as used here means "without value," "without honor," or "worthless." It is the type of affection that produces despicable, degrading, disgraceful and disgustingly shameful behavior. Having *subverted* the truth and having *avoided* God in their thinking (aversion), ungodly people begin to *pervert* (change or distort) the natural order.

Sodomy, which is anal intercourse, is perverted sex. Why? Because in the natural order of things, the anus was not designed to accommodate the penis (or any other elongated object used to produce friction). The cells lining the anus are too thin to withstand that kind of activity. Many blood borne infections can be contracted in the practice of sodomy. This is the origin of the so called "gay bowel syndrome."[16]

Inversion of the Truth

> *And likewise also the men, leaving the natural use of the woman, burned in their lust one toward another; men with men working that which is unseemly, and receiving in themselves that recompence of their error which was meet.*
>
> Romans 1:27

Inversion means to "reverse the order" or to "turn upside down." Here we see that homosexuality is behavior that is more than just perverted. It is behavior that literally turns God's natural order upside down. It strikes at the very life-sustaining, life-producing mechanism that God has ordained to propagate the human race from one generation to the next. If everyone practiced homosexual sex, the human race would be extinct in about two generations. It's really that simple.

A homosexual couple appeared on CNN Headline News a few months ago. They wanted to adopt a child, and their reason: as a couple, they were infertile! By definition, infertility is the inability to conceive or to induce conception. This is a classic example of inverting the truth, also known as redefining the truth. If a person were to plant an apple seed in a pot of sawdust and then declare the seed to be defective when it did not grow, one would think that person to be very foolish. The seed is not defective, it is just not being planted in the right kind of environment! Likewise, the homosexual who claimed infertility, is simply not planting his "seed" in the right kind of soil. He was *inverting*, or redefining, established truth.

Diversion from the Truth

> *Who* changed the truth *of God into a lie,* and worshiped and served the creature *more than the Creator, who is blessed for ever. Amen.*
>
> Romans 1:25 (emphasis added)

Diversion is distraction from the primary course, a breaking of focus. It is a fact of life that we were created with the capacity to know God and worship Him. We were created to worship. We will by nature worship something or someone. Rather than worship the true God, fallen man created substitute gods that were diversions from the one true God. These diversionary gods suited their taste and they began to worship them. These objects of worship (diversions), as noted in Romans 1:23, are historically consistent with the worship instituted by many ancient societies including: Babylon, Egypt, Greece, Rome and India.

> *And changed the glory of the incorruptible God into an image made like to* corruptible *man, and to birds, and fourfooted beasts, and creeping things.*
>
> Romans 1:23 (emphasis added)

Romans 1:24 reveals that diverting from true worship results in (sexual) uncleanness. Men began to engage in behaviors that were sexually unclean and spiritually defiling. They chose and fashioned gods that suited their lust. (For the historical analysis of fallen man's spiritual decline into sexual idolatry, see Volume 1, Chapter 3.)

> *Wherefore God also* gave them up to uncleanness *through the lusts of their own hearts, to dishonour their own bodies between themselves.*
>
> Romans 1:24 (emphasis added)

MILLENNIAL CONTROVERSY

As we move into the twenty-first century, one of the most critical issues that will face the church has to do with church doctrine regarding sexual sin in general, and homosexuality in particular. This issue of homosexual acceptance and gay rights is being waged within the church. Consider:

- In January 1999, sixty-eight Methodist ministers sanctioned the union of two lesbians.[17]
- The 5.2 million member Evangelical Lutheran church in America allows ordination of homosexuals.[18]
- The Episcopal church has been debating for thirty years whether to ordain homosexuals.[19] A church commission set up to study the issue has refused to take a position on same sex unions.[20]
- Estimations are that 25 percent of the Episcopal dioceses now ordain gay men and women.[21]
- The United Church of Christ permits the ordination of non-celibate homosexuals.[22]
- In a survey conducted among Catholic priests, about 60 percent said they knew of at least one priest who had died of AIDS. Thirty-three percent said they knew priests who where living with HIV or AIDS. Catholic priest are dying of AIDS related illness at a rate four times that of the general population.[23]
- Every major denomination will be forced to deal with the issue of gays within their midst.

The homosexual debate is expected to dominate the church conventions of the United Methodist, Presbyterian and Episcopal denominations.[24] Reconstructionist Judaism, the Unitarian Universalist Association and the United Church of Christ have all sanctioned same sex marriages.[25]

Biblical Christianity, Old or New Testament, has never condoned or sanctioned the homosexual lifestyle or any other sexual sin. The gospel is the "power of God unto salvation." Through Jesus Christ, the homosexual can be delivered from his/her sinful sex style and deception. The biblically correct Christian attitude toward the homosexual sex style is the same attitude that we should have toward any sinner who needs salvation. We love the sinner, but we reject the sinful behavior (even as God loves the sinner and rejects the sinful behavior).

There appears to be an all-out assault aimed at the doctrinal integrity and purity of the Word of God upon which the church is founded. As it says in Jude:

> *Beloved, when I gave all diligence to write unto you of the common salvation, it was needful for me to write unto you, and exhort you that ye should earnestly* contend for the faith *which was once delivered unto the saints. For there are certain men crept in unawares, who were before of old ordained to this condemnation, ungodly men, turning the grace of our God into* lasciviousness, *and denying the only Lord God, and our Lord Jesus Christ.*
>
> Jude 3,4 (emphasis added)

Church approval of the homosexual sex style is a sure sign that many of those who are in leadership position are no longer "earnestly contending for the faith." Jude apparently saw this coming assault upon the doctrinal purity of the church. It is as Jude articulated in verse 4: The grace of God is being turned into lasciviousness. Lasciviousness is the removal of all boundaries, limitations, and restraints. It is lust unrestrained. It is doing what we please, in open defiance to the Word of God.

LABELS

Homosexual behavior is often defended by labeling those who disagree with it as homophobic bigots and hatemongers. We are described as not having the "compassion" of Jesus. In reality, those who reject our message are the one's suffering with the phobias. They are what I call "gospelphobic" and "Biblephobic." These are individuals that suffer from acute to chronic fear of the Gospel of Jesus Christ. These people have an irrational fear of the preaching of the "whole" Bible!

Those who use the "compassion" argument to justify homosexuality have little understanding of Scripture. Indeed, Jesus was very compassionate, but his compassion for the sinner cannot be separated from the sinner's need to seek and receive forgiveness of his or her sin.

> *And Jesus said unto her, Neither do I condemn thee: go and* sin no more.
>
> John 8:11 (emphasis added)

> *Jesus…said unto him, Behold, thou art made whole,* sin no more.
>
> John 5:14 (emphasis added)

In these Scriptures we see that Jesus' compassion for the sinner is only expressed within the context of forgiveness of sin—sin from which the sinner must repent. True forgiveness can only be expressed within the context of repentance (of sin). Jesus' compassion for the homosexual sex style is expressed in His capacity to forgive the homosexual of his homosexuality. The homosexual, as any other sinner, can only take advantage of Jesus' compassion to forgive by repenting (turning away and rejecting) of their sin.

This attempt to legitimize the homosexual lifestyle in the church is equivalent to "turning the grace of God into lasciviousness." Lasciviousness is the New Testament word that is used to describe all manner of sexual sin, including, but not limited to, adultery, fornication, incest, sodomy, rape and homosexuality. Lasciviousness is also the failure to restrain and place godly boundaries upon ungodly thoughts and desires. Paul states that this is tantamount to "denying the Lord God and Jesus Christ." This is apostasy. Apostasy, by definition, is abandoning (departing) the Christian doctrine or faith. In 1 Timothy we read:

> *Now the Spirit speaketh expressly, that in the latter times some shall depart from the faith, giving heed to seducing spirits, and doctrines of devils.*
>
> 1 Timothy 4:1 (emphasis added)

Seducing Spirits

In this passage from 1 Timothy, the word "depart" implies that these individuals were once joined to the church. You can't depart from something you were never a part of. Sexual sin and its deceptive lure have caused many to depart from the faith by rejecting the Word of God. It is important to understand that we cannot name the name of Christ and habitually practice sexual sin (see 1 John 2:4).

> *Nevertheless the foundation of God standeth sure, having this seal, The Lord knoweth them that are his. And, Let every one that nameth the name of Christ depart from iniquity.*
>
> 2 Timothy 2:19

The God of the Bible requires that we choose our sin or His Savior. We cannot have both. We are rapidly approaching a period in church history whereby men are giving heed to "seducing spirits" and "doctrines of devils." In 1985, fifty leading religious scholars formed the Jesus Seminar. Their goal: revise Christian creeds and undermine biblical Christianity.[26] This new Christianity would depict Jesus as a "compassionate" teacher and emphasize forgiveness and freedom over punishment and piety. It would also endorse all forms of "protected recreational sex among consenting adults."

Chapter Summary

1. In Old Testament times, homosexuality (same sex unions) was an activity that was associated with the worship of false gods.
2. "Lesbianism" (female homosexuality) is a term that dates back to ancient Greek poetess Sappho who lived on the island of Lesbos.
3. In Romans chapter 1, the apostle Paul refers to homosexuality as a vile affection.

4. The apostle Paul rejects homosexuality as a viable lifestyle choice. His rejection of this practice is partially based on "natural law" theory.

5. Man, created in the image of God, has a natural attraction for the woman. This attraction has been biologically and spiritually engrained into his personhood. The introduction of sin greatly distorted this (godly) image. This (image) distortion came to manifest itself in attitudes, actions and behaviors that were ungodly (not like God). Fornication, adultery and homosexuality are behaviors that reflect a distortion of the image that man originally possessed in the beginning.

6. The act of homosexuality violates the "natural" design of the sexual body.

7. In the beginning, God designed and equipped the woman with the tools that would permit the implantation, fertilization and the germination of her husband's sperm (seed).

8. The rectum was not designed to accommodate the penis.

9. Ultimately, fallen man's rejection of the "natural" use of the woman is rooted in his rejection of God Himself.

10. Romans 1:27 indicates that homosexual behavior is learned or acquired at some point and time after birth. In other words, people are not born that way.

11. New Testament Bible doctrine is consistent with Old Testament Bible doctrine in rejecting the sin of homosexuality.

12. In rejecting God, and embracing (sexual) idolatry, fallen man's disposition toward the truth was altered. The five terms below describe mankind's disposition towards God's revealed truth.
    - Subversion: to overthrow or destroy; to undermine that which is already established.
    - Aversion: the act of avoiding or turning away from.
    - Perversion: to deviate from the norm: to distort, twist, or misinterpret, to change the meaning of.
    - Inversion: to turn upside down, to reverse the order, to move away from.
    - Diversion: the act of distracting the attention.

13. As we enter the twenty-first century, one of the most critical issues that will face the church will be the doctrine of sexual purity. There will be great pressure from worldly forces to

impose unbiblical sexual standards upon the church. In particular, homosexuality will become more and more controversial as many churches struggle with accepting or rejecting this lifestyle.

Chapter Six

MASTURBATION

Masturbation is defined as stimulation of the sex organs resulting in orgasm (sexual release). Masturbation my be achieved by manual manipulation, instrumental stimulation (dildos, vibrators, etc.) or by sexual fantasies. The word is of Latin derivation (*masturbatus* or *masturbari*) and is apparently a combination of two Latin words: *manus*, meaning "hand," and *stuprare*, meaning "defile" or "deflower." Thus, the literal meaning of the word "masturbation" is "to defile by use of the hand." Masturbation may be practiced by male or female, adolescent or adult.

As I travel to teach the principles in Volume 1, the most frequently asked questions have to do with masturbation. Is it right or wrong? What does the Bible have to say about it? What position should the church take on this issue? New Testament Scriptures do not specifically address this issue; that is to say, the word "masturbation" is not specifically addressed. What about the Old Testament? There are at least two Scriptures that are often quoted in reference to masturbation:

*And Judah said unto Onan, Go in unto thy brother's wife,
and marry her, and raise up seed to thy brother. And Onan
knew that the seed should not be his; and it came to pass,
when he went in unto his brother's wife, that he spilled it
on the ground, lest that he should give seed to his brother.
And the thing which he did displeased the LORD: wherefore he slew him also.*

Genesis 38:8-10

*When men strive together one with another, and the wife of
the one draweth near for to deliver her husband out of the
hand of him that smiteth him, and putteth forth her hand,
and taketh him by the secrets (penis): Then thou shalt cut
off her hand, thine eye shall not pity her.*

Deuteronomy 25:11,12

If we carefully study the first passage, we see that Onan was not masturbating at all. He was actually practicing *coitus interruptus*. This is a birth control technique practiced by many couples who do not want to have children. Sexual intercourse is engaged in up to the point of male ejaculation, at which time the man withdraws himself from the woman's vagina.

In some dictionaries, "onanism" is defined as masturbation. This, in my view, is not correct. Onan, whose name means "strong," was engaging in the pleasures of sexual intimacy with Tamar while at the same time willfully neglecting his *responsibility* to impregnate her. Too many men want the joys and pleasures of the sex act but refuse to take on the responsibility of fatherhood and child rearing. God never sanctions sex without commitment and responsibility.

SACRED OBJECTS

The second passage of Scripture (Deuteronomy 25:11,12) refers to the woman who, in the act of fighting her husband's enemy, grabs the enemy by the "secrets" (penis). Her punishment is severe ("cut off her hand"). In this context, there is nothing sexual about what she did; she was not trying to sexually stimulate the man. In defend-ing her husband, she was apparently trying to incapacitate his enemy. I believe that this Scripture is placing emphasis on the *sacred nature* of the man's sex organ (penis) and the unauthorized touching of that organ, even in the most dire circumstance. The unauthorized touching of sacred or hallowed objects is a very serious matter that can get you hurt or even killed. For example, in 2 Samuel 6 Uzzah put forth his hand to keep the ark of the covenant from falling. He died instantly for touching a *sacred object*, even though his motive in so doing was noble.

Petting is the manipulation or caressing of another's sex organ. It is also referred to as sexual "foreplay." I spoke at a meeting sponsored by a large Pentecostal denomination a few years ago, and one of the Bishops of that denomination publicly stated that there was nothing wrong with "petting." For a church bishop to sanction this type of sexual activity among single youth is a disgrace.

For married couples, sexual foreplay (petting) is good, righteous and holy, but for those who are not married, this type of touching is "unauthorized" and a violation of spiritual law. As Deuteronomy 25:11-12 and 2 Samuel 6 points out, unauthorized touching of sacred objects can get you into a lot of trouble.

So what does the Bible teach about masturbation? Let me say this, there are many topics that the Bible does not specifically address. For instance, the Bible does not specifically address the issue of cigarette smoking. However, the Bible does lay down principles that we can use to discern whether an activity or behavior is good or bad, right or wrong, moral or immoral. In the case of masturbation, I believe that there are biblical principles that will help us form a righteous opinion.

MASTURBATION: ANALYSIS, BIBLICAL GUIDELINES AND PRINCIPLES

According to a 1994 sex survey of Americans aged eighteen to fifty-nine, approximately 60 percent of men and 40 percent of women said that they had masturbated in the past year.[1] It was once thought that people engaged in masturbation because there was an absence of a sexual partner. The assumption was that masturbation was employed as a substitute for sex with a partner to release sexual tension. This may be true in some cases, but how does one explain the large number of people who practice masturbation and have readily available sex partners? The same question can be asked about those who commit adultery. Why do some people commit adultery when they have spouses who are being sexually intimate with them? Adultery, as with masturbation, cannot be for the sexual release alone. I believe that the Scripture can shed light on these questions.

Concupiscence

> *That every one of you should know how to possess his vessel in sanctification and honour; Not in the lust of* concupiscence, *even as the Gentiles which know not God.*
> 1 Thessalonians 4:4,5 (emphasis added)

> *Mortify therefore your members which are upon the earth; fornication, uncleanness, inordinate affection,* evil concupiscence, *and covetousness, which is idolatry.*
> Colossians 3:5 (emphasis added)

I believe that the key to understanding the sin of masturbation is found in what the apostle Paul calls "evil concupiscence." Masturbation is a behavior that has its origins in what the Bible calls "evil concupiscence." By definition, concupiscence is the ungodly, passionate, sexual desire that originates in, and is stimulated by, the mind. The Scripture teaches that sexual defilement of any kind originates in the mind.

> *For out of the heart proceed evil thoughts, murders, adulteries, fornications, thefts, false witness, blasphemies.*
> Matthew 15:19

Concupiscence is an interesting word. It appears to be derived from the combining of two words: "conscience" and "cupid." Cupid was the Roman god of sexual love. According to ancient myth, one arrow from cupid's bow was supposed to inflame sexual passion and desire in an individual. The Latin word *cupido* means "sexual desire." The conscience is the inner mental faculty which allows us to:

1. Discriminate between right and wrong.
2. Give rise to our thoughts.

When we combine these two words (cupid and conscience), we can more clearly understand what Paul was trying to communicate when he uses the phrase "evil concupiscence," that is, the passionate, sexual desire that is induced by exposing the mind to images that are sexually explicit in nature.

Evil concupiscence is the mental straying that leads to the ungodly behavior of masturbation. In Romans 1:27, the apostle Paul uses the word "lust" within the context of ungodly sexual behavior. In the Greek, this word is *orexis* which means to "excite the mind." When one begins to study masturbation and other ungodly expressions of sexual behavior, it becomes evident that there is a great deal of sexual idolatry, originating in the mind, that is rooted in pornographic activity.[2] There is, indeed, a great deal of masturbation that takes place in pornographic movie houses.

It is important to understand that masturbation is only the behavior or by-product of a mind that has been pornographically stimulated. There are many masturbators who cannot reach orgasm without pornographic images to aid their mental fantasies.[3] In men, sexually arousing thoughts can lead to penile erection.[4] One of the keys to dealing with masturbation is addressing why we allow impure, sexually arousing thoughts into our minds. One of the primary sources of sexual arousal (stimulation) for those who masturbate is pornography.[5]

> But every man is tempted, when he is drawn away of his own lust, and enticed. Then when lust hath conceived, it bringeth forth sin: and sin, when it is finished, bringeth forth death.
>
> James 1:14,15 (emphasis added)

Once the floodgate of the mind has been opened to sexual idolatry, ungodly soul ties seem to develop. The heart (soul) becomes more vulnerable to sexual sin. As the masturbator focuses on pornographic images, his heart is further deceived. As the heart becomes more entangled, the masturbator acts out his sexual fantasy in the form of masturbation. Masturbation is one of many sinful sexual behaviors that fall in the category of evil concupiscence.

But for Adam there was not found an help meet for him.

Genesis 2:20

The statement that no help was "found" for Adam implies that a search was made. I believe Adam was searching for help, and loneliness may have driven his search. I believe that Adam began to search the animal kingdom for "help." Instinctively, he knew that a dog could not be his best friend. I believe that he began to search himself and discovered that he was not able to "help" himself.

This is the essence of masturbation: a man or woman attempting to sexually fulfill themselves without a "help meet"/"counterpart." This activity is not consistent with God's divine strategy for sexual fulfillment. Perhaps Adam came to the conclusion that masturbation was not a suitable or proper consideration for him, and he rejected it as such.

In essence, masturbation is a man or woman having sex with him/herself. It is self-directed, self-administered sexual gratification. In a sense, a man having sex with himself (masturbation) is not much different than a man having sex with another man (homosexuality). In both cases a man is seeking sexual gratification from a male. From this standpoint, masturbation is self-directed, self-administered homosexual behavior. It is homosexuality in the "singular." Therefore, if homosexuality is immoral, then so is masturbation. If a man sexually stimulating another man is immoral and unbiblical, then so is a man sexually stimulating himself (masturbation). In this regard, masturbation and homosexuality are two closely related sins.

There are those who maintain that masturbation is merely practicing "safe sex." It is true that the spread of sexually transmitted diseases are greatly reduced, but this behavior is not without spiritual consequences.

Thou shalt not lie with mankind, as with womankind: it is abomination.

Leviticus 18:22

The word "lie" as used here connotes sexual intimacy or sexual relations. A male or female who seeks sexual release from a person of the same sex (homosexuality) or who seeks sexual release from him/herself (masturbation) is in violation of this spiritual law.

Seducing Spirits

Recently, a pastor of a church whose denomination has traditionally placed heavy emphasis on holy living told me that he did not discourage masturbation to those he counseled. He believed that masturbation was an acceptable alternative to extramarital sex. I believe that this kind of erroneous thinking is pervasive and has become the norm for many churches.

> *Beloved, when I gave all diligence to write unto you of the common salvation, it was needful for me to write unto you, and exhort you that ye should earnestly contend for the faith which was once delivered unto the saints.*
>
> Jude 1:3

To teach that masturbation is an acceptable alternative to extramarital sex is a mockery in itself. If the gospel of Jesus Christ is the "power of God unto salvation" (Romans 1:16), then it should be able to deliver an individual from any ungodly sexual urges, including masturbation. If not, then it cannot deliver an individual from homosexuality, adultery, fornication, or any other sexual sin. In regards to the doctrine that pertains to sexual relations, there is a great need for the church to "earnestly contend for the faith that was once delivered to the saints."

> *For there are certain men crept in unawares, who were before of old ordained to this condemnation, ungodly men, turning the grace of our God into lasciviousness, and denying the only Lord God, and our Lord Jesus Christ.*
>
> Jude 1:4

As I see it, unless there is widespread repentance, many churches will be deceived and swept away by a spirit of apostasy.

> *Now the Spirit speaketh expressly, that in the latter times some shall depart from the faith,* giving heed to seducing spirits, *and doctrines of devils.*
>
> 1 Timothy 4:1 (emphasis added)

Apostasy is defined as a falling away, a withdrawal, or defection. The Bible teaches about those who were once a part of the church and have ceased following sound doctrine. We are living in a critical hour. We have entered a new millennium. The spiritual atmosphere is changing. The church will continue to be pressured to "conform" to the world's standard of sexuality. The church will be pressured more and more to accept all manner of sexual sin as part of the biblical norm.

Even now, some churches are yielding to political and societal pressure and are ordaining homosexual priest and pastors to lead congregations. Even now, some churches are performing same sex marriages. Even as I write, many churches are struggling with whether to sanction "domestic partners" and elevate these kinds of relationships to the same level as legitimate, Bible-sanctioned, heterosexual marriage.[6]

Masturbation: Hidden Sexual Idolatry

But I say, that the things which the Gentiles sacrifice, they sacrifice to devils, and not to God: and I would not that ye should have fellowship with devils.

1 Corinthians 10:20

We need to understand the spiritual implications of the sex act. *Sex is a spiritual act.* When we engage in this act, we touch aspects of the spiritual realm that we know not of. The sex act, when it fulfills its true purpose, is a wonderful sacrament. Sex is a sacrament that should glorify God. When the sex act is abused and perverted it becomes a "sacrifice unto devils." In essence, this is precisely what masturbation is. Like all sexual sin, it is an ungodly sexual covenant that brings the masturbator in "fellowship" with unseen spiritual forces.

In addressing the sexual idolatry of his day, the prophet Isaiah condemns those who have entered into these ungodly, secret sexual covenants:

Behind the door and the doorpost you have directed your thoughts; *Abandoning me, you have gone up on the* couch

you made so wide. You have made a covenant with them,
you have loved bedding with them; *you have chosen lust.*
                    Isaiah 57: 8 (The Tanakh; emphasis added)

When one begins to look beneath the surface and more closely
examine the issue of masturbation, one can see that it is not a safe
and harmless means of attaining sexual release. Masturbation is an
act of psychological defilement. Isaiah 57:8 seems to indicate that the
thought life of those given to sexual sin is defiled. The mind of the
masturbator is consumed by ungodly sexual fantasy, which is usually
pornographic in nature. These types of hidden, mental activities, if
not cast down, will eventually lead to covenants with unclean spiritual forces (2 Corinthians 10:5). These forces can exert a tremendous, negative influence upon one's life to the point where the
masturbator becomes enslaved by his own lust.

This passage of Scripture also illustrates that God is intimately
familiar with your thought life. Evil thoughts can be a source of
offense to Him. It is clear from Scripture that God will hold us
accountable for the very thoughts that we think.

The thoughts *of the wicked are an abomination to the
LORD.*
                    Proverbs 15:26a (emphasis added)

*And GOD saw that the wickedness of man was great in the
earth, and that every imagination of the* thoughts *of his
heart was only evil continually.*
                    Genesis 6:5 (emphasis added)

In Genesis 6:5, evil thoughts led to wicked behavior. The wicked
behavior led to God's decision to destroy the earth with water. My
point is that you cannot separate the act of masturbation from the
pornographic thoughts that encourages the behavior. In Matthew
15:18-20, Jesus teaches that the process of defilement begins in the
mind, with the thoughts.

*But those things which proceed out of the mouth come forth
from the heart; and they defile the man. For out of the heart*

proceed evil thoughts, murders, adulteries, fornications, thefts, false witness, blasphemies: These are the things which defile a man.

Matthew 15:18-20a

Sexual Fantasy

It has been said that the most powerful human sex organ is the brain. The use of thought and mental imagery is what sets humans apart from animals and is important within the context of sexuality. Sexual fantasy may be defined as the sexual use of the imagination.[7] It is the act of forming mental images for the purpose of sexual arousal. Sexual fantasies are those mental experiences that arise from one's own imagination. There are typically two sources of sexual fantasies:

1. Past sexual encounters.
2. Erotic books, drawings, photographs, movies, videos, etc.[8]

Past Sexual Encounters

One of the problems many married couples have to deal with are the recurring fantasies that manifest concerning past sexual encounters (sexual encounters they may have had prior to getting married). Images of past sexual encounters may manifest from time to time, especially during moments of sexual intimacy with their present spouse. In one study, more than 70 percent of men and women reported using fantasy while having sex.[9] This can create real problems in a marriage, particularly when these fantasies concern past sexual relationships. Private fantasies of past sexual encounters, while being sexually intimate with your current spouse, may decrease the trust and intimacy in that relationship.[10] When a man or woman constantly fantasizes about past sexual encounters, this is an indication that a strong *ungodly soul tie* is present and needs to be broken. Pastors who counsel married couples should be aware of this potential roadblock and be prepared to help these couples overcome them scripturally.

Sexual Fantasy and Masturbation

Sexual (erotic) fantasy typically serves to enhance sexual arousal during masturbation.[11] The association of fantasy and masturbation is well-documented. One study found that 89 percent of males who had masturbated used fantasies as a source of stimulation while masturbating.[12] It is important to point out the relationship between sexual fantasy and masturbation because there are Christians who believe that masturbation is a healthy, harmless practice that has no spiritual consequences. Masturbation, because of the mental idolatry involved, is a practice that is condemned by Scripture:

> *But I say unto you, That whosoever looketh on a woman to lust after her hath* committed adultery *with her already* in his heart.
>
> Matthew 5:28 (emphasis added)

I want to reemphasize that the issue goes beyond the physical act of masturbating. Masturbation reflects the condition of the heart and the mind of the masturbator. The words of Jesus are key:

> *But those things which proceed out of the mouth* come forth from the heart; *and they defile the man. For* out of the heart proceed evil thoughts, *murders,* adulteries, fornications.
>
> Matthew 15:18,19 (emphasis added)

Those who think that masturbation is a harmless act, fail to recognize the *inner* defilement that it represents. They also fail to recognize that a heart and mind that are yielded to sexual idolatry can never please God. The masturbator commits adultery in his or her heart. This act violates the seventh commandment (Exodus 20:14) and reflects an attitude of rebellion toward God that resides within the heart.

When the masturbator is under the mental influence of a sexual fantasy, he or she becomes "fascinated" with an ungodly "fleshly lust" that will war against the soul.

> *Dearly beloved, I beseech you as strangers and pilgrims, abstain from fleshly lusts, which war against the soul.*
>
> 1 Peter 2:11

As the masturbator's sexual fantasy grows, so does his or her "fascination" with the object of his or her lust. The word "fascinate" or "fascination" is an interesting one. It means to cast a spell or to enchant. This is the effect of sexual idolatry because it brings the masturbator under its powerful sway (Hosea 4:11). It is interesting to note that the word fascination is derived from the ancient Latin word *fascinum.* The Roman fascinum was a charm, shaped like a penis, that was worn around the neck for good luck.[13] The masturbator is deceived and ensnared by the sexual fantasies that he allows to flood his mind as he seeks sexual release.

Bible-Based Sexual Fantasy?

I do not believe that all sexual fantasy in every context is evil any more than I believe that all sexual intimacy in every context is evil. For instance, sexual intimacy within the context of marriage is not evil but holy, healthy and biblical.

> *Let thy fountain be blessed: and rejoice with the wife of thy youth.*
>
> Proverbs 5:18

Generally speaking, for a husband *to think of his wife* in sexual terms, in my view is holy, healthy and biblical. I believe that God intended for a husband and wife to have sexual thoughts for each other. These kinds of thoughts and feelings were divinely inspired from the beginning and are foundational for a holy, healthy and biblical marriage.

> *Let her be as the loving hind and pleasant roe; let her breasts satisfy thee at* all times; *and be thou* ravished always *with her love.*
>
> Proverbs 5:19 (emphasis added)

> *Thou hast* ravished *my heart, my sister, my spouse; thou hast ravished my heart with one of thine eyes, with one chain of thy neck.*
>
> Song of Solomon 4:9 (emphasis added)

> *Therefore shall a man leave his father and his mother, and shall* cleave *unto his wife: and they shall be one flesh.*
>
> Genesis 2:24 (emphasis added)

These Scriptures describe a loving, mutually satisfying, sexual relationship between husband and wife that includes sexual thoughts for each other. In Proverbs 5:19, the writer uses the words "all times" and "always." These words refer to a continuous or perpetual event. Even when spouses are apart, their minds should be continuously filled with warm, loving, intimate thoughts of each other.

The Hebrew word translated "ravished" (3823) in Song of Solomon 4:9 makes reference to a heart that has been totally captivated. It is a heart that is filled with pleasure to the point of "intoxication." The Bible commands us to become intoxicated with the love (marital intimacy) of our spouses. When one is intoxicated, one is under the psychological influence of that which one is intoxicated by. Intoxication often times leads to addiction, which is precisely what marital intimacy (sex) was designed to bring about. Sex, within the confines of marriage, was designed to establish a bond of psychological, emotional, spiritual and physical interdependency. This marital bond (soul tie) was intended to be established and maintained for a lifetime.

This is the essence of the "Law of Cleaving" (Genesis 2:24), that is, the establishment of a permanent bond that was to be the foundational basis of the nuclear family.[14] In general, thoughts of a sexual nature that are directed toward one's own spouse are biblical, wholesome, holy and acceptable. Thoughts of this type pass the standard established by the Holy Spirit in the book of Philippians.

> *Finally, brethren, whatsoever things are true, whatsoever things are honest, whatsoever things are just, whatsoever things are pure, whatsoever things are lovely, whatsoever things are of good report; if there be any virtue, and if there be any praise, think on these things.*
>
> Philippians 4:8

There is nothing more true, more honest, more just (righteous), more pure, more lovely, more virtuous, or more praise worthy than a husband and wife being sexually intimate with each other. This is God's way. This is the biblical perspective.

> *I sleep, but my heart waketh: it is the voice of my beloved that knocketh, saying, Open to me, my sister, my love, my*

dove, my undefiled: for my head is filled with dew, and my locks with the drops of the night. I have put off my coat; how shall I put it on? I have washed my feet; how shall I defile them? My beloved put in his hand by the hole of the door, and my bowels were moved for him. My beloved is white and ruddy, the chiefest among ten thousand. His head is as the most fine gold, his locks are bushy, and black as a raven. His eyes are as the eyes of doves by the rivers of waters, washed with milk, and fitly set. His cheeks are as a bed of spices, as sweet flowers: his lips like lilies, dropping sweet smelling myrrh. His hands are as gold rings set with the beryl: his belly is as bright ivory overlaid with sapphires. His legs are as pillars of marble, set upon sockets of fine gold: his countenance is as Lebanon, excellent as the cedars. His mouth is most sweet: yea, he is altogether lovely. This is my beloved, and this is my friend, O daughters of Jerusalem.

Song of Solomon 5:2-16

In a moment of quiet contemplation, Solomon's bride engages in warm and affectionate thoughts of her husband. This passage of Scripture further illustrates the idea that the Bible endorses the type of fantasy that is directed toward one's spouse. This is a holy and acceptable expression that is a key element in the husband and wife "cleaving" to one another in lifelong union.

Chapter Summary

1. Masturbation is the stimulation of the sexual organ, usually resulting in orgasm.
2. Masturbation may be achieved by manual manipulation or instrumental stimulation (dildos, vibrators, etc.). It is usually aided by sexual fantasies.
3. The act of masturbation, as with most sexual sins, is lust that originates in the mind (Matthew 15:19). The New Testament Greek word for lust is *orexis* and it means to "excite or inflame the mind."
4. Masturbation is acting upon those mental images that have "inflamed" or aroused the flesh.

5. When we meditate and focus upon unclean thoughts that we have allowed to enter our mind, we will begin to act upon those thoughts. Masturbation is just one way in which unclean thoughts are acted upon.

6. Evil concupiscence is the New Testament way of describing the source of the mental straying that leads to the sexual sin of masturbation.

7. Evil concupiscence is (mental) idolatry.

8. Pornography, sexual fantasy and masturbation are related.

9. Those who view masturbation as a harmless act fail to recognize the rebellious disposition of the heart (toward God), that this behavior reflects. They fail to recognize the (mental) idolatry that is involved in this behavior (see Colossians 3:5).

10. Fantasizing about past sexual experiences may be detrimental to a marriage.

11. Recurring sexual fantasies about past sexual encounters is an indication that an ungodly soul tie has been established and needs to be broken.

12. All sexual fantasy is not inherently evil. Within the context of holy matrimony, fantasizing about one's spouse is healthy, holy and biblical (see Song of Solomon 5:2-16).

13. Masturbation is one of those sexual sins that "war against the soul" (see 1 Peter 2:11).

14. Here are some keys to dealing with the sin of masturbation:
    a. Acknowledge it as sinful and repent.
    b. Clean up the thought life, getting rid of and avoiding all sexually explicit material.
    c. Break ungodly soul ties.

Finally, brethren, whatsoever things are true, whatsoever things are honest, whatsoever things are just, whatsoever things are pure, whatsoever things are lovely, whatsoever things are of good report; if there be any virtue, and if there be any praise, think on these things.

Philippians 4:8 (emphasis added)

Chapter Seven

SEX DRIVE AND ACHIEVEMENT DRIVE:
DIVINELY UNITED

And God blessed them, and God said unto them, Be fruit-ful, and multiply, and replenish the earth, and subdue it: and have dominion over the fish of the sea, and over the fowl of the air, and over every living thing that moveth upon the earth.

Genesis 1:28

This chapter will emphasize these important facts:

- God's divine purpose is intimately connected to our sexuality.
- In the beginning, God placed two "divine motivators" within Adam:
  - a. A "sex drive."
  - b. An "achievement drive."
- These two "motivators" are linked to each other in that as we live sexually pure, we are able to reach our full achievement potential in the earth.

- As Adam's help meet, Eve was created and designed to be a stabilizing force in Adam's life as she:
  1. Ministered to his sex drive.
  2. Inspired him to great heights of achievement and accomplishment.

And God blessed them, and God said unto them, Be fruitful, *and* multiply, *and* replenish *the earth, and* subdue *it: and have* dominion *over the fish of the sea, and over the fowl of the air, and over every living thing that moveth upon the earth.*

Genesis 1:28 (emphasis added)

God has a divine purpose for each of us. His purpose is closely connected with our sexuality. In Genesis 1:28 God first commanded Adam to be fruitful, multiply and replenish the earth. Second, Adam was to subdue and have dominion over the earth. These five words are key to understanding God's divine purpose for mankind: fruitful, multiply, replenish, subdue and dominion.

Be Fruitful, Multiply and Replenish: Sex Drive

These three words make it clear that God expected Adam and Eve to function as sexual creatures within the earth realm. As sexual creatures, God endowed Adam with what is commonly called a "sex drive." This sex drive was to be an important and powerful influence in Adam's life. Through his sex drive, Adam would produce sons and daughters who would shape future events. It is essential that we understand that God's purpose for Adam was intimately connected with Adam's God-given ability to express himself sexually.

Subdue and Have Dominion: Achievement Drive

The Hebrew word for subdue is *kabesh* (3533), meaning to "conquer," "subjugate," or "disregard." This word implies that there would be obstacles and problems in life for Adam to overcome. God called Adam to conquer and subjugate. When something is subjugated, it is brought under control. What does "disregard" have to do with subduing? When life's problems and obstacles became overwhelming to the point that they seemed to be prohibiting Adam from accomplishing the will of God, Adam was to "disregard" them. Adam was not to deny the existence of obstacles, but he was not to allow these obstacles to dictate whether or not he succeeded in doing God's will. When the obstacle said, "No, you cannot," Adam was to disregard the negative and say, "Yes I can, and I will."

This is important because life is filled with obstacles that are constantly telling you that you cannot achieve this or that. The obstacles may be anything from prejudice to being raised in a single parent home. These obstacles were not to stop Adam, who was commanded and expected, with God's help, to disregard the obstacle and overcome anything that tried to hinder the will of God in his life.

The Hebrew word for dominion is *radah* (7287), meaning to "tread down," "rule," or "prevail against." This word also implies that there would be forces resisting Adam in his quest to fulfill the will of God in the earth. God's expectation was that Adam would crush all opposing forces that might try to hinder him. He was to put them under his feet, the place of submission. Jehovah expected Adam to subdue and take dominion because God had placed within Adam what I call the achievement drive.

Sex Drive and Achievement Drive: The Two Divine Motivators

The sex drive was to compel Adam to take on the marital commitment and replenish the earth with godly offspring. The sex drive afforded Adam the opportunity to experience an intimacy (between husband and wife) like no other on the face of the earth. On the other hand, the achievement drive compelled Adam to accomplish great things, to be successful in reaching his full potential by exerting himself. It was to motivate him in developing his intellect and in establishing a solid work ethic. God placed in Adam the ability to do, to become and to overcome. God gave Adam a strong desire to be a goal-oriented success and to take on responsibility. These two drives were to play important roles in the fulfillment of the divine purpose in the earth.

It is crucial that you realize:

• Your sex drive and your achievement drive are divinely connected.

- Your ability to subdue and take dominion in the earth will depend on how you submit your sex drive to God.
- If you do not live sexually pure, you will undermine your ability to achieve, succeed and walk in the fullness of God's purpose.
- Your sexuality and your ability to subdue and take dominion in the earth are divinely connected.

More specifically, if you submit your sex drive to the holy dictates of God's Word, you will greatly enhance your ability to take dominion in the earth realm. Conversely, if you do not submit your sex drive and allow it to be governed by God's Word, your ability to subdue and take dominion in the earth will be greatly hindered. (I will give biblical examples of this principle later.)

God placed a sex drive in Adam and connected his sex drive with a drive to achieve. This achievement drive was to inwardly motivate Adam to be successful, to take on responsibility and to overcome opposition. These two divine motivators (sex drive and achievement drive) were to complement each other by assisting Adam in the fulfillment of God's divine plan in the earth. These motivators would enable Adam to become a stable, socially responsible individual who could shoulder the responsibility of marital commitment and fatherhood and still achieve great things in the earth.

Testosterone

> *And God blessed them, and God said unto them, be* fruit- *ful, and* multiply, *and* replenish *the earth....*
>
> Genesis 1:28 (emphasis added)

The Effect of Testosterone on the Sex Drive

Testosterone is a hormone that is classified as an androgen (male) hormone because it is produced more abundantly in the male species. In fact, men have ten times more testosterone than women.[1] Testosterone is produced in the male testicle and is responsible for promoting sperm production, growth of pubic hair and all the secondary sex characteristics in the male. The male secondary sex characteristics include: facial hair growth, chest and armpit hair growth, lowering of the voice and broadening of shoulder and chest muscles.

Among the many effects that testosterone has upon the body, the most interesting has to do with its effect upon male *behavior*. The presence or absence of this hormone has profound effects on male sexual behavior.[2] Research on male rats shows that sexual behavior and testosterone blood levels decline after castration. Among human males, sexual interest and the potential for sexual activity are highest at the age when testosterone levels are highest (ages fifteen to twenty-five).[3] This is why the Holy Spirit, speaking through the apostle Paul, makes this statement:

> *Flee also youthful lusts....*
>
> 2 Timothy 2:22

The high levels of testosterone in the blood stream of fifteen- to twenty-five-year-old males makes this a very practical and relevant piece of advice from the apostle. The true test of a mature Christian is to avoid sexual temptation. There is no victory in exposing oneself to sexual situations for the sake of testing one's ability to resist sin! From a biological standpoint, men were designed in such a way that we are greatly affected when we expose our minds to pornographic images. The height of deception is to believe that you can look at adult magazines and watch adult movies (X-rated/NC-17) and not be affected by it. We must learn to flee youthful lust.

Men with low testosterone levels generally have lower than average frequencies of erection and sexual activity, although both frequencies increase after many of these men received testosterone injections.[4]

I make mention of these facts to point out that testosterone affects the male sex drive. Testosterone has another important function that relates to God's original plan at creation. It has to do with the effect that testosterone has upon male *social behavior*.

The Effect of Testosterone on the Achievement Drive

> *...Subdue it: and have dominion over the fish of the sea, and over the fowl of the air, and over every living thing that moveth upon the earth.*
>
> Genesis 1:28

Testosterone is also responsible for activating aggressive behavior in males. Most of the fighting that takes place within animal species is activated by sex hormones.[5] In many species, reproductively mature males fight one another vigorously during the mating season. This fighting is aimed at securing (protecting) territorial boundaries and maintaining the right to mate with the females. Castrated males fight very little, but testosterone injections restore the aggressive behavior. Studies conducted on professional athletes show that testosterone rises in anticipation of competition and rises further following a victory.[6] One researcher theorizes that testosterone levels rise in professional athletes with each victory which, in turn, promotes further competitiveness.[7]

Not only do testosterone levels rise before athletic competition, other human research shows that testosterone levels also rise before intellectual competition.[8]

Testosterone levels rise in chess players prior to a chess match. In the victor, there is a sharp increase of testosterone and there is a sharp decrease of testosterone in the defeated chess player.[9] These are the same patterns of testosterone increase and decrease that are seen in athletic competition.

It is a divinely instilled feature, partially hormonal in origin, for males to take on the role as aggressors, achievers, competitors, conquerors and subduers of their environment. This, I believe, is related to the innate drive for achievement that God placed within Adam from the beginning. God placed in Adam the desire to accomplish, achieve, set goals, develop a work ethic, take on responsibility and be successful in this life. However, we are living in a culture where too many young men have made excuses for their underachievement, lack of work ethic and laziness. It was not so in the beginning. This ability to take dominion over and subdue the earth (achievement drive) was connected to Adam's ability to be fruitful and multiply (sex drive).

Biologically and hormonally we can see that these two drives— sex drive and achievement drive—are linked. This was ordained from the beginning when God placed in Adam the necessary hormonal and biological elements that would help in motivating him to:

1. Subdue and take dominion (achievement drive).
2. Be fruitful, multiply and replenish (sex drive).

One of the hormonal links that motivated and enabled Adam to subdue (achievement drive) and replenish (sex drive) appears to be testosterone. This biological fact is consistent with the spiritual truths revealed in Scripture. Testosterone was designed to play a key role in motivating Adam to achieve, that is, *subdue* and *take dominion*, and to be sexual, that is, be *fruitful*, *multiply*, and *replenish* the earth.

Adam: Created to Take Dominion and Achieve

And God said, Let us make man in our image, after our likeness: and let them have dominion *over the fish of the sea, and over the fowl of the air, and over the cattle, and over all the earth, and over every creeping thing that creepeth upon the earth.*

Genesis 1:26 (emphasis added)

Consider the scope and magnitude of what God called Adam to do. Adam was to take dominion over many aspects of God's creation.

The Fish of the Sea

This was not a command to make a fishing pole and go down to the local creek. Think about it: If Adam was to do this, ultimately, he had to build ships. In order to build a ship you must have an understanding of design, structural engineering and mechanical engineering. To do this you must master geometry, trigonometry and biometrics. To safely navigate that ship, you need an understanding of oceanography and navigation. Dominion over the fish of the sea implies that Adam, at some future point, would need to build submarines. In that case he would need to understand the physics of gas pressure differentials, hydrostatic forces, physiology and blood-gas dynamics.

The Fowl of the Air

The only way for Adam to have dominion over the fowls of the air was to build airplanes and fly. To do this he needed an understanding of physics, complex math, Newton's law of motion and the laws governing gravity and flight. He would have to understand aviation science and mechanical engineering. Ultimately, this challenge called for Adam to build space ships. To travel in space, Adam would eventually need to know something about astronomy, astrophysics, calculus and complex geometric equations.

The Cattle of the Field

Adam was to have dominion over the cattle of the field. This included all four-legged beasts. Consider the educational disciplines Adam had to master: agriculture, horticulture, animal science, zoology, biology, anatomy, physiology, neurology, pathology, histology, veterinary medicine, microbiology, surgery, internal medicine, immunology, chemistry, pharmacology and genetics.

All The Earth

To have dominion over all the earth, Adam would eventually need to conquer and understand geology, geophysics, atomic science, nuclear science, natural science, geothermal science and nuclear physics, just to name a few.

Every Creeping Thing

Adam's dominion over every creeping thing included reptiles and insects. This meant that Adam would need to study herpetology (reptiles) and entomology (insects).

When you place the command to "have dominion" in the above context, one can begin to see the magnitude of what God was calling Adam to do. God had placed within Adam the intellect to master all of these disciplines and use that knowledge to overcome any force that would hinder the will of God in his life. Adam was an awesome being, endowed with awesome abilities to achieve, accomplish and overcome. God placed this tremendous potential to achieve within Adam from the beginning.

In God's economy, when a man fulfills God's mandate to subdue and take dominion (achievement drive), he then earns the right to be fruitful and multiply (sex drive).

GOD'S PRIORITY: ACHIEVEMENT BEFORE SEX

And out of the ground the LORD God formed every beast of the field, and every fowl of the air; and brought them unto Adam to see what he would call them: and whatsoever

Adam called every living creature, that was the name thereof. And Adam gave names to all cattle, and to the fowl of the air, and to every beast of the field; but for Adam there was not found an help meet for him.

Genesis 2:19,20 (emphasis added)

I believe that these two verses are important in explaining God's motivation in prioritizing these two divine motivators in Adam's life. Before Adam was allowed to engage his sex drive, God required that Adam commit to a certain level of achievement, accomplishment, personal development and success that was God ordained (achievement drive). This standard is still practical in today's society. Young people need to heed this Scripture when it comes to choosing a marriage partner.

Young women in particular should be especially careful to set high standards for the men they choose to marry and make babies with. Young women should not waste their time on young boys who have not developed themselves to the point of what I call "godly achievement." The marriage relationship cannot survive on the sex drive alone. There has to be something more substantive and practical to sustain a relationship over the long haul.

What is godly achievement? Rather than defining what it is, I will list those things that indicate a young man has or is striving toward godly achievement.

1. He has repented of his sin and Jesus is Lord of his life.
2. He has an education. He has advanced technical training or college-level training.
3. He has realistic, achievable goals and objectives for his life.
4. He has a stable job or means of financial support.

This list is by no means all-inclusive, but it is a good place to start. If a man can't adequately support himself, he cannot adequately support a family. If he cannot adequately support a family, he is not ready for love, marriage, or sex.

It has been said, "Where there is no *finance*, there can be no *romance*." There is great truth and revelation in this statement.

Achievement First

In Genesis 2:19, we see that Adam was challenged by God to take on the awesome responsibility of naming all of the animals. Adam accepts the challenge. In Old Testament culture, when you named a thing you were defining its nature, character and purpose. Before you can define the nature of an animal, you must first take the time to study it. In naming all these creatures, Adam had to first invest a tremendous amount of time, energy and effort in study and observation.

In properly naming the creatures that God had brought before him, Adam had achieved a task that took patience, discipline, skill and hard work. In this sense, we can see the God given achievement drive being manifest in Adam's life. Adam becomes a disciplined problem solver who had to develop a consistent work ethic in achieving what God had called him to do. We should note that Adam achieved this great and noteworthy task *before* he was introduced to the woman.

> And Adam gave names to all cattle, and to the fowl of the
> air, and to every beast of the field; but for Adam there was
> not found an help meet for him.
>
> Genesis 2:20

In verses 23 and 24 God brings the man and woman together as husband and wife, *after* Adam had made a commitment to subduing and taking dominion. In doing so, God establishes sexual expression within the context of heterosexual marriage and sets a standard that would prioritize a certain level of responsibility and achievement *before* sex and marriage. Achievement drive followed by sex drive. It is as if God said to Adam, "First you must become an 'achiever,' who will be responsible in developing a disciplined work ethic, then you may express yourself sexually, within the confines of marriage."

Before Eve was allowed to become Adam's help meet, which includes being his sexual companion, Adam had to develop a work ethic. God knew that it was important for Adam to develop a strong work ethic prior to taking on the responsibility of husband and father. Adam was an achiever and provider before he became a husband and father. Our culture has rejected this standard. We are living in a society that promotes and encourages sexual activity before marriage and before young people are emotionally, socially, psychologically, or financially stable. One of the most devastating trends in our society is the prevalence of males who are eager to engage in sex, but have not developed a godly work ethic or taken on the responsibility of providing for the babies they helped to make. Many men (young boys) want the sex, but don't want the responsibility of subduing, providing and protecting.

God's way is for a man to reach a certain level of maturity—a maturity that will allow him to achieve and take on the responsibility of subduing and taking dominion—then enter into marital intimacy. In God's economy, when a man rejects his God-given responsibility to achieve, subdue and take dominion, he forfeits his right to engage his sex drive. God requires men to achieve and take dominion before engaging in sex. This is an important point because God doesn't want non-achievers to reproduce after their own kind (species).

EVE: THE PERFECT HELP MEET

After Adam proved that he was a mature, responsible male with a solid work ethic, God introduces His daughter to him. Eve was impressed with Adam's:

- Drive To Achieve
- Work Ethic
- Intellectual Development
- Commitment to God
- Spiritual Depth

Too many young women in our society value the wrong things in a man. Many young women are impressed by a man's sexual prowess (as opposed to his achievement prowess) but not with his work ethic or willingness to take on responsibility and achieve. These women discover, too late, that these men may be able to make babies, but they are unwilling or unable to pursue gainful employment. These men will have sex, but they will not take on the responsibility of marriage, home and family. It is important to note that God never intended for His daughter (Eve) to marry or become intimate with a non-achieving, non-working, undisciplined bum!

I believe that God created and designed Eve not only to minister to Adam's sex drive, but also to inspire Adam to greater heights of achievement. Eve was the most unique creature on the planet. No other creature on earth could minister to Adam's physical and emotional needs. Adam had great potential locked within him, and Eve would be the earthly inspiration who would play a key role in unlocking and unleashing his inner greatness. No one can inspire a man like a woman. Even as as I was growing up, a game of basketball or football on the playground would always become more intense and competitive when the ladies came out to watch. Why? We were trying to impress the girls with our physical attributes on the field of play. Instinctively, we would try harder to outperform each other in the presence of females. I believe that this behavior is not only culturally instilled, but was also divinely instilled in the beginning.

Eve was to be a source of inspiration, stability and strength as she ignited Adam's sex drive and inspired his achievement drive. In becoming "one" with Eve, the physical seed within Adam would be implanted and birthed in the earth. Even so, Eve was endowed with the ability to inspire Adam to "birth forth" great accomplishments in the earth.

Eve was given a tremendous responsibility in shaping society as she helped Adam maintain a godly balance between his drive to achieve and his sex drive. In essence, Eve could inspire Adam to great heights of achievement and accomplishment (see Proverbs 31), or she could be a destructive force that could be a source misery and failure (see Proverbs 5:4,5,22, 6:26,32, 7:26).

Because God created Adam with these two divine motivators, Eve, by her very design, wields a tremendous amount of influence upon him. As we mentioned earlier, a woman can be a source of godly achievement or ungodly destruction.

Destruction: A Whorish Woman

Remove thy way far from her, and come not nigh the door of her house: Lest thou give thine honor unto others, and thy years unto the cruel: Lest strangers be filled with thy wealth; and thy labors be in the house of a stranger; And thou mourn at the last, when thy flesh and thy body are consumed.

Proverbs 5:8-11

But whoso committeth adultery with a woman lacketh understanding: he that doeth it destroyeth his own soul. A wound and dishonour shall he get; and his reproach shall not be wiped away.

Proverbs 6:32,33

Let not thine heart decline to her ways, go not astray in her paths. For she hath cast down many wounded: yea, many strong men have been slain by her. Her house is the way to hell, going down to the chambers of death.

Proverbs 7:25-27

The Bible is consistent in its teachings on sexual immorality and its destructive effects. These three Scriptures have a common theme: the whorish woman and her destructive effects upon a man. What is a whorish woman? A whorish woman is a woman who uses her sexual body to enflame, ensnare and entrap. The whorish woman is viewed as the hunter (predator), conqueror and the destroyer. The man is viewed as the hunted (prey), conquered and destroyed. A whorish woman can do this by taking advantage of the divine sex drive that God placed within the man. If men had no sex drive, the whorish woman would be powerless to destroy because much of her appeal to the man is rooted in his sex drive.

Note the destructive power of the whorish woman. The key to her destructive ability is sexual immorality. Look at what she destroys in the man:

- Wealth and labors: A whorish woman can destroy a man's work ethic and motivation to toil, strive and be successful.
- Flesh and Body: A whorish woman (or man) is the fountain from which many venereal diseases spring forth.
- Soul: A whorish woman can destroy a man emotionally, even to a point in which a man has no desire to live, much less be all that God created him to be.
- Strength: A whorish woman can weaken a man at the very core of his being, even to a point in which he will not be able to pursue his mandate to subdue and take dominion in the earth.

The whorish woman embodies a *spirit* and an *attitude* that seeks to frustrate God's original plan for human sexuality. As you recall, God's original plan for Adam was that he would be a man who was balanced, both as an achiever and as a sexual being. Adam's life was to be centered around subduing and taking dominion in the earth. In order to do this, God placed within Adam an achievement drive and a sex drive. It is important to note that God first required Adam to become a committed achiever.

God wanted Adam to develop a solid work ethic and a goal-oriented attitude. In effect, Adam was to develop into a man who was willing to take on the responsibilities of a mature, committed individual. Adam had to first develop a work ethic and a sense of responsibility before he could entertain his sex drive. Sexually, he would be fulfilled within the holy bonds of covenant marriage. Marriage is an awesome responsibility that takes a great deal of sacrifice and commitment. A commitment to godly achievement lays the ground work for a successful marriage and family life.

The whorish woman (spirit of whoredom) ignores the need for a man to develop as an achiever first and offers to meet the man's sexual needs without the encumbrances of covenant marriage. Essentially, she offers sex without sacrifice, sex without commitment and sex without obligation. When a man's sex drive is engaged before his achievement drive has been set in motion, the man is on a collision course with disaster. Why? Because:

- God's divine order is disrupted.
- The divine incentive that a man needs to fulfill his purpose is taken away.
- God's protective covering (covenant marriage) that provides the proper environment for sexual expression is removed.

The spirit of whoredom (sexual immorality) is destroying a generation of youth. Young boys who have no concept of what it means to be committed or responsible, are having sex on a regular basis. These boys are fathering children that they are not capable of raising or nurturing. A woman needs to understand that she becomes an instrument of destruction when she yields herself sexually to a man who has not matured enough to commit to a work ethic, covenant marriage and family.

Without the woman, man could not be all that God desired for him to be. There is a delicate balance here. For a woman to engage in sex with a male without the benefit of covenant marriage undermines God's divine plan. Sex without covenant marriage destroys much of the divine incentive to achieve (subdue and dominate). Sexual sin can destroy a man's potential (and drive) to achieve and accomplish. This is the danger and destructive nature of a whorish woman:

> *For by means of a whorish woman a man is brought to a piece of bread: and the adulteress will hunt for the precious life.*
>
> Proverbs 6:26

> *For she hath cast down many wounded: yea, many strong men have been slain by her.*
>
> Proverbs 7:26

Consider a man being made as worthless as a "piece of bread." Consider the strong men that have been slain by the spirit of whoredom. These where men who could have accomplished great things and achieved noble heights. These were men of great potential. But the whorish woman killed the will and incentive to achieve in these men. This underscores an important point. When many of these young men experience sexual intimacy apart from covenant marriage, much of the divine incentive to achieve is destroyed.

Sex outside of marriage caters to the self-centered, self-indulgent and self-satisfying nature of the fallen humanity. When one engages in premarital or extramarital sex, irresponsible, unfaithful and immature behavior is reinforced. These individuals are often unstable and unable to develop the kind of qualities (commitment, responsibility, accountability, sacrifice, delayed gratification, etc.) that are necessary for developing and maintaining stable, nuclear families and homes.

If young women would raise their standards, men would rise to those standards. This is what I mean. If women would require that men take on responsibility, develop a work ethic and be committed to the things of God *before* developing an intimate relationship with them, then both the women and the men would be better off—and so would society as a whole.

Even in the animal kingdom, the female of the species sets high standards before she mates with the male of her species. Notice how the males must fight and take dominion over the territory, defeat all challengers and subdue all opposition before he can mate with the female. (Note the divinely established pattern, first take dominion [achieve], then mate). Only after the male "achieves" does the female allow him the privilege to mate with her. It's as though the female of the species sets the standard, and the male must meet those standards that she has set. This assures her that her offspring will have the gene pool of a strong and determined father.

In the animal kingdom, the "achiever" (overcomer, subduer and conqueror) gets to mate. In the human economy, too often the nonachiever gets to mate. Too often, women set little or no standards for their prospective mate. Young men today do not need to have a car, house, education, job, trade, insurance, or manners to impress weak-minded, desperate women. These women set standards that are so low that the men are not challenged to any appreciable level of achievement or accomplishment. Even so, these men still get to mate. If women would uphold the same standard that is found in the animal kingdom, our society would be much better off.

To Subdue or Not to Subdue

Earlier in this chapter I made a statement that needs further clarification. I stated that "if you submit your sex drive to the holy dictates of God's Word, you will greatly enhance your ability to take dominion in the earth realm. Conversely, if you do not submit your sex drive and allow it to be governed by God's Word your ability to subdue and take dominion in the earth will be greatly hindered."

Sex is a spiritual act. When we violate the spiritual laws that govern human sexuality, we open our lives up to ungodly influences that hinder the fulfillment of God's plan. I want to illustrate this point by reviewing three biblical examples of individuals who never fulfilled their God-given purpose/potential because of sexual sin: Reuben, Esau, and Samson.

Reuben: Son of Jacob

> *Reuben thou art my firstborn, my might, and the beginning of my strength, the excellency of dignity, and the excellency of power. Unstable as water, thou shalt not excel; because thou wentest up to thy father's bed; then defiledst thou it: he went up to my couch.*
>
> Genesis 49:3,4

As the first-born male, Reuben was destined to be blessed above and beyond all of his brothers. As the first-born son of Jacob, he was granted the opportunity to be the one through whom the Messiah would eventually come. Tragically, it never came to pass. The potential blessing that was to come upon his life was so great, that it had to be divided between Joseph and Judah.

> *Now the sons of Reuben the firstborn of Israel, (for he was the firstborn; but, forasmuch as he defiled his father's bed, his birthright was given unto the sons of Joseph the son of Israel: and the genealogy is not to be reckoned after the birthright. For Judah prevailed above his brethren, and of him came the chief ruler; but the birthright was Joseph's.*
>
> 1 Chronicles 5:1,2

Think about it. Joseph became the second most powerful man in the world. In a de facto sense, Joseph was the most powerful man in the world. Judah became the ancestor of Jesus Christ, for He is the "Lion of the tribe of Judah." Reuben was in position to accomplish what Joseph accomplished. Conceivably, Jesus could have been known as the "Lion of the Tribe of Reuben." Neither came about because of a sexual indiscretion recorded in Genesis.

> *And it came to pass, when Israel dwelt in that land, that* Reuben went and lay *with Bilhah his father's concubine: and Israel heard it. Now the sons of Jacob were twelve.*
>
> Genesis 35:22 (emphasis added)

Reuben's behavior was reckless and incestuous. The word "lay" makes reference to a man having unlawful sexual relations with a woman. It is a very impersonal way of stating that the woman was basically used for sexual gratification only. This situation degrades both the woman, the man and the sex act to the level of dumb beasts. When the sex act is lawful, the Bible uses the expression "knew" (for example, he "knew" his wife).

In the case of Reuben, this sexual sin is particularly disgusting because it was his father's wife that he seduced. Thus, his sin was incestuous. Reuben did not have to defile his father's couch; there were many other women that he could have had in marriage. Reuben's behavior exposes a reckless disrespect and callousness that made him unfit to attain the birthright or the blessing. His actions show a total disregard for the things of God. From God's perspective, this behavior was tantamount to uncovering his father's nakedness.

> *The nakedness of thy father's wife shalt thou not uncover:*
> *it is thy father's nakedness.*
>
> Leviticus 18:8

No doubt, Reuben's behavior was designed to assert his position as the next leader of the clan. As first-born son, he had a legitimate claim to taking over as the next leader. Like most people, Reuben failed to understand that there is a right way and a right time for God to elevate. Reuben, because he was unwilling to wait on God's timing, chose the wrong means of self-elevation.

> *Reuben thou art my firstborn, my might, and the beginning*
> *of my strength, the excellency of dignity, and the excellency*
> *of power.* Unstable *as water,* thou shalt not excel; *because*
> *thou wentest up to thy father's bed; then defiledst thou it:*
> *he went up to my couch.*
>
> Genesis 49:3,4 (emphasis added)

There are two things that Jacob says about Reuben's character and future:

1. Unstable: The Hebrew word here is *pachaz* (6349), meaning "to bubble or become frothy." The idea that is being conveyed is

that of water reaching its boiling point. In my high school chemistry class, I was taught that boiling water is highly unstable and begins to evaporate rapidly. Water vapor is here one second and gone the next. It does not stay around very long. Such is the life of one given to sexual sin, their life is filled with meaningless, superficial relationships that have no longevity or sustaining power. The word also alludes to the emotional instability that consumed Reuben's life. Sexually promiscuous people live on a continuous emotional rollercoaster. The more they yield to their lust, the more empty, meaningless and lonely they become. This downward spiral becomes a vicious cycle.

2. Unable to excel: The Hebrew word is *yathar* (3498), meaning "exceed, cause to abound, to make plenteous, or to remain." Reuben's life never reached the potential that God had destined for him. Such is the life of those who are given to sexual sin. Sexual sin and success are not compatible. The two don't go hand in hand. Sexual sin robs an individual of their full potential. Those given to sexual sin will never become all they could or should be. This is the great tragedy of Reuben's life. His life was one of missed opportunity and regret about what could have or should have been. Sexual sin offers instant gratification, but it robs the sinner of future blessings and ultimately, fills the sinner with regret and remorse.

In summary, Reuben humiliated his father and disqualified himself of great future blessings. Tragically, Reuben's destiny was unfulfilled because of sexual sin.

Esau: Son of Isaac

Esau was the oldest son of Isaac. Because his father was Abraham's child of promise, Esau was in line to become the ancestor of the Savior of the world. But he sold his birthright to his younger brother Jacob.

> *And Esau said, Behold, I am at the point to die: and what profit shall this birthright do to me? And Jacob said, Swear to me this day; and he swear unto him: and he sold his birthright unto Jacob. Then Jacob gave Esau bread and*

pottage of lentils; and he did eat and drink, and rose up,
and went his way: thus Esau despised his birthright.

Genesis 25:32-34

There is a New Testament Scripture that is even more revealing as to the underlying reason why Esau lost his position of honor.

Lest there be any fornicator, *or* profane *person, as Esau,*
who for one morsel of meat sold his birthright.

Hebrews 12:16 (emphasis added)

Paul informs us that Esau was a *pornos* (fornicator). Esau was primarily a person who was motivated and consumed by his sexual lust. He was one who was given to sexual and sensual pursuits, as is evident in the fact that he married two heathen Canaanite women (Genesis 26:34). In part, it was his indulgence in forbidden sexual practices that led him to sell his birthright. Sensual people, or individuals who are controlled by their physical appetites, see little or no need to be concerned about godly, spiritual matters. These kind of people can't see beyond their immediate self-gratification. These kind of people are not concerned about the future consequences of their present day behavior. It does not surprise me, then, that Esau would walk away from his birthright for a bowl of beans.

Not only was Esau a fornicator, but he was also "profane." This word implies that Esau had no regard for things sacred to God. This is usually the case with those who are given to sensual pursuits. "Profane" also implies that Esau had no respect for sacred boundaries and that he was constantly breaching those boundaries that God had established. Esau placed little or no value on what God valued. Esau would readily tread upon that which was holy in a defiant show of his lack of respect for the things that mattered to God. Esau is another tragic example of one who never fulfilled his potential because of sexual sin.

Samson: Judge of Israel

Judges chapter 16 records the tragic demise of a man full of potential and promise. From his birth and early childhood, Samson had been dedicated to the Lord. A Nazarite vow, a special vow of separation, had been proclaimed upon his life even before he was born.

Samson was only one of three men who are known to have had this vow declared upon them before they were born and dedicated to God for life. The other two were the prophet Samuel and John the Baptist.

A Nazarite vowed to live separated unto God for His service. They had to abstain from wine and other intoxicating drinks. They were to be under the influence of the Spirit of God only. A Nazarite refused to cut his hair. This was a visible symbol of his dedication and consecration to God. The Nazarite could not come into contact with dead bodies, even for burying dead family members. But even with such a great consecration and endowment of strength, Samson never reached the full potential that God had in store for him.

Of Samson, the argument can be made that he was the strongest and mightiest failure to ever live. His sexual sin finally caught up with him in the person of a woman named Delilah. For a full account of this tragedy, see Judges chapter 16. The destructive effects that sexual sin has upon a person is evident in Samson's life.[10]

> But the Philistines took him, and put out his eyes, and brought him down to Gaza, and bound him with fetters of brass; and he did grind in the prison house.
> Judges 16:21 (emphasis added)

Ultimately, sexual sin will render a person *blind, bound* and *broken.* Samson, the strongest man in the Bible, is another tragic example of potential that was never fulfilled because of sexual sin. Samson's life should serve as a warning to all. Look at what Samson lost:

1. His sight.
2. His anointing.
3. His reasoning.
4. His freedom.
5. His hair (consecration).
6. His reputation.
7. His legacy.
8. His strength.

Presidential Impeachment

I have attempted to show how God ordained the *sex drive* and the *achievement drive* to complement each other in fulfilling the divine plan in the earth. In examining the lives of Esau, Reuben and Samson, we can clearly see how sexual sin can hinder a person's destiny and undermine the fulfillment of divine purpose for their life. In contemporary America, we have seen first hand how a person's future legacy can be destroyed and undermined by sexual sin. Consider the impeachment and Senate trial of President William Jefferson Clinton. A recent news article stated:

> "No matter what else happens in the last two years of his term, assuming he serves out his term, Clinton will be known in large part not for what he *accomplished* in office but for simply managing to hold onto it—a legacy of survival, not *achievement*. The sense of *a legacy lost, an opportunity squandered*, is the ghost that looms over the White House...."[11] (emphasis added)

Chapter Summary

1. God's divine purpose for each of us is intimately connected to our sexuality.
2. God expected and commanded Adam to function as a sexual creature within the earth realm and therefore endowed Adam with a sex drive.
3. The sex drive may be defined as the instinctive desire and attraction to the opposite sex for companionship and sexual intimacy. It is the inward biological urge that motivates one to become sexually intimate.
4. God also placed another desire within Adam: a desire to accomplish, excel and to be successful in overcoming opposition. It is called the achievement drive. The achievement drive is what motivated Adam to subdue and to take dominion in the earth.
5. Adam's sex drive and his achievement drive were divinely connected.
6. Adam's ability to subdue and take dominion (achievement drive) in the earth was dependent upon his willingness to

submit his sex drive to the dictates of God's Word. Plainly stated, sexual sin and promiscuity will greatly undermine one's ability to subdue, conquer, overcome and achieve their full potential in life.

7. These two divine motivators, sex drive and achievement drive, were intended to assist Adam in the pursuit and fulfillment of God's divine plan in the earth.

8. As a help meet, Eve was endowed with those qualities that would assist Adam in:
   a. constructively channeling his sex drive.
   b. inspiring him to great heights of achievement.
   Eve was to help bring stability and balance in both of these areas.

9. Testosterone, the predominant male hormone, plays an important role in both the sex drive and the achievement drive.

10. Divine priority dictated that Adam first become an "achiever" after which he could express himself sexually within the confines of holy matrimony. Adam was to first develop a strong work ethic and sense of responsibility (achievement drive) before he married and expressed himself sexually (sex drive).

11. The whorish woman seeks to undermine and destroy the achievement drive by engaging the man in illegal and unlawful sexual intercourse.

12. Illicit sexual intercourse can lead to personal failure. It can also undermine one's personal potential to achieve (see Proverbs 7:26).

13. Violation of the spiritual laws that govern human sexuality will expose one's life to ungodly spiritual forces. These spiritual forces may delay, hinder, or block the fulfillment of God's divine plan for your life.

14. Sexual idolatry can be emotionally destabilizing and personally destructive.

15. Esau, Reuben and Samson are three Old Testament examples of individuals whose lives never reached their full potential because of sexual sin.

Chapter Eight

SOUL TIES

*But every vow of a widow, and of her that is divorced,
wherewith they have bound their souls, shall stand against
her.*

Numbers 30:9

In Chapter 7 of Volume 1, we discussed soul ties. I would like to
briefly review the highlights of that chapter so that we can expand
upon some of those ideas.

- Soul ties were defined as the psychological, emotional and/or
  physiological dependency that develops when a person yields
  him/herself to another person or thing.
- Sex was designed by God to be an addictive act.
- Sexual intimacy is a common means whereby soul ties
  develop.
- Soul ties may be divided into two categories: *godly* and
  ungodly.

- Ungodly soul ties (UST) can bind an individual to dangerous people and habits.
- In order to gain freedom from the past, ungodly soul ties must first be broken.

God created mankind—spirit, soul and body. There is more to you than meets the eye. Consequently, when we engage in consensual sex we are not only engaging our physical bodies in the sex act, we are also engaging our soul and our spirits. Sexual intimacy touches every aspect of our being.

> *Thou hast* ravished my heart, *my sister, my spouse; thou hast* ravished my heart *with one of thine eyes, with one chain of thy neck. How fair is thy love, my sister, my spouse! how much better is thy love than wine! Your ointments are more favorable than any spice.*
>
> Song of Solomon 4:9,10 (emphasis added)

In this passage, the Bible graphically illustrates the powerful emotional effect that sexual intimacy has upon an individual. The Bible also admonishes us to "be thou *ravished* always with her love" (Proverbs 5:19, emphasis added). The word translated "ravished" is the Hebrew word *shagah* (7686), and it speaks of being intoxicated or being emotionally captivated by a thing. Sexual intercourse can be as intoxicating as any drug. God, in all His wisdom, designed us to be sexual creatures. In the same context, He has merged our hearts (emotions) with our sex drive in such a way that we become emotionally and psychologically "bonded" with our sexual partner. This was God's plan and intent from the beginning. Sex was meant to be an "intoxicating" experience that was to enhance the marital bond.

> *Therefore shall a man leave his father and his mother, and shall* cleave *unto his wife: and they shall be one flesh.*
>
> Genesis 2:24 (emphasis added)

This godly soul tie provides an emotional bond within the marriage relationship. It "binds" a man and woman beyond the physical, into the realm of the soul, heart and emotion. This soul tie makes it impossible for a man to truly love more than one woman at a time. One reason the "safe sex" message is so inadequate is that condoms may protect you from some sexually transmitted diseases (STDs), but they will not protect your heart from the emotional devastation that can result when you engage in sexual sin. Condoms were not designed to protect your spirit from the spiritual defilement that sexual sin produces.

Sacred Vows: Sacred Covenants

But every vow of a widow, and of her that is divorced, wherewith they have bound their souls, *shall stand against her.*

Numbers 30:9 (emphasis added)

In Numbers chapter 30, Moses institutes an important but often overlooked statute regarding sacred vows and oaths. These particular vows and oaths have a peculiar effect upon the soul. These sacred covenants "bind the soul." The expression "bound her soul" is used at least ten times in Numbers chapter 30. It is important to note that the Bible recognizes and acknowledges the reality of "soul ties." There are covenants that can have profound effects upon the soul.

In verse 9 we see that widows and divorced women, as a result of their "vows," have developed soul ties and, if not dealt with, "shall stand against [them]." The word "vow" in the Hebrew is *neder* (5088). These are sacred objects that have been offered up to God. I want to highlight this verse because I believe that it has relevance in today's contemporary society. I believe that this verse speaks to our culture. A culture that devalues marriage, condones adultery, encourages divorce and is flippant about "casual sex."

Marriage is a holy, sacred institution. The vows of marriage are spiritual in nature. Covenant marriage is the means that God has established whereby we can engage in "undefiled" sexual relations. The sex act itself is a sacred, blood covenant act.[1]

I believe that Numbers 30:9 highlights:

1. The importance of the marriage covenant.
2. The sacred nature of the sex act.
3. The profound impact that the sex act has upon the soul.
4. The personal consequences of violating sacred covenants.

A culture that devalues marriage, condones adultery and encourages casual sex will eventually have a society full of people who have forged *illegal sexual covenants*. These illegal sexual covenants lead to the formation of ungodly soul ties that can emotionally cripple and spiritually hinder an individual for years. When we engage in sexual intercourse, we are making a sacred vow that will "bind" the soul. Sexual covenants were meant to be eternal and enduring; this is why God established covenant marriage. Marriage was to protect the sanctity and the integrity of these vows (sexual covenants). Sexual covenants, because of their potential devastation, must be protected within the covenant restraints that marriage provides. God did not establish marriage to keep us from having fun. He established marriage to protect us from the potential emotional and psychological devastation that ungodly soul ties can inflict upon us.

When we sexually "join" ourselves to another (in consensual sex), a very powerful, yet unseen, soul tie develops.[2] If these ungodly soul ties are not broken, they can afflict us emotionally for a life time. Ungodly sexual covenants (vows) have many men and women emotionally tied to their past, unable to walk in the full liberty and purpose that God has intended.

SEX AND THE SOUL

The impact that sexual intercourse exerts upon the soul cannot be understated.

> *Let her be as the loving hind and pleasant roe; let her breasts satisfy thee at all times; and be thou ravished always with her love.*
>
> Proverbs 5:19

In this Scripture, a wise father is instructing his son in sexual matters. Specifically, he admonishes his son to engage only his wife in sexual intimacy. There are three words used in this verse that allude to the profound impact sexual intercourse has upon the soul.

- Loving: from the Hebrew *ahab* (158), meaning "to have sexual affection for."

- Satisfy: from the Hebrew *ravah* (7301), meaning "to make drunk."
- Ravish: from the Hebrew *shagah* (7686), meaning to "reel" or to "intoxicate."

In creation, God merged our heart (emotions) with our sex drive in such a way that, as we are sexually intimate, we become emotionally bonded to, enraptured with and intoxicated by our sex partner. God designed sexual intimacy to act as a powerful, emotionally intoxicating experience that was to bind a man and woman together for a lifetime. Even though the author of Proverb 5:19 did not realize it, he was describing, in part, what happens at the hormonal level when a man and a woman engage in sexual intercourse.

Research has shown that certain chemicals (hormones) are released during the sex act. These hormones have an affect upon the way we feel.[3] In men and women *oxytocin, vasopressin* and chemicals called *endorphins* are released into the blood stream during sexual foreplay (petting) and sexual intercourse (orgasm).[4]

Oxytocin

Experiments indicate that oxytocin is the hormone that stimulates the emotional bonds to one's sexual partner and to their offspring as well. Oxytocin is thought to bind to areas in the brain that are involved with emotion. Studies conducted at the University of Maryland show that, after certain rodents engaged in sexual intercourse, oxytocin is released into the females brain, literally bonding her to the male.[5] If the female is deprived of oxytoxin, she finds her mate no more appealing than any other male.[6] This research indicates that oxytocin acts as a powerful chemical messenger that can influence behavior and emotions.[7]

Endorphins

Endorphins are powerful drugs that have an analgesic/narcotic affect much like the addictive drug opium.[8] Endorphins are released during the sex act and are believed to be responsible for the euphoric, intoxicating and addictive nature of sexual intimacy. Endorphins also act as pain killers and can induce a state of contentment and relaxation.[9]

Sex was designed by God to be an addictive act. I did *not* say that God wants us to become "sex addicts," but, apparently, God *does* want a man to become addicted to having sex with his one and only wife!

> *Let her be as the loving hind and pleasant roe; let her* *breasts satisfy thee at all times; and* be thou ravished always with her love.
>
> Proverbs 5:19 (emphasis added)

There is a big difference in a man being addicted to sex and being addicted to sex with his own wife. The intent was that a man, after being sexually intimate with his wife, would desire to have sex *only* with her. He was to spend his life *cleaving* to that one woman in holy matrimony.

Research has shown that mankind's capacity for "loving emotions" is related to our biochemical makeup.[10] The sex act was designed with monogamy in mind. It was God's intent that a man would become "addicted" to his wife to the point of "cleaving" to her for a lifetime of love and commitment.

Vasopressin

In nature, the California mouse is an example of an animal whose monogamous (single sex partner) habits appear to be hormonally related. Studies show that when a male California mouse is separated from his mate and put into a box with another female he will violently avoid having any contact with that female.[11] Researchers believe that vasopressin is largely responsible for this monogamous behavior in some rodents.[12] Oxytocin is thought to bind to areas in the brain that are involved with emotion; vasopressin has a similar effect upon the male who prefers his mate's company above all others. The California mouse has the right idea: *faithfulness to one sex partner, for life.*

SEX: A PHYSICAL AND EMOTIONAL ACT

Feelings of sexual love have been shown to affect the whole body. It can increase the heart rate, respiratory rate and induce sexual arousal (erection). These sensations are all made possible by the vagus nerve (10th cranial nerve).[13] This nerve transports signals from the brain to the heart, lungs and sexual organs. It also responds to the release of oxytocin and serves as the pathway between the sexual organs and the brain for the feelings of arousal and satisfaction after sexual intimacy.[14]

SOUL TIES AND THE BRAIN

In creation, God designed us in such a way that our brain is stimulated when these chemicals (oxytocin, vasopressin and endorphins) are released during sexual intercourse. When these chemicals stimulate the brain, certain emotions are triggered that will initiate *strong soul ties*. This complex system of hormone release and stimulation has a powerful physiological, psychological and emotional effect upon us. In describing the volatile nature of sexual intercourse, the author of Proverbs writes:

> *Can a man take* fire *in his bosom, and his clothes not be burned? Can one go upon hot coals, and his feet not be burned?*
>
> Proverbs 6:27,28 (emphasis added)

By divine design, sexual intimacy kindles fires of passion that can emotionally overwhelm us. It was God's intent that husband and wife develop an inseparable, emotional addiction that was to bind them together as life partners. Indeed, there is a hormonal and biological basis for the development and the maintenance of soul ties. A few of the hormones that are involved in this complex reaction are:

- Oxytocin.
- Vasopressin.
- Endorphins.
- Testosterone.
- Estrogen.

People should realize the dangers of casual sex, that is, sex that has no strings of marital commitment attached. When you engage in sex outside of marriage, you set certain laws in motion (spiritual, emotional and biological) that were intended to function within the confines of holy matrimony. To give oneself sexually (spirit, soul and body) to someone, without the safeguard of a committed marital relationship, is a very dangerous proposition. There are psychological, emotional and physiological strings attached that may devastate your life for years. When we engage in sexual intercourse, certain fires of passion are ignited that may kindle for many years.

In order to keep these fires under control, and within safe boundaries, God instituted holy matrimony. One man, one wife for life. A *controlled fire* can keep a house warm and cozy. An *uncontrolled fire* can destroy a house and everything in it. Marriage was intended to function as a "fire wall" that would keep the fires of our sexual passions regulated, in check and under control.

> *Can a man take fire in his bosom, and his clothes not be burned? Can one go upon hot coals, and his feet not be burned?*
>
> Proverbs 6:27,28

To sexually commit is to emotionally commit. To emotionally commit to someone that is not maritally committed to you can wound and scar you for years. It can drastically alter your future and undermine your destiny. Many feel remorse and regret for having given themselves sexually to one who was not committed to them in marriage. The 1960's Sexual Revolution has birthed forth a generation of individuals who have been emotionally and psychologically scarred by sexual idolatry.

Breaking Ungodly Soul Ties

> *Every vow, and every binding oath to afflict the soul, her husband may establish it, or her husband may make it void.*
>
> Numbers 30:13

In Volume 1 I offered some practical, biblical tips on breaking ungodly soul ties.[15] I would like to expand upon this idea. Once again I want to examine a few words in this verse from Numbers. The word translated "afflict" is the Hebrew word *anah* (6031), meaning "to browbeat, to depress, to chasten oneself, to defile, hurt, or weaken."

This is precisely the effect that ungodly soul ties have upon an individual. These soul ties can be a source of severe emotional depression, low self-esteem and remorse. Ungodly soul ties may be a hidden source of deep hurt and emotional anxiety. These are just some of the emotional consequences of sexual sin. When we break or violate the laws that govern human sexuality, we often pay a heavy emotional price. See Volume 1, Chapter 5 for more information on the "laws governing human sexuality."

The word "afflict" in Numbers 30:13 helps us to understand that past, ungodly sexual covenants have a negative impact upon the soul. Those who propagate worldly philosophy would have us believe that we can engage in ungodly sexual relations without paying a price. However, ungodly sexual covenants:

1. Will be judged by God, and we will be held accountable for the sexual covenants that we enter.
2. Can impact future relationships.
3. Must be dealt with if we are to be free to fulfill God's purpose.

LAWS: TO BLESS OR TO CURSE

A law may be defined as an established rule that governs how a particular thing functions or works. Laws are important. In the realm of natural sciences, we know that there are laws that govern the universe (e.g., law of gravity, law of motion, laws of thermodynamics, etc.). In the legal realm, there are laws that dictate how we are to govern our behavior. Without laws, we would not understand how the universe functions. Without laws we would live in a chaotic, violent-filled society. We need both natural law, to understand the universe, and moral law, to guide our behavior. It is important to note that God's moral law is in harmony with the natural laws He set in motion to govern the universe. A recent Newsweek article reported that a growing number of scientists now believe that many modern scientific discoveries support the very nature and existence of God.[16]

I emphasize this point because without laws, we have no understanding of God or the universe He created. In Volume 1 I put forth the thesis that there are laws that govern human sexuality. These laws are found in God's Word, the Bible. In our discussion on soul ties, we have been examining the Law of Cleaving found in Genesis 2:24.

> *Therefore shall a man leave his father and his mother, and*
> *shall cleave unto his wife: and they shall be one flesh.*
>
> Genesis 2:24 (emphasis added)

The Law of Cleaving, like all of God's moral and natural laws, was set in motion for our good. However, God's laws (moral and natural), even though they were meant for our benefit (blessing), can be to our detriment (destruction). God's laws can be a blessing or a curse. How can this be? How can a law bless you, and the same law curse you? I will give the answer and then illustrate it from Scripture. The answer is simple. The key is your attitude or disposition in regards to the law in question. If you choose to *obey* the law, then that law will be a *blessing* to you. If you choose to *disobey* the law, that same law will *curse* you (Isaiah 1:19,20). In this regard, the law has two sides, a blessing side and a cursing side. Your obedience, or disobedience, will determine which side of the law you experience. The Bible illustrates this principle very clearly.

> *And Moses charged the people the same day, saying, These*
> *shall stand upon mount Gerazim to bless the people, when*
> *ye are come over Jordan; Simeon, and Levi, and Judah, and*
> *Issachar, and Joseph, and Benjamin: And these shall stand*
> *upon mount Ebal to curse; Reuben, Gad, and Asher, and*
> *Zebulun, Dan, and Naphtali.*
>
> Deuteronomy 27:11-13 (emphasis added)

After rehearsing the law that God had given him with the people, Moses instructs them to perform a symbolic yet highly important act. He instructs six tribal representatives to stand on Mt. Gerazim and six tribal representatives to stand on Mt. Ebal. Why did Moses do this? To symbolically illustrate to the people that the law of God has two sides, as represented by these two mountains. On one side of the law were blessings, symbolized by Mt.Gerazim. On the other side were cursings, symbolized by Mt. Ebal. Moses was illustrating to the people that they had to choose one or the other.

God's law was not (and is not) going to change. God had already set it in motion. If the Israelites wanted to experience the blessing side of the Law, they had to choose obedience, or Mt. Gerazim.

However, if they wanted to experience the cursing side of the Law, they could choose to disobey (Mt. Ebal). In effect, Moses was saying, "The choice is up to you, but realize that your choice (obedience or disobedience) will determine whether the law works for your good (blessing) or for your detriment (cursing)." In this regard, the law is like a quarter, on one side is "heads" and on the other side is "tails." This is an extremely important concept: The law, like the coin, has two sides.

Let's illustrate this principle using the law of gravity. God set the law of gravity in motion, as all natural laws, for our benefit. The law of gravity keeps us planted on the ground. We now know that gravity holds the world, atoms, molecules and perhaps even the universe in place.[17] This wonderful law that is designed to bless us can be to our detriment. How? By violating the rules that govern this law. If one jumps from a seventeen story building without a parachute, the law of gravity dictates that the pavement below will kill you instantly.

In 1986 I attended a scientific conference in Toronto, Canada. While studying in the lobby of the hotel, I witnessed the death of a young woman who had jumped from the seventeenth floor of that building. I stood over her mangled body and assisted those who carried her away. I only mention this tragic story to illustrate how an individual can violate the law of gravity and be destroyed by doing so.

Another example is the law of motion, discovered by Sir Isaac Newton. We function in this law on a daily basis as we drive to work or go shopping in our car. This law functions to our benefit, but this same law can also destroy us if we violate it. If you drive your car into a brick wall at 100 miles per hour, the same law that functioned to take you to work will kill you instantly. Why? Because you foolishly violated the law.

It is important to note that laws function whether we understand them or not. Laws function whether we agree with them or not. It's the same with God's moral laws that are found in the Bible. You may not like, understand, or agree with them, but they are still in *effect*. If you violate them, it will be to your detriment.

The *Law of Cleaving* was set in motion by God, in part, to bond a husband and wife in a monogamous relationship. This law was established for our benefit. If we violate the principles that govern this law, it will be to our detriment. How do we violate the Law of Cleaving? By engaging in sexual relations outside the protective bonds of holy matrimony (marital commitment). When we disobey the Law of Cleaving, we experience the other side of this law that brings a curse.

What is the other side of the Law of Cleaving? I call it the Law of Yielding and Bondage.[18] The Law of Cleaving that was meant to bless you now presents itself as the Law of Yielding and Bondage. At this point, an ungodly soul tie may be established that can curse and destroy you emotionally, as previously explained. Keep in mind that the coin (law) has two sides to it: "heads" on one side and "tails" on the other. In this spiritual example, it's the Law of Cleaving on one side, and the Law of Yielding and Bondage on the other.

Law of Cleaving.
Side 1 (heads)

Law of Yielding and Bondage.
Side 2 (tails)

You don't really break God's laws in the sense that they stop functioning. They keep functioning as God intended. What happens is that you reap the consequences for violating the order that God has established. God's laws (moral and natural) were designed to function within His divinely established order. These laws uphold God's order. When we break these laws and violate divine order, tragedy usually results.

> *For because ye did it not at the first, the LORD our God made a breach upon us, for that we sought him not after the due order.*
>
> 1 Chronicles 15:13(emphasis added)

In this passage, King David is referring to an incident that is recorded earlier in 1 Chronicles:

And the anger of the LORD was kindled against Uzza, and he smote him, because he put his hand to the ark: and there he died before God.

1 Chronicles 13:10

In this passage of Scripture a man named Uzza dropped dead when he tried to keep the ark of the covenant from falling to the ground. The ark was being transported in a manner that was not consistent with divine order. In 1 Chronicles 15:13 David is explaining why Uzza died: he violated God's order.

When we violate the laws that govern human sexuality, we violate the due order that God has established, and we will ultimately reap the consequences for these violations. In a sense, you don't break the law, the law breaks you. The woman who jumped from the seventeenth floor did not break the law of gravity, the law of gravity broke her.

Breaking Ungodly Soul Ties

Every vow, and every binding oath to afflict *the soul, her husband may* establish *it, or her husband may make it* void.

Numbers 30:13 (emphasis added)

The next word I want to focus on in this verse is "establish." It is translated from the Hebrew word *quwm* (6965). It means "to continue, confirm, strengthen, or cause to endure." I believe Scripture is teaching us a very important point about ungodly soul ties. Many people have developed ungodly soul ties because of past sexual relations and, as a result, that ungodly soul tie may now be hindering their present relationship. Multiple sexual partners prior to marriage is a very common feature of a sexually promiscuous society.

It is important that husbands and wives understand that what may be hindering their marriage is an ungodly soul tie from a past sexual indiscretion by one or both partners. Let me say this, *the fewer sexual relations that you have prior to marriage, the better off your marriage (and life) will be.* Many married couples have to deal with recurring fantasies as a result of sexual encounters that they may have experienced prior to getting married. These fantasies may manifest during moments of intimacy with their current spouse. Sexual covenants of the past are not as easily walked away from as many would have us believe.

How do we deal with these ungodly soul ties that have developed as a result of past sexual sin? The answer, in part, is found in the third and final word that I want to focus on in Numbers 30:13: "void."

The Hebrew word here is *parar* (6565), meaning "to break, cast off, dissolve, cause to cease, or make of none effect." Numbers 30 mentions at least two individuals that have the authority to *parar* (break) the bonds of the soul. They are *the father of a daughter* and *the husband of a wife*.

The Father of a Daughter

> *These are the statutes, which the LORD commanded Moses, between a man and his wife, between the father and his daughter, being yet in her youth in her father's house.*
>
> Numbers 30:16

Research indicates that one of the most important factors in stabilizing a young girl's life is the positive influence of a father's love and affirmation.[19] A study of almost fifteen thousand teens shows that girls with involved fathers are more likely to delay sex and are less likely to use drugs or alcohol.[20] Other studies show that children without fathers more often have lowered academic performance, have more cognitive and intellectual deficits, have increased adjustment problems and are at higher risks for psychosexual developmental problems.[21]

For many women, the lack of a nurturing parent (especially the lack of a father), particularly in the early adolescent years, is the underlying basis for what may later become (sexually) promiscuous behavior.[22] Scientific research now supports the importance of fathers, just as the Bible always has. A father may very well be the single largest contributing factor to his daughter's emotional security or her sexual promiscuity.[23] The Bible is clear on this point.

> *Do not prostitute thy daughter, to cause her to be a whore; lest the land fall to whoredom, and the land become full of wickedness.*
>
> Leviticus 19:29

Note that God holds the father accountable for causing his daughter to become sexually promiscuous (a whore). In Genesis 34, one can see the impact that Jacob's neglect had on his daughter Dinah and the resulting tragedy.[24] When fathers do not invest the time to nurture their daughters, many young girls grow up emotionally scarred.

In a study conducted by the American Association of University Women (AAUW), twenty-one hundred girls between the ages of eleven and seventeen said that the number one struggle they faced was the pressure to engage in premarital sex.[25] These girls said that the pressure came from:

1. Boys.
2. Other girls.
3. Friends.
4. Media.

Many of these girls are not emotionally mature enough to deal with the pressures to engage in premarital sex. Many fall prey to sexual immorality. They are often searching for the love that their parents, specifically their fathers, never provided. According to another survey, about 66 percent of babies born to teenage girls were fathered by adult males.[26] It appears that many of these young people are "looking for love in all the wrong places."

According to Jonetta Barras, author of *What Ever Happened to Daddy's Little Girl?*, fathers teach girls how to relate to men and how to maneuver in a male-dominated society. Fathers assist their daughters in becoming comfortable with who they are as girls and later as women.[27] When fathers are absent, daughters miss out on important insights into how men are, how men can be and how men should be.[28] It is important that fathers establish standards and set expectations so that their daughters know how to discern "good" men from "bad" men.[29]

I believe God intended for fathers to stand as the first line of defense in protecting their daughters from the sexual temptations that exist in the world. Without this kind of intervention from a father figure, women are at risk for developing ungodly soul ties. Early and continuous paternal involvement in a daughter's life is key in helping to prevent the development of these ungodly soul ties that are established as the result of sexual sin.

The Husband of a Wife

Numbers 30:16 asserts the authority a husband has in breaking the effects of ungodly soul ties that his wife may have acquired prior to marriage. A husband, through ignorance or neglect, may allow certain soul ties to persist and hinder his marriage. On the other hand, a spirit-filled husband, through godly counsel and Holy Spirit guidance, can dissolve or break ungodly soul ties that are hindering his wife and affecting his marriage.

THE NEED TO BREAK UNGODLY SOUL TIES

Soul ties that develop as the result of past ungodly sexual covenants can be psychologically and emotionally crippling. These kind of soul ties are rooted in blood covenants because sexual intercourse is a blood covenant act. Before a man can engage in penile-vaginal intercourse, his penis (organ of sacred covenant) must first become erect. Erection cannot take place until blood enters the penis. In this sense, without blood, the sex act is not possible.[30] Scripture teaches us that "the life of the flesh is in the blood" (Leviticus 17:10). Blood symbolizes a person's life. When you have sexual intercourse with a person, you are symbolically partaking of and sharing that person's very life—past, present and future.

We know this to be the case because many blood-born infections are transmitted via sexual intercourse. If your sex partner has an STD, which he or she contracted from a previous sexual relationship, you may contract that disease. In a sense, you are becoming one with every person that your sex partner has become one with. Sexual intercourse is not only a means of transmitting physical diseases, it can also be a vehicle whereby "spiritual" diseases are transferred.

> "AIDS has a long and indeterminate incubation period, you and your partner can carry the virus and spread it around with perfect innocence, perhaps ten or more years. Thus, you are not only having sex with your partner, *you are also having sex with everybody your partner has had sex with for the past decade or more.*"[31] (emphasis added)

This is one of the tragedies of ungodly sexual covenants. They have a lasting effect, and they can affect you with the sexual covenants of your sex partner's past. Sex is more than a physical act. It is also a spiritual act that impacts us at the spiritual core of our beings. Having sex with someone is like sharing a needle with that person: Anyone using the same needle will be sharing the blood (life) of anyone that previously used that needle. Sexual intercourse is no different! When you become one in sexual intercourse, you become all that the person is. Ungodly sexual covenants bind us to things that we may be unaware of or don't understand. This highlights the need to confess our past sins and receive forgiveness and healing for ungodly sexual covenants of the past.

GODLY PASTORS AS SPIRITUAL FATHERS

There are situations that exist in which a young person has lost their virginity and there is no father or other spiritual authority in the home to break the influence of an ungodly soul tie that may be present. In these situations, godly pastors who are trained to hear from God are extremely important. As a "spiritual father," these pastors have the God-given authority to break ungodly soul ties in the lives of the young people (or older people) that are within their spiritual house. Through the Word of God, and by the Spirit of God, godly shepherds can lead and influence a young person in such a way as to help them avoid and overcome the sexual pitfalls that exist in the world.

CHAPTER SUMMARY

1. A soul tie may be defined as a psychological, emotional and/or physiological dependency that a person may develop toward another person or thing.
2. Sexual intimacy is a common means whereby soul ties develop.
3. Soul ties may be divided into two categories:
    a. Godly soul ties.
    b. Ungodly soul ties.
4. Ungodly soul ties may bind a person to dangerous people and/or habits.
5. The godly soul tie was divinely ordain to be the emotional, psychological and spiritual basis for binding husband and

wife in holy matrimony. Marriage was designed, in part, to protect us from the devastating effects of ungodly soul ties.

6. A culture that devalues marriage, condones adultery and encourages casual sex will eventually become a society filled with people who will be devastated by the effects of ungodly soul ties.

7. The development of ungodly soul ties can be emotionally destructive and may hinder or prevent the fulfillment of God's purpose in a person's life.

8. At creation, God united our hearts (emotions) with our sex drive. The intent was that, as we are sexually intimate with an individual, we also would become emotionally bonded to that person as well.

9. Soul ties that develop during sexual intimacy have a biological/hormonal basis. During sexual intercourse, certain hormones are released within the body. These hormones affect the way that we feel and are involved in the formation of soul ties. God designed our bodies in such a way that, as we engage in sexual intimacy, we become emotionally and psychologically bonded to our sexual partner. This is how God intended husband and wife to cleave in lifelong commitment.

Therefore shall a man leave his father and mother, and shall cleave *unto his wife: and they shall be one flesh.*
Genesis 2:24 (emphasis added)

10. Sexual intercourse was designed by God to be an "addictive" act. The intent was for husband and wife to develop an inseparable, emotional and spiritual bond that was to keep them together as life partners.

11. The 1960's Sexual Revolution birthed forth an entire generation of individuals who have developed ungodly soul ties because of sexual sin.

12. Ungodly soul ties of the past may hinder your present marriage.

13. Fathers are an important first line of defense in protecting their daughters from sexual temptation.

14. Righteous, God-fearing husbands have been given the authority to break the ungodly soul ties that his wife may have acquired prior to marriage.

15. Sexual immorality, and the resultant ungodly soul ties that develop, will bind us to unseen spiritual forces that may hinder the will of God from being executed in our lives.

16. Godly, Spirit-filled pastors may play a key role in:
    - Protecting his or her spiritual sons and daughters from certain sexual pitfalls.
    - Breaking the ungodly soul ties that may already exist.

Chapter Nine

URBAN STRONGHOLDS
TAKING BACK THE CITIES

Between the early 1940's and mid to late 1960's, an estimated five million African Americans left the fields and farms of the deep south and headed north for the big cities.[1] Many were searching for greater economic opportunities; some were in search of civil and legal rights that they had been denied under well-established Jim Crow laws.

There is some speculation that this mass exodus may have begun as early as 1927, after the catastrophic Mississippi River flood of that year. Whatever did, or did not, motivate this mass exodus can be debated, but one thing is certain: This great influx of African Americans into the cities of the north changed city life forever in many ways. Race relations were changed. The political and cultural landscape was altered for both city and suburb alike. With this shift in population, issues like busing, integration and civil rights became points of contention. America was once again forced to deal with her race problem.

One of the most formidable challenges the great migration precipitated relates to the family structure of many black households. In the late 60's, about 25 percent of black families were headed by women with no husbands.[2] These were families where the male was absent because of divorce, separation, or desertion and did not include families with illegitimate children who never had a father present.[3] By 1991, black illegitimacy in some areas had reached 68 percent.[4]

We can present much more data to make the case, but the point that I'm really trying to make is that the structural makeup of many urban families has been partially responsible for many of the social problems that have developed within some inner cities over the past few decades. The crime, poverty, neighborhood decay and weaknesses in the educational institutions are all related, in part, to a weakened family structure. Why did these problems become so magnified in the urban areas? After all, many of these families were similarly structured in the rural areas from which they came. I believe that it relates, in part, to the differences that existed at that time in the spiritual climates of the city and the country.

Apparently, the city was not as tolerant of certain family weaknesses as the rural setting was. The city environment was harder on "fatherless" homes than rural environments were. I don't mean to imply that the rural setting is the place for fatherless families, but that the social demographics of the city made it much more difficult for single parent or fatherless homes to thrive, much less survive. City life was not as kind to fatherless homes as country life or rural life had been. City life magnified, and even exploited, the inherent weaknesses of fatherless families. In 1965, Daniel Patrick Monihan, then Urban Affairs Advisor to President Johnson, recognized and articulated the dimensions of the crisis:

> "At the heart of the deterioration of the fabric of Negro society is the deterioration of the Negro family. It is the fundamental source of weakness of the Negro community at the present time. Unless this damage [the deterioration of the Negro family] is repaired, all the effort to end discrimination, poverty and injustice will come to little."[5]

> *Righteousness exalteth a nation: but sin is a reproach to any people.*
>
> Proverbs 14:34

Sin, particularly sexual sin, will bring a reproach on any ethnic group, at any time. Much of the reproach (poverty, crime, illiteracy, premature death, social deprivation, etc.) present in many urban areas, relates to the weakened family structure, fatherless homes in particular. Sure enough, racism and discrimination have taken their toll, but the main problem relates to family breakdown (fatherlessness). Issues like out of wedlock births, unwed mothers and fatherless homes cannot be dealt with without addressing the issue of sexual sin and sexual immorality. This includes adultery, fornication, homosexuality and incest.

> *Righteousness exalteth a nation: but* sin *is a reproach to any people.*
>
> Proverbs 14:34 (emphasis added)

In writing this chapter, I am attempting to look at how sexual morality, or the lack thereof, can destroy *any* ethnic group. Once sexual sin becomes the culturally accepted norm, the effects can be devastating and long-term. I want to focus on the spiritual climate of the inner cities in general and how those unseen spiritual forces of sexual idolatry can work to undermine a people and its culture.

Urban renewal will not take place with government funds alone. Thirty years of heavy government investment totaling five trillion dollars by some estimates, has had some impact, but not nearly enough. We have thirty to thirty-five years of history to verify this fact. The government cannot and will not establish the kind of biblical morality that will translate into the kind of family structure that is needed for family survival, urban or other wise. After thirty years of heavy government investment, many inner city communities have worsened. This is a job for the church. The church must become more actively involved in preaching, teaching and modeling a gospel that will:

1. Rebuild families.
2. Reverse the influence of sexual idolatry on urban culture.
3. Restore the biblical standard for holy living.
4. Reject and resist the worldly philosophies that have brought about this spiritual and cultural devastation.

What Went Wrong?

There has been much discussion and analysis over the years as to what is wrong with America's inner cities and how to fix them. Getting to the root causes of the crime, poverty, drug addiction, family disintegration and general hopelessness has seemingly evaded both politicians and social scientists. Much of what we see in the inner cities is merely a reflection of the general moral failure of our country as a whole. No doubt, problems are magnified in our cities because:

1. There are more people living in closer proximity.
2. There are higher levels of unemployment and poverty.
3. There are issues of personal and communal accountability that have not been adequately addressed.

There are profound spiritual issues that need to be examined. This chapter highlights some of the spiritual forces that must be dealt with when one is seeking to affect significant change in these areas. Political and economic solutions, though helpful, are not enough. As we seek to "win back" the cities, we must be able to pull down certain spiritual strongholds that influence many of these urban areas. Some of these unseen strongholds:

1. Exert negative influences upon urban social institutions (i.e., church, home and school).
2. Exert negative influences upon the urban culture in general.

There are spiritual strongholds of sexual idolatry that must be confronted and dismantled. Any serious attempt to transform the urban landscape must address the issue of sexual idolatry and the spiritual forces that instigate it. I am not saying that suburban areas are not experiencing problems associated with sexual idolatry and sexual sin. What I am saying is that there needs to be more emphasis placed on this aspect of urban society because of the seriousness of the problem that exists in many of these areas. Even though the problem seems to have improved a little in recent years, some urban areas still have an out of wedlock birth rate approaching 60 percent.

No community, urban or suburban, can prosper and thrive with this kind of out of wedlock birth rate. The mind-set and behavioral patterns that are responsible for this kind of sexual promiscuity must be changed. If significant change is to take place, the spiritual influences that are propagating these behaviors within the culture must be "cast down" with the Word of God.

> *For the weapons of our warfare are not carnal, but mighty through God to the pulling down of strong holds; Casting down imaginations, and every high thing that exalteth itself against the knowledge of God, and bringing into captivity every thought to the obedience of Christ.*
>
> 2 Corinthians 10:4,5

I grew up in the inner city. At an early age I was exposed to the destructive consequences of the drug trade, and like many, I witnessed the addiction and premature death that it generated. In 1985, my wife and I moved into a high crime area of a major U.S. city. For nine years, I became reacquainted with the complex problems that plague our cities. The apartment complex in which we lived for three years became a major focal point for much of the drug activity in our neighborhood. Crack cocaine was openly sold in the lobby of our apartment complex. With any illegal drug trade, there are turf wars. My wife and I witnessed those wars and their sometimes fatal consequences.

From our apartment, we could see the drug trafficking on the streets and the futile attempts by the police to stop it. We could see prostitutes walking the street in the early morning hours being picked up by their customers. Broken homes, family disintegration, spousal abuse, teen pregnancy, domestic violence and premature death gripped the neighborhood.The local funeral home was one of the most prosperous businesses in the neighborhood.

In a real sense, the problems that inner cities are facing today are not unlike those in Bible times. Indeed, "there is nothing new under the sun" (Ecclesiastes 1:9).

I believe that many of the problems that we have seen in many inner cities are spiritual in nature (at the core) and will not be solved without applying spiritual solutions. Second Kings 17 illustrates some spiritual parallels and principles that are important in helping us understand:

1. The origin of certain urban strongholds.
2. The nature of certain urban strongholds.
3. The solution to pulling down these urban strongholds.

And the king of Assyria brought men from Babylon, and from Cuthah, and from Ava, and from Hamath, and from Sepharvaim, and placed them in the cities of Samaria instead of the children of Israel: and they possessed Samaria, and dwelt in the cities thereof. And so it was at the beginning of their dwelling there, that they feared not the LORD: therefore the LORD sent lions among them, which slew some of them. Wherefore they spake to the king of Assyria, saying, The nations which thou hast removed, and placed in the cities of Samaria, know not the manner of the God of the land: therefore he hath sent lions among them, and, behold, they slay them, because they know not the manner of the God of the land. Then the king of Assyria commanded, saying, Carry thither one of the priests whom ye brought from thence; and let them go and dwell there, and let him teach them the manner of the God of the land. Then one of the priests whom they had carried away from Samaria came and dwelt in Bethel, and taught them how they should fear the LORD. Howbeit every nation made gods of their own, and put them in the houses of the high places which the Samaritans had made, every nation in their cities wherein they dwelt. And the men of Babylon made Succothbenoth, *and the men of Cuth made* Nergal, *and the men of Hamath made* Ashima, *And the Avites made* Nibhaz *and* Tartak, *and the Sepharvites burnt their children in fire to* Adrammelech *and* Anammelech, *the gods of Sepharvaim. So they feared the LORD, and made unto themselves of the lowest of them priests of the* high places, *which sacrificed for them in the houses of the high places. They feared the LORD, and served their own gods, after the manner of the nations whom they carried away from thence.*

2 Kings 17:24-33 (emphasis added)

Here we see the unfolding of a satanic strategy to "possess" Samaria, the capital of the ten northern tribes of Israel. Second Kings 17:7-23 reviews the reasons Jehovah God sent the ten northern tribes into exile, the primary reason being sexual idolatry or sex worship. Jehovah God used the Assyrian nation to execute this judgment of exile. The strategy that the king of Assyria implemented to "possess" Samaria was twofold:

1. Deportation—remove the children of Israel and send them to lands that were already under Assyrian control.
2. Importation—transplant people from other nations that were under Assyrian control and allow them to inhabit the land.

This strategy was successful because it removed God's people and any influence they might exert by remaining in the land and replaced them with heathen nations. Note: When godly churches leave urban areas, they take with them the godly influence that can aid in transforming that area. These heathen nations, as we will readily see, brought with them their customs, ways and religions. It is these religious (spiritual) influences and the devastating effect that they had upon the land that I would like to bring into focus.

Let me first say this: The deities that these heathen nations worshipped had a profound effect upon the spiritual, social, cultural and moral climate of the land. *Who and how we worship affects culture, culture affects laws, and laws affect social order.* Second Kings 17:34 states that the heathen nations did not worship the Lord nor adhered to His statues, ordinances, laws, or commandments. Ultimately, the gods that a nation chooses to worship have a profound effect upon that culture's laws, ordinances and customs.

As a side note, it should be pointed out that when a person moves from one location to another, that individual takes certain things along with them. They take with them their problems, sins, mind-set, attitudes, past histories and their gods (system of worship).

SEVEN HEATHEN DEITIES

In 2 Kings 17, the heathen nations brought with them their cultures and religions. Let us examine who and how these heathens worshiped. The table below identifies the nation, the deity worshiped, and clues to how that worship was practiced.

Nation	Deity	Worship Defined
Babylon	Succoth-benoth. (tent of women)	whorehouses. prostitution
Cuth	Nergal	lion deity. violence, war
Havites	Ashima	goat deity
Havites	Nibhaz	dog deity
Havites	Tartak	mule deity
Sepharvites	Anammelech. Adrammelech	Fire god (Molech). child sacrifice

I. Babylon

And the men of Babylon made Succoth-be'noth...

2 Kings 17:30a (emphasis added)

The literal Hebrew translation is "tents of the daughters" or "booths of women." These were places where the worshiper engaged in sexual sin, a place where sex was worshiped as god. These Babylonians brought their favorite deity with them. These tents, or shrines, were nothing more than (spiritual) whorehouses where illicit sexual intercourse was sanctioned. The presence of these tents indicates how deeply rooted sexual sin and sexual promiscuity were engrained into Babylonian culture. Casual sex was a way of life.

II. Cuth

...and the men of Cuth made Nergal...

2 Kings 17:30b (emphasis added)

Nergal was the "god of battles."[6] His symbol was a lion with the head of a man. In nature, the lion is the ultimate predator. A vicious and violent creature by nature, he survives by destroying others. The Cuthites worshiped Nergal. Keep in mind that people conform to the image of who and what they worship (Psalms 135:18). We can assume, with reasonable certainty, that the Cuthite culture was given to excessive violence.

Even though we have seen a recent drop in some violent crimes, American society has grown more and more violent over the past thirty-five years or so. This is not just an urban problem, it is a nationwide epidemic. Consider the rise in:

• Domestic violence.
• Youth and school violence.
• Gang violence.

Like the Cuthite culture of biblical times, American society has too many sociopathic/sexiopathic "predators" in her midst.

III. Hamath

...and the men of Hamath made Ashi'ma.

2 Kings 17:30c (emphasis added)

Ashi'ma was symbolized by and worshiped in the form of the goat.[7] Since ancient times, the goat has served as a symbol of sexual vigor. The famed Greek historian Herodotus, upon visiting Egypt, recorded the use of goats in the worship rituals in one the temples at Mendes, Egypt. He reported that these goats were trained and used to engage in sexual intercourse with temple prostitutes in public exhibitions of worship.[8]

The word translated "goat" is *saiyr* (8163), meaning "hairy or shaggy goat." The reference is clearly to demonic creatures that would dance among the ruins of Babylon and Edomite cities (see Isaiah 13:21, 34:14).[9] "He goat" or "hairy goat" is what the name commonly refers to, but in Leviticus 17:7 ("goat demons") and 2 Chronicles 11:15 ("satyrs") the reference is clearly to some object of idolatrous worship.[10] This assertion is reasonable, given the use of this animal as an object of sexual idolatry in ancient Egypt. The key to understanding sexual idolatry is realizing that there are unseen spiritual agents that influence the worship of these idols. The demonic reference is also indicated in Revelation 18:2.

In Greek and Roman mythology, satyrs were the goat-like companions of Dionysius, the god of wine and sexual love.[11] The Greek gods and the Hebrew "saiyr" are symbols of idolatry and the demon powers they represent.[12] Worship of this deity illustrates the hold that gross sexual immorality and perversion had upon the Hamathites. The culture had become infected with sexual idolatry to the point that sex was deified and worshiped. When sex becomes god, cultural and social decay soon follows.

IV. Avites

….and the Avites made Nibhaz *and* Tartak…

2 Kings 17:31a (emphasis added)

Nibhaz was worshiped in the form of a dog.[13] In ancient Israel, the dog was not man's best friend. To call someone a dog was to insult them in the most derogatory way. Here is why:

There shall be no whore of the daughters of Israel, nor a sodomite of the sons of Israel. Thou shalt not bring the hire of a whore, or the price of a dog, into the house of the LORD thy God for any vow: for even both these are abomination unto the LORD thy God.

Deuteronomy 23:17,18

In the ancient East, the term dog was made in reference to impure or profane persons, usually men. Here in Deuteronomy 23:17,18 the term "dog" is used in connection with sodomites. A sodomite is a male prostitute or male homosexual. Even today, men who have an uncontrolled and unrestrained sexual appetite are sometimes referred to as dogs. Given the biblical and historical association of dogs and what they represent, it appears that male prostitution, homosexuality and other sexual perversions (sins) may have permeated Avite culture and society. It was truly a culture that had "gone to the dogs!"

The second object of worship for the Avites was Tartak. Tartak may have been worshiped in the form of a mule (ass).[14]

For she doted upon their paramours, whose flesh is as the flesh of asses, and whose issue is like the issue of horses.

Ezekiel 23:20 (emphasis added)

In Ezekiel 23:20, the eagle-eyed prophet rebukes the nation of Israel for her spiritual whoredom in following after the gods of Egypt. The prophet uses sexually explicit (graphic) words to describe the spiritual idolatry (whoredom) of Israel. In essence, he accuses God's people of:

1. Being in heat (sexually inflamed), that is, "too hot to trot."
2. Pursuing another paramour (sexual lover).
3. Being captivated by the size of the sex organs of Egypt's gods.

If this language is offensive to you, I suggest you direct your anger and comments at the prophet Ezekiel since he wrote it.

The thing I want to highlight is Ezekiel's reference to the ass (mule) and its sexual endowment. This reference is an indication of the sexual and sensual nature of the worship that may have been associated with the worship of Tartak by the Avites. The animal symbolism that is represented by these gods (lion, goat, dog, mule) is only indicative of the sexual and sensual nature that surrounded their worship. Throughout the ancient world, the sex organs were worshiped in the form of some animal.[15]

It was the worship of these deities and the resultant sexual sin that was responsible for much of the social, moral and cultural decay of ancient Israel (Samaria). It was the worship of these deities and the resultant sexual sin that presented such a great stronghold upon the land and its inhabitants.

V. Sepharvites

> ...and the Sepharvites burnt their children in fire to Adrammelech and Ana'melech...
>
> 2 Kings 17:31b (emphasis added)

Anammelech (meaning "Anu is king") and Adrammalech (meaning "Adar is king)" were worshiped by the Ammonites under the name of Molech. This deity was honored by sacrificing children on fiery altars.[16] Palestinian excavations have uncovered evidences of infant skeletons in burial places around heathen shrines. Hebrew law prohibited worship of Molech (Leviticus 18:21, 20:1-5). Solomon built an altar to Molech at Topheth in the valley of Hinnom. Manasseh (c. 696-642 B.C.), in his idolatrous orgy, also honored this deity (2 Kings 21:6). The prophets sternly denounced this form of heathen worship (Jeremiah 7:29-34; Ezekiel 16:20-22, 23:37-39; Amos 5:26).

In the culture's worship of these merciless and destructive gods, the children were targeted for sacrificial destruction. What kind of society would tolerate the killing of its most vulnerable members? What kind of society would legally permit murdering innocent children and throwing their bodies in the fire? What kind of society would legally permit abortion on demand for any reason? What kind of society would permit the barbaric practice of "partial birth abortion"?

- A society whose culture has been corrupted by sexual idolatry and sexual perversion.
- A society that glorifies and worships sexual perversion and sexual immorality.
- A society that has become self-centered and caught up in self-gratification.
- A society that has embraced "lying vanities" as the philosophical basis for their moral choices.
- A society whose culture has been saturated with violence and immorality.

It was the worship of these deities and the resultant sexual practices that were responsible for much of the moral and cultural decay that existed in ancient Samaria. I believe that these same spiritual entities, exerting the same ungodly spiritual influences, exist throughout our country today.

CULTURAL IMPACT

In this chapter, I have focused on these deities and the cultural impact they exert upon many urban areas. I have attended Christian conferences in which the primary theme was taking the inner cities for Christ. I have noticed that very little is being said about coming against the spiritual entities of sexual idolatry that are affecting the culture and influencing the customs in many of these areas.

In the past, most urban renewal efforts have emphasized the importance of political, economic and/or social reform. These kinds of reforms will take place when "spiritual revival" comes to these areas and impacts the culture, thereby transforming the customs. This can come only through the Word of God, energized by the Spirit of God. The church should be in the business of being the salt and light that will impact society's culture in a meaningful way. If urban areas are to be transformed and renewed, we need a spiritual strategy. The Bible speaks of taking the city:

> A wise *man scaleth the* city *of the* mighty, *and casteth down the strength of the confidence thereof.*
>
> Proverbs 21:22 (emphasis added)

Many of the problems that urban America is suffering from are spiritual at their core. Spiritual problems need spiritual solutions. These problems will take wise men and women of God who have the mind of God. If the urban areas are to be "scaled" (broken through), and the "mighty" (spiritual tyrants) are to be defeated, there must be revival. When the influence of these spiritual tyrants is broken, cultural changes will take place. *Spiritual change must proceed cultural change.*

The City Reflects the Nation

It should be pointed out that the problems of urban America only reflect the problems that exist in America as a whole. Sexual idolatry and sexual sin is not a "city" problem. In general, over the past thirty years or so, America has fallen deeper into the pit of sexual idolatry and sexual sin. Since the 1960's Sexual Revolution, this trend has accelerated nationwide. Recent data shows that, since 1930, the out of wedlock birth rate has risen by as much as 600 percent.[17]

Too often, the problems that have existed in the cities have been ignored as being problems that are restricted to the cities. This is *not* the case. Sexual sin is everywhere. Sexual sin exists on Wall Street and Main Street. School violence is *not* restricted to inner cities. The recent string of school shootings in affluent suburban areas bears out this truth. Drug usage is *not* restricted to urban America. Drug addiction and usage is plaguing the suburbs and rural America as well. Recent data indicates that drug abuse is increasing at faster rates for rural teens than for urban teens. Furthermore, rural eighth graders are 104 percent more likely to use amphetamines, 83 percent more likely to smoke crack and 50 percent more likely to use cocaine.[18]

No ethnic or racial group is immune from these unseen spiritual forces and the cultural and social devastation that they exert upon a community. No ethnic group has a hegemony on sexual sin (or any other sin for that matter). It is important to point out that the problems that exist in urban America only reflect the problems that exist in America as a whole. Years ago, I heard a wise man make this statement:

> "If you want to know what suburban America will look like in the future, all you have to do is go into the worst section of urban America, and you will see."

CHAPTER SUMMARY

1. Between 1940 and the mid 1960's, there was a massive population shift in the racial makeup of many northern U.S. cities.
2. This population shift was a direct result of African Americans migrating from southern rural areas to northern urban settings.
3. The urban climate was not as tolerant of certain family weaknesses as the rural climate was.
4. Fatherless homes and single parent homes were at a greater disadvantage in urban centers.
5. In 1965, the Monihan Report, a federally commissioned study, identified the deterioration of the black family as the most significant threat to black social order.
6. Issues such as out of wedlock births, unwed mothers, fatherless homes and the spread of AIDS cannot be adequately addressed without dealing with sexual immorality.
7. Though important, urban renewal will not take place with government funding alone.
8. Many of the problems that exist in some urban municipalities are spiritual in nature. These problems must be solved with spiritual solutions.
9. If the urban landscape is to be truly transformed, the spiritual strongholds of sexual idolatry must be pulled down.

10. Second Kings 17:24-33 records the removal of God's people from Samaria and the repopulation of the land with heathen nations and their cultures and religions.

11. These cultures and religions embraced sexual idolatry and resulted in further spiritual, social and moral decline.

12. In America today, like Samaria of old, many urban areas are culturally and spiritually handicapped by the widespread sexual idolatry that is so prevalent.

13. Sexual idolatry is responsible for many of the social and cultural ills that plague both urban and suburban communities.

14. No ethic or racial group is immune from the devastating effects that sexual idolatry has upon family, community and nation.

15. We need spiritual solutions to be applied to spiritual problems.

Appendix

KEY TERMS DEFINED

abomination: Activities or behaviors that are particularly disgusting to God. These are activities that jeopardize the security and well-being of society in general. Some sexual abominations include: bestiality, incest, pedophilia, statutory rape and homosexuality.

abortion: Any deliberate procedure that removes or induces the premature expulsion of the unborn child from the uterus.

achievement drive: The God-given desire to accomplish, excel and to be successful in overcoming opposition. The achievement drive is that which motivated Adam to subdue and to take dominion in the earth.

accumulation of sin theory: The idea that the ground (earth) can register the sins of wicked inhabitants. These sins may accumulate over a period of many years when the bodies (bones) of the wicked are returned to the earth (see Genesis 4:10,11; Job 20:11).

addiction: The habitual or compulsive use of habit-forming drugs or habit-forming activities.

adultery: Sexual relations with someone other than your spouse. It is taken from the Greek *moicheia* (see Matthew 15:19; Mark 7:21).

apostasy: To abandon the faith or to reject what one previously held to be true.

Baby Boom generation: Members of the Baby Boom generation were born between 1945-1960. No period in history has defined and impacted this generation like the turbulent 60's, a period of great social, political and cultural change. One of the most significant events of the 1960's was the so-called Second Sexual Revolution. Many Boomers embraced the Sexual Revolution, and the Sexual Revolution, to a great degree, has defined the morality and character of the Boomers.

Balaam (lord of the people): Balaam was a false prophet soothsayer (Joshua 13:22) who was summoned by the Moabite king Balak to curse the Israelites before they entered Canaan (Numbers 22:5–24:25; Deuteronomy 23:4,5). Balaam instructed Balak to corrupt God's people by seducing them to fornicate with Moabite Baal worshipers.

bestiality: Sexual intercourse with animals. The practice of bestiality in conjunction with many of the nature religions, Baalism in particular, is well-documented. Bestiality is closely associated with zoophilia which is the sexual attraction to animals (see Volume 1, Chapter 3; Leviticus 18:23, 20:13; Deuteronomy 27:21).

Biblephobia: An irrational hatred or fear of the preaching/teaching of the whole Bible.

circumcision: The surgical removal of the foreskin of the male penis.

civilization: The development of a people and its culture to a point of advanced social/political organization and technological, scientific, religious and artistic achievement.

constellation: The constellations are twelve groups of stars visible in the clear night sky. These constellations can be seen on the inner surface of a huge sphere surrounding the earth called the celestial sphere. There are twelve zodiacal signs that represent these constellations:

Aries.	Gemini.
Leo.	Libra.
Saggitarius.	Aquarius.
Taurus.	Cancer.
Virgo.	Scorpio.
Capricorn.	Pisces.

copulate: Sexual intercourse; to become united in sexual intercourse.

covenant: An agreement or contract entered (willfully) by two or more individuals. There are natural covenants and there are spiritual covenants.

critical mass (of sin): That point in which the land becomes saturated with unrepentant sin of the past and present inhabitants. When this happens the land rejects the inhabitants and the judgment of God may be manifest in the form of earthquakes, drought, famine, pestilence, disease and political unrest.

cultural decay: The regression and/or disintegration of a nation's political, judicial, educational, legal and social institutions. Cultural decay has its origins in corrupt worship systems.

culture: The total pattern of human behavior that is manifest in speech, thought and actions. A people's culture defines its social order, its likes and dis-likes, what it deems as appropriate or inappropriate, acceptable or unacceptable.

customs: Societal behavioral patterns that are accepted as the norm. The daily practices, activities and behaviors of various peoples that are culturally inspired.

Possible Steps to Custom Development

1. Cultural dissemination: Ideas and philosophies are generated and pub-licly disseminated.
2. Cultural desensitization: Ideas and philosophies are publicly practiced; "coming out of the closet."
3. Cultural assimilation: Ideas gradually become attitudes and behaviors that are accepted by the public as harmless or as having "social redeem-ing value."
4. Cultural indoctrination: Ideas and philosophies are further dissemi-nated and propagated via educational institutions and the media.
5. Cultural legalization: Ideas and philosophies become law, and the behavior, no matter how socially destructive, is no longer punishable by law.

DNA: Deoxyribonucleic Acid, the molecule that carries all of the biologic information that will dictate the "physical traits" of the offspring. In humans, DNA is naturally passed on from one generation to the next via sexual repro-duction. DNA was discovered in 1953 by the American biochemist James Watson and British biophysicist Francis Crick.

doctrine of Balaam: The doctrine of Balaam represents those worldly ideas and philosophies that come to weaken the biblical doctrine of moral purity and sanctification from within. The doctrine of Balaam is a doctrine of *compromise* with sin, *complicity* with sinners, *complacency* toward sin and *compliance* with worldly standards. The doctrine of Balaam encourages fornication, adultery and other sexual sins within the house of God.

endorphins: One of the chemicals that are released by the brain during sexual intercourse. These opium-like chemicals are natural pain relievers. They are released to help relieve stress and may be responsible for the "addictive" nature of sexual intercourse.

estrogen: A hormone secreted, primarily, by the ovary. It is involved in the maintenance and development of female reproductive organs, secondary sexual characteristics and the menstrual cycle.

evil concupiscence: Sinful, sexual desire that is induced by exposing the mind to images that are sexually explicit in nature. It appears to be derived from the combining of two words: "conscience" and "cupid." Cupid was the Roman god of sexual love. According to ancient myth, one arrow from cupid's bow was supposed to inflame sexual passion and desire in an individual. The Latin word *cupido* means "sexual desire." The conscience is the inner mental faculty which gives rise to our thoughts.

foreplay: The mutual sexual stimulation that takes place before sexual intercourse.

fornication: From the Greek work *porneia*, making reference to illicit sexual intercourse in general. At present the word refers to those unmarried individuals who engage in sexual intercourse.

genes: Biologic molecules that contain DNA, the genetic blueprint of life.

G.I. generation: The so-called G.I. generation is made up of those individuals born between 1901 and 1924. World War II helped to define and mold the character of this generation. This generation will be remembered for their great courage and sacrifice in saving the world from Nazism. They have been called the greatest generation of the twentieth century.

gospelphobia: An irrational hatred or fear of the gospel of Jesus Christ.

high places: Elevated sites usually found on the top of mountains or hills. They were areas consecrated to the worship of pagan deities.

homophobia: The fear of homosexuals; dislike for those who practice homosexuality.

homosexuality: From the Greek word *arsenokoites*, homosexuality refers to same sex unions or any activity that involves males engaging in sexual intimacy with males. Female homosexuality is referred to as *lesbianism*.

idolatry: The worship of false gods.

incest: Sexual intercourse between persons too closely related to marry legally.

Industrial Revolution: Describes the historical transformation of society by the industrialization of the economy. During this period, there was systematic application of scientific knowledge to the manufacturing process. The Industrial Revolution rapidly transformed this nation from a predominantly farm-based economy to a manufacturing-based economy. The Industrial Revolution arrived in America in the late nineteenth century. By the early 1900's, the United States had overtaken Britain in the output of iron, coal and the consumption of raw cotton. In the midst of this era of technological change, God was preparing the church for a great spiritual outpouring, the Azusa Revival.

lasciviousness: Lasciviousness is the New Testament word that is used to describe all manner of sexual sin including, but not limited to, adultery, fornication, incest, sodomy, rape and homosexuality. Lasciviousness is the failure to place godly restraints and boundaries upon ungodly thoughts and desires.

Law of Cleaving: Found in Genesis 2:23, this law functions to bind a husband and wife in lifelong commitment. It is the emotional and spiritual union that is forged and strengthened when a husband and wife become one sexually (physically). The Law Of Cleaving is the spiritual glue that is to hold a marriage and home together.

Law of Yielding and Bondage: One of the spiritual laws that govern human sexuality. It maintains that "whatever you yield your body to enslaves you." "To whomever you yield your members to will bring you under its power." That to which you yield your body will enslave you. This law is found in Romans 6:16.

lesbian: A female homosexual.

masturbation: Masturbation is defined as the erotic stimulation of the sex organs resulting in orgasm (sexual release). Masturbation my be achieved by manual manipulation, instrumental stimulation (dildos, vibrators, etc.), or by sexual fantasies.

millennial mission: The church must seek to combine spiritual power and the anointing with education and expertise. The church must stress the need to achieve academic excellence without compromising the standard message of sanctification and holiness. The church must rededicate itself to raising up a generation of spirit-filled believers who have the education and expertise to "occupy" until Jesus returns.

millennial motto: "Salvation that leads to sanctification and education that leads to occupation!"

millennial outpouring: As we enter into the new millennium, we will begin to witness the end and the start of three major cycles that are spiritually relevant: a 100-year cycle, a 1000-year cycle and a 2000-year cycle. These three cycles speak to this generation prophetically.

100 speaks of grace and divine enablement.

1000 speaks of the glory of God revealed.

2000 speaks of a prophetic outpouring that will come upon the church.

monogamy: The practice of being married to one person for a lifetime.

necrophilia: Sexual contact with dead bodies.

oxytocin: A chemical produced in the brain. It is released in non-pregnant women during sexual intercourse (orgasm). Oxytocin is released in lactating mothers and facilitates the release of milk from the mammary glands. In the female, oxytocin has been linked to the "emotional bonding" of the female to both her sex partner and her baby.

partial birth abortion: The medical term used for this barbaric procedure is "intact dilation and extraction" (D&X). This procedure is used in pregnancies that are too advanced to be terminated by suction. The procedure is performed by bringing the unborn, feet first, into the birth canal. The skull is punctured with a sharp instrument and the brain is sucked through a catheter.

pedophilia: The act or desire to engage in sexual intercourse with children. Adults engaging in sex with young children.

petting: Touching or caressing the sexual organs of another. It is sometimes referred to as foreplay.

Phinehas: The son of Eleazar and grandson of Aaron. During the wilderness wandering Phinehas killed Zimri, a leader of Israel and Cozbi, a Midianite woman whom Zimri had brought into the camp. This action ended a plague by which God had judged Israel for committing sexual sin with Midianite prostitutes who were dedicated to the worship of Baalpeor. For such zeal, Phinehas and his descendants were promised a permanent priesthood (see Exodus 6:25; Numbers 25).

pornography: Sexually explicit and/or obscene pictures, movies, books, magazines, etc. that serve to arouse sexual desire.

precept: A rule that imposes a standard of conduct or action.

profane: Without regard for sacred things; showing contempt and hatred for the things that are important to God.

regeneration: The attaining of a new spiritual nature (life). It is the inward transformation that causes a complete revolution of the individual from inside out. Regeneration is an important aspect of the gospel message. As children of Adam, we are alienated from the life of God (Ephesians 4:18) and have a corrupt nature. This type of spiritual transformation represents a "rebirth" or being "born again." In regeneration, the born-again believer receives a new set of "spiritual" genes (DNA).

reverse evangelization: The world evangelizing the church. This is manifest when one sees the church embracing worldly methods and philosophies. In essence, the church becomes more worldly rather than the world becoming more churchly (see Romans 12:2).

righteous gene pool: A spiritual term that is used to describe the presence of godly influences within the spiritual DNA of a people, family, or person. It is manifest as righteous acts of obedience to the things that please God.

sensual: Related to the physical senses; preoccupied with sexual or physical pleasures.

sex drive: The instinctive desire and attraction to the opposite sex for companionship and sexual intimacy. It is the inward biological urge that motivates one to become sexually intimate. The sex drive and achievement drive are divinely connected (Genesis 1:28).

sexiopathic: Sexually maladjusted, deviant, or otherwise perverted.

sexual fantasy: The sexual use of the imagination. It is the act of forming mental images (situations or experiences) for the purpose of sexual arousal. Sexual fantasies are those mental experiences that arise from one's own imagination. There are typically two sources of sexual fantasies: past sexual encounters and erotic books, drawings, photographs, movies, videos, etc.

Sexual Revolution: A defined period in history characterized by a significant and radical departure from the Judeo-Christian ethic of sexual fidelity within the context of marriage. Twentieth century America has experienced two such periods: the 1920's and the 1960's.

Sexually Transmitted Disease (STD): Diseases that are transmitted via sexual intercourse. There are more than thirty known diseases or entities that are sexually transmitted.

sodomy: The unhealthy and unsanitary practice of anal intercourse. It is derived from the biblical story of Sodom and Gomorrah (see Genesis 19).

soul tie: The psychological, emotional and/or physiological dependency that develops when a person yields him/herself to another person or thing. Sexual intimacy is a common means whereby soul ties develop. Soul ties may be divided into two categorize: godly and ungodly. Ungodly soul ties can bind an individual to dangerous people and habits.

spiritual DNA: The means by which "spiritual" traits are transferred from parents to children; the means by which "spiritual covenants" are transferred from parents to future generations.

statute: A legislative act that declares, commands, or prohibits something.

statutory rape: The crime of having sexual intercourse with a female or male under the age of consent, which may be sixteen, seventeen, or eighteen, depending upon the state.

stronghold: A fortress or militarily strategic area that is occupied by enemy forces.

suburban: A region on the outskirts of the city.

testosterone: The predominant male hormone that is produced in the testicle and is responsible for promoting sperm production, growth of pubic hair and all the secondary sex characteristics in the male. Male secondary sex characteristics include: facial hair growth, chest and armpit hair growth, lowering of the voice and broadening of shoulder and chest muscles. It is also partly responsible for aggressive male behavior.

tradition: Customs of the past that are passed down from generation to generation.

truth: Reality as defined by the Word of God (John 1:1) which is revealed in Jesus Christ, the Son of God (John 14:6). Romans 1 articulates at least five attitudes that fallen man held toward God's revealed truth. They are:

> **Subversion:** to overthrow or destroy; to undermine that which is already established.
>
> **Aversion:** the act of avoiding or turning away from.
>
> **Perversion:** to deviate from the norm; to distort, twist, or misinterpret; to change the meaning of.
>
> **Inversion:** to turn upside down; to reverse the order; to move in the opposite direction.
>
> **Diversion:** that which acts to occupy or distract one's attention.

urban: Comprising the city; characteristic of the city.

vasopressin: A hormone produced and secreted by the brain. It is believed to be released during sexual intercourse and is responsible for regulating blood pressure. In animal studies, vasopressin has been shown to be linked to "emotional bonding" in males.

worship: The act of reverence or devotion to a deity. Worship defines how we relate to or identify with God.

Endnotes

Chapter 1

1. Sex and The Bible: A Biblical Perspective of Human Sexuality (vol.1), D. Conaway, Treasure House Pub., 1996, p.34-40.
2. CBN News 2/27/97
3. Lange's Commentary On Holy Scripture vol.1; Leviticus , Zondervan Pub., 1960, p.143.
4. US News and World Report; 8/14/95, p.51.
5. Ibid.
6. Ibid.
7. USA Today; 3/28/96, p.2A.
8. Our Sexuality 4th Ed.; Crooks and Baur, Benjamin/Cummings Pub. Co., 1990, p.752.
9. US News and World Report; 2/10/97, p.44.
10. Ibid.
11. Ibid.
12. Ibid.
13. Ibid.
14. U.S. News and World Report; 3/27/00, pp.36-44.
15. Ibid.
16. Ibid.
17. U.S. News and World Report; 1/19/98, pp.20-25.
18. USA Today; 3/1/00, p.10D.
19. USA Today; 3/17/00, p.1.
20. Sex and The Bible: A Biblical Perspective of Human Sexuality (vol.1), D. Conaway, Treasure House Pub., 1996, p.34-40.
21. Ibid; p.44.
22. Ibid.
23. New Bible Dictionary 2nd Fd.; J.D.Douglas, et.al., Tyndale Pub., 1987, p.31.
24. Pictorial Encyclopedia Of The Bible vol.1; M. Tenney, Zondervan, 1980, p.141.
25. The 12 Ceasars; Gaius Tranquillus, Penguin Books, 1957, p.31-32.
26. Ibid; p.88.
27. Ibid; p. 131.
28. Ibid; p.161.
29. Ibid; p.198.
30. Ibid; p. 223.
31. Ibid.
32. Ibid; p.290.
33. Ibid; p.309.
34. World Civilizations 4th Ed. Vol.1, E.M. Burns and P.L. Ralph, W.W. Norton and Co., 1969, p.287-288.

35. Ibid; p.299.

36. USA Today; 5/24/99, p.D8.

37. Ibid.

38. Ibid.

39. The Black Family: Sex Life Of The African and American Negro; Essays and Studies: Robert Staples (editor); Wadsworth Pub., 1971, p.111.

40. The Decline and Fall Of The Roman Empire, vol.2,; Gibbon's, Washington Square Press, N.Y. 1972.

41. The Black Family: Sex Life Of The African and American Negro; Essays and Studies: Robert Staples (editor); Wadsworth Pub., 1971, p.110.

Chapter 2

1. *The Tanakh: The Holy Scriptures*, Jewish Pub. Society, NY, NY 1988 p.928.

2. Sex and The Bible: A Biblical Perspective of Human Sexuality (vol.1), D. Conaway, Treasure House Pub., 1996, p.23.

3. Ibid; p.105-121.

4. Ibid.

5. Ibid; p.64.

6. US News and World Report; 11/9/98, p.59-63.

7. Ibid.

8. Ibid.

9. Ibid.

10. Principles Of Medical Genetics; T. Gelehrter and F. Collins, Williams and Wilkins pub., p.4, 1990.

11. Nelson Bible Dict., Thomas Nelson Pub. 1986.

12. Sex and The Bible: A Biblical Perspective of Human Sexuality (vol.1), D. Conaway, Treasure House Pub., 1996, p.127.

13. Ibid; p.106.

14. Ibid; p.31-46.

15. Cancer Watch; Vol.1, Num.1, January 1992.

16. Sex and The Bible: A Biblical Perspective of Human Sexuality (vol.1), D. Conaway, Treasure House Pub., 1996, p.53-77.

17. Principles Of Medical Genetics; T. Gelehrter and F. Collins, Williams and Wilkins pub., p.4, 1990.

18. USA Today 6/9/98 p.6D.

19. Principles Of Medical Genetics; p.4.

20. Sex and The Bible: A Biblical Perspective of Human Sexuality (vol.1), D. Conaway, Treasure House Pub., 1996, p.63.

21. Personal communication: Pastor Emeka Nwankpa; Nigeria, Africa.

22. Responding to the Homosexual Agenda: Prison Fellowship Ministries, 1997, pp.9-13.

23. Ibid.

24. Molecular Cell Biology 2nd Edition; Darnell, J.; Lodish, H.; Baltimore, D.; Scientific American Books, 1990, pg. 86-87.

25. Personal communication: Pastor Emeka Nwankpa; Nigeria, Africa.

26. Encyclopedia Of Psychological Problems; C. Narramore, Zondervan Pub., 1966,p.127.

27. Sex and The Bible: A Biblical Perspective of Human Sexuality (vol.1), D. Conaway, Treasure House Pub., 1996, pg.38.

28. Lander and Weinberg: Science, Bol. 287, pp.1777-1782, 3/10/2000.

29. Sex and The Bible: A Biblical Perspective of Human Sexuality (vol.1), D. Conaway, Treasure House Pub., 1996, p.112.

Chapter 3

1. Sex and The Bible: A Biblical Perspective of Human Sexuality (vol.1), D. Conaway, Treasure House Pub., 1996, p.42.

2. Ibid.

3. Ibid, p.203-204.

4. CNN Headline News 1/30/00 (from Kansas City Star article).

5. Sex and The Bible: A Biblical Perspective of Human Sexuality (vol.1), D. Conaway, Treasure House Pub., 1996, p.42-44.

6. NBC News Report 2/5/00.

7. Focus On The Family Magazine, Aug.98, p.2.

8. US News and World Report; 8/19/96, p.8.

9. The Christian Century; 9/23/98, vol.115, p.856 (1).

10. CNN Headline News 1/30/00 (from Kansas City Star article).

11. The Christian Century; 9/23/98, vol.115, p.856.

12. Ibid.

13. Sex and The Bible: A Biblical Perspective of Human Sexuality (vol.1), D. Conaway, Treasure House Pub., 1996, p.37-42.

14. Ibid; p.137.

15. Personal Communication From Pastor Raphael Green; Metro Christian Worship Center, St. Louis, Mo.

16. Dake's Annotated Reference Bible; F.J.Dake, DBS Pub., 1990, p.386.

17. US News and World Report; 12/7/98, p.23.

18. US News and World Report; 1/19/98, p.20-25.

19. USA Today Weekend; 1/9/98, p.12.

20. US News and World Report; 8/19/96, p.8.

21. US News and World Report; 1/19/98, p.20-25.

22. US News and World Report; 1/19/98, p.31.

23. US News and World Report; 7/19/99, p.46-47.

Chapter 4

1. Sex and The Bible: A Biblical Perspective of Human Sexuality (vol.1), D. Conaway, Treasure House Pub., 1996, p.38.

2. US News and world Report; 7/19/99, p.46-47.

3. US News and World Report; 8/19/96, p.8.

4. CNN Headline News 1/30/00 (from Kansas City Star article).

5. US News and World Report; 2/14/00, p.50.

6. God's Generals: R. Liardon, Albury Press, 1996, p.137.

7. Biblical Mathematics: E.F. Vallowe, Ed Valowe Evang. Assoc., 1984, p.199.

8. God's Generals: R. Liardon, Albury Press, 1996, p.137.

9. Biblical Mathematics: p. 232.

10. US News and World Report; 8/16/99, p.32.

11. "Constellations of the Zodiac," Microsoft, Encarta 97 Encyclopedia 1993-1996.

12. Witness Of The Stars, E.W. Bullinger, Kregel Pub. 1967, p.84.

13. "Constellations of the Zodiac," Microsoft® Encarta®2001 Encyclopedia. © Microsoft Corporation. All rights reserved. Reprinted with permission from Microsoft Corporation.

Chapter 5

1. Sex and The Bible: A Biblical Perspective of Human Sexuality (vol.1), D. Conaway, Treasure House Pub., 1996, p.38-40.

2. US News and World Report; 4/21/97, p.78.

3. Sex and The Bible: A Biblical Perspective of Human Sexuality (vol.1), D. Conaway, Treasure House Pub., 1996, p.128-130.

4. Integrating Treatment Of Unwanted Male Homosexual Attractions: Clinical Interventions, paper presentation; NARTH Annual Conference, L.A., Ca. 10/23/98.

5. The Prevalence of Childhood Sexual Assault; Amer. Jour.of Epidemiology, 126, 6:1141, December, 1987.

6. Sex and The Bible: A Biblical Perspective of Human Sexuality (vol.1), D. Conaway, Treasure House Pub., 1996, p.128-131.

7. The 12 Ceasars, p.181-241.

8. Barnes Notes On The New Testament; A. Barnes, Kregel Pub., 1978, p.554.

9. A Meta-Analytic Examination of Assumed Properties of Child Sexual Abuse Using College Samples; Psychological Bulletin, July 1998, vol.124 (1), p.22-53.

10. Sex and The Bible: A Biblical Perspective of Human Sexuality (vol.1), D. Conaway, Treasure House Pub., 1996, p.54.

11. Sex and The Bible: A Biblical Perspective of Human Sexuality (vol.1), D. Conaway, Treasure House Pub., 1996, p.44.

12. Sex and The Bible: A Biblical Perspective of Human Sexuality (vol.1), D. Conaway, Treasure House Pub., 1996, p.44.

13. US News and World Report, 7/19/99, p.46-47.

14. Sex and The Bible: A Biblical Perspective of Human Sexuality (vol.1), D. Conaway, Treasure House Pub., 1996, p.173-185.

15. Ibid, p.31-46.

16. Ibid, p.128-131.

17. Kansas City Star 1/29/00.

18. Ibid.

19. Ibid.

20. USA Today 2/14/00, p.3a.

21. Kansas City Star 1/29/00.

22. Ibid.

23. Ibid.

24. US News and World Report 4/10/00, p.50.

25. Ibid.

26. US News and Wold Report, 8/4/97.

Chapter 6

1. Sex In America: A Definitive Survey; Robert T. Michael et. al., Little, Brown and Co. 1994, p.158.

2. Lover's Guide Encyclopedia; D. Massey, Thunder's Mouth Pub., 1996, p.126.

3. Ibid.

4. The Sexual Brain; S. LeVay, Bradford Book, MIT Press, 1993, p.48.

5. Lover's Guide Encyclopedia; p.126.

6. US News and World Report; 7/19/99, p.46-47.

7. Lover's Guide Encyclopedia; p.126.

8. Our Sexuality 4th Ed.; Crooks and Baur, Benjamin/Cummings Pub., 1990, p. 286.

9. Lover's Guide Encyclopedia; p.126.

10. Our Sexuality 4th Ed.; p.292.

11. Ibid; p.286.

12. Human Sexuality 2nd Ed.; Wade and Cirese, HBJ Pub., 1991, p.319.

13. The Latin Sexual Vocabulary; J. N. Adams, Duckworth and Co. Ltd., 1982, p.63.

14. Sex and The Bible: A Biblical Perspective of Human Sexuality (vol.1), D. Conaway, Treasure House Pub., 1996, p.91.

Chapter 7

1. Healthy Adam On Testosterone: M. Segell; MSNBC.com Health Section, Jan.1999.

2. Biological Psychology; 3rd Ed., J. Kalat, Wadsworth Pub., 1988, p.305.

3. Ibid.

4. Ibid.

5. Ibid; p.308.

6. Sex On The Brain; D. Blum, Penguin Books, 1998, p.171.

7. Ibid.

8. Ibid.

9. Ibid.

10. Sex and The Bible: A Biblical Perspective of Human Sexuality (vol.1), D. Conaway, Treasure House Pub., 1996, p.85-103.

11. USA Today 1-15-99.

Chapter 8

1. Sex and The Bible: A Biblical Perspective of Human Sexuality (vol.1), D. Conaway, Treasure House Pub., 1996, p.110.

2. Sex and The Bible: A Biblical Perspective of Human Sexuality (vol.1), D. Conaway, Treasure House Pub., 1996, p.92-93.

3. The Sexual Brain; S. Levay, MIT Press; Cambridge, Mass., 1993, p.71-81.

4. Ibid.

5. USNews and World Report; 2/17/97, p.59.

6. Ibid.

7. Ibid.

8. Anatomy and Physiology 2nd Ed.; Seely, Stephens and Tate, Mosby Pub.,1992, p.553.

9. USNews and World Report; 2/17/97, p.59.

10. USNews and World Report; 2/17/97, p.58.

11. The State News; Lansing, MI., 11/9/99, D. Blum.

12. Sex on the Brain, D. Blum, Penguin Books, 1997, p.114-115.

13. USNews and World Report; 2/17/97, p.60.

14. Ibid., p.60.

15. Sex and The Bible: A Biblical Perspective of Human Sexuality (vol.1), D. Conaway, Treasure House Pub., 1996, p.99.

16. Newsweek; 7/20/98, p.46-52.

17. Ibid; p.48.

18. Sex and The Bible: A Biblical Perspective of Human Sexuality (vol.1), D. Conaway, Treasure House Pub., 1996, p.56.

19. CNN Headline News; 6/18/98.

20. USA Today; Health Section, 8/24/98.

21. Research On The Essential Characteristics of the Father's Role For Family Well-Being: Focus On The Family Magazine, August 1995, p.4.

22. The Promiscuous Woman: M. Searf, Psychology Today, July 1980, p.78-87.

23. Sex and The Bible: A Biblical Perspective of Human Sexuality (vol.1), D. Conaway, Treasure House Pub., 1996, p.98.

24. Sex and The Bible: A Biblical Perspective of Human Sexuality (vol.1), D. Conaway, Treasure House Pub., 1996, p.93-98.

25. USA Today; 9/15/99.

26. US News and World Report; 8/14/95, p.51.

27. USA Today 6/7/00, p.7d.

28. Ibid.

29. Ibid.

30. Sex and The Bible: A Biblical Perspective of Human Sexuality (vol.1), D. Conaway, Treasure House Pub., 1996, p.110.

31. US News and World Report; 1/12/87, p.61-62.

Chapter 9

1. The Promised Land: The Great Black Migration and How It Changed America; N. Lehman, Knopf Pub., 1991.

2. The Black Family: Essays and Studies; R. Staples (editor), Wadsworth Pub., 1971, p.344.

3. Ibid.

4. Slouching Towards Gomorrah; R. Bork, Harper Collins Pub., 1996, p.155.

5. The Black Family: Essays and Studies; R. Staples, Wadsworth Pub., 1971, p.61.

6. Dake's Reference Bible; F.J. Dakes, Dake Bible Sales, 1990, p.410.

7. Ibid; p.410.

8. Sex and The Bible: A Biblical Perspective of Human Sexuality (vol.1), D. Conaway, Treasure House Pub., 1996, p.35.

9. Unger's Bible Dictionary, PC Study Bible for Windows version 2.1, Bible Soft, 1993-1995.

10. Ibid.

11. "Satyr," Encarta 97 Encyclopedia, Microsoft, 1993-1996.

12. Unger's Bible Dictionary, PC Study Bible for Windows Version 2.1, Bible Soft, 1993-1995.

13. Dake's Reference Bible, p.410.

14. Ibid.

15. Sex and The Bible: A Biblical Perspective of Human Sexuality (vol.1), D. Conaway, Treasure House Pub., 1996, p.34-40.

16. Unger's Bible Dictionary, PC Study Bible for Windows Version 2.1, Bible Soft, 1993-1995.

17. CNN Headline News; 1999.

18. Study conducted by: Center on Addiction and Drug Abuse: "No Place to Hide" Presented on the 700 Club, 2/16/00.

Other Publications By The Author

Sex And The Bible:
A Biblical Perspective Of Human Sexuality
Treasure House Pub., 1996. Paperback 204 pages.

Copies of Sex And The Bible: A Biblical Perspective Of Human Sexuality may be purchased from:

- Purity Press Publishers
  P.O. Box 252
  Okemos, Michigan 48864
  517-381-2373

- Metro Christian Worship Center Church; St. Louis, Missouri
  314-772-8444

- Black Light Publishing
  P.O. Box 5369
  Chicago, Illinois 60680
  Phone: 773-826-7790

- Purchase online at:
  Amazon.com

Sex is a Spiritual Act
Order Form

Postal orders: Purity Press Publishers
P.O. Box 252
Okemos, Michigan 48864-0252

Telephone orders: (517) 381-2373

Please send *Sex is a Spiritual Act* to:

Name: _____

Address: _____

City: _____ State: _____

Zip: _____

Telephone: (_____) _____

Book Price: $16.95
Make checks payable to: Purity Press Publishers (PPP)

Shipping: $2.00 for the first book and $1.00 for each additional book
(up to ten books) to cover shipping and handling within the
US, Canada, and Mexico. International orders add $6.00 for
the first book and $2.00 for each additional book. Allow 2-4
weeks for delivery.

Special discounts for bulk orders.

Or order from:
Amazon.com

or

ACW Press
5501 N. 7th Ave. #502
Phoenix, AZ 85013

1-800-931-BOOK

or contact your local bookstore